TUESDAY

E. L. TODD

Fallen Publishing

Tuesday

Editing Services provided by Final-Edits.com

CHAPTER ONE

Two Years Later

Francesca

Like every morning, it was chaos.

Workers were preparing breakfast and lunch on one side of the bakery, where an enormous line wrapped around the store and headed out the door. Every table was filled with customers, and when one was finally vacated, someone snatched it before the busser got there. The line for the baked goods was just as long. We stopped playing music in the shop because it was always so loud you couldn't hear anything anyway.

I was in the cake kitchen going over a new design for a wedding cake. It was an unusual creation, but it had strong significance to the couple. I was open-minded to anything, and since it was their special day, I would do whatever I possibly could to give them what they wanted.

"Frankie." Liz came from the front. Her black t-shirt was caked in flour, and a gleam of sweat was on her forehead.

"What's up?" I didn't take my eyes off my binder.

"Some guy wants to put in a large catering order. He says it's for a work conference. And he wanted me to tell you it's Matt."

Matt had become an acquaintance from all his visits to the bakery. He was my first customer when I had my grand opening, and he still came in here twice a week. "I'll be there in a second."

"Okay." Liz returned to the chaos.

After I grabbed my notebook, I headed to the front. The closer I got, the louder it became. The noise level was always at its peak. Whenever I was here in the morning, it was dead silent—but it didn't feel right.

Matt's eyes lit up when he saw me. "Busy day, huh?"

"It's always busy." I gave him a quick smile then nodded to the rear. "You want to talk in my conference room?"

"What?" He leaned forward like he hadn't heard me. It was impossible to have a conversation in this place.

I waved him toward the back, and we headed up the stairs until we reached the hallway and entered the conference room.

"I can hear myself think again." He walked with one hand in the pocket of his suit. A shiny watch was on his wrist, and he smelled like Hugo Boss.

"Sometimes I wear ear plugs."

He chuckled. "Good thinking."

We sat down at the table, and I pulled out the catering menu. "What do you have in mind?"

"Well, it's for a charity banquet."

I didn't like the sound of that. "How many people?"

He cringed like he knew I didn't want to hear the number. "Six hundred."

I shook my head slowly. "That's a lot of people, Matt."

"I know. But your stuff is unbelievable. They'll go crazy over it."

I gave him a soft smile. "I appreciate the compliment. But…I'm not sure if I have the manpower to do that and supply goods for the bakery at the same time."

"What if I pay you double?"

That's not what I was fishing for. "No, of course not."

Tuesday

He leaned over the table, his handsome face almost childlike as he begged. "Come on, Francesca. Help me out."

I sighed because I knew I was going to regret this. "Fine."

He smiled, highlighting his nice cheekbones and straight teeth. "Thank you. I really appreciate it."

I held the pen to the paper and took down his order. I'd definitely have to call in all my workers overnight to get this job done. My business had grown so much that I seriously considered expanding or opening another shop.

"Do you have plans on Saturday?"

"I'm working." I held up the notes to him. "And I'm working *all* day."

"But what about in the evening?" Matt was a nice guy. He was polite and thoughtful, and he was good-looking. He'd discreetly asked me out a few times, and when I said no, he dropped it—for a while.

"I'll be exhausted." I tried to turn him down easily. Sometimes, I wondered if he loved my bakery that much or if it was just an excuse to talk to me.

A quick glimpse of disappointment flashed across his eyes before it disappeared. "You're right. I doubt you'll be able to stand when you're finished."

He gave me a smile that said there were no hard feelings.

"Well, I'll see you then. I should get back to work." I rose from the table with the order in my hand.

"Me too. If I stay here too long, I'll eat something I shouldn't." His hand moved to his stomach.

"Like you have anything to worry about..."

We headed downstairs and back into the fray of the crowd.

"I'll see you later, Matt."

"Bye, Francesca." He gave me a quick wink before he walked out and headed back to work.

I migrated through the crowd and returned behind the counter.

"Frankie?" Liz was at my side again.

"What's up?"

"Marie is here to see you."

My heart throbbed in my chest and excitement shot through me. "Where is she?"

"I put her in the cake kitchen. Wasn't sure where else to leave her."

"Thank you." I quickly migrated through the workers in the kitchen and headed to the back.

Marie was there, pacing back and forth like she couldn't stand still. She wore a black pencil skirt and a pink blouse. Her blonde hair reached past her shoulders. My eyes immediately went to her left ring finger.

When she noticed me, she practically screamed. "Frankie!" She held up her left hand. "Look who's getting married!"

"Oh my god!" I screamed then hugged her tightly. "Congratulations. I'm so happy for you."

"It was so romantic. It was right on the beach."

I grabbed her left hand and examined the ring even though I'd already seen it. "It's beautiful. He did a good job."

"We're going to be sisters—officially."

"I know…it's great." I squeezed her shoulder. "You guys are perfect together. I'm so happy."

Suspicion moved into her eyes. "You already knew, didn't you?"

"You think Axel wouldn't tell me?" I asked incredulously. "I helped him pick out the ring."

"No wonder it's so perfect," she said with a laugh. "I can't believe you were able to keep it a secret."

"I tried not to think about it."

She examined her ring with affection. "He totally caught me off guard. I just turned around and he was on his knee in the sand. I cried…"

Axel caught me off guard too. I had no idea he could be romantic. "That's very sweet."

"I can't believe my day is finally here!" She screamed in the middle of my kitchen.

Happiness moved through my heart. Marie deserved nothing but the best. When she and Axel started fooling around, I never expected it to go anywhere. I thought he would just break her heart and leave. But I was wrong—thankfully.

"You'll be my maid of honor?" She squeezed my hand.

"Do you really need to ask?" I said sarcastically. "And it better be me. I'd kick your ass if it wasn't."

She chuckled. "Great. I was thinking we'd have an engagement party."

"That's a good idea. I'll put it together for this weekend."

Her eyes lightened in awe. "Wow, you're already a great maid of honor."

I shrugged. "I try."

She felt the ring on her finger then grew serious. The aura in the room noticeably darkened, and all the joy that was once in her cheeks disappeared. I felt the coldness enter my body, freezing me. "There's something we need to talk about…"

I knew exactly what this was regarding. "Marie, I know he's going to be there, and it doesn't bother me in the least."

Relief was in her eyes. "Axel was going to ask him to be his best man…but we won't if it's too uncomfortable for you. We would never do that to you."

I hadn't seen or heard from Hawke in two years. The break up was hard on me, and I spent three months just trying to get by. It was like someone ripped out one lung, and I was forced to survive without it. I spent most of my days crying and lying in bed. I managed to pass my classes because Marie did all my work. They both saw me at my worst, and their concern was appropriate. "I'm fine, Marie. It's your day, and you shouldn't worry about anyone but yourself."

"Shut up," she said. "My day is about you too. I want you to be comfortable."

After the first six months of being apart, it got easier. I finally focused on opening my bakery and moving on with my life. I was still angry with Hawke, but eventually that passed. I'd been in a happy place for a long time now. Seeing him didn't bother me in the least. If he could move on and forget about me, I could do the same. "I couldn't care less that he's going to be there. He's just another person to me now."

"But Axel and I know how you felt about him..."

"Two years ago, Marie. I've dated other guys and have moved on. Seriously, I'll be fine."

She still seemed unsure. "Because he doesn't have to be in the wedding at all. He can just be a guest."

And give him that satisfaction? Hell no. "Marie, put him in the wedding. He's Axel's best friend. He belongs there."

"Maybe you should take a few days to think about it..."

I put my hands on my hips and glared at her. "Marie, if I couldn't handle this, I would be upfront about it. I—"

"No, you wouldn't."

Okay, I wouldn't. "I really am fine. I don't miss him, and I never think about him. Why would I mourn over someone who packed his shit and just took off like that? Why would I think about someone so selfish? I thought what we had was true and real, but it obviously wasn't. I've had enough time to forget about him and move on. You know I have a thing with Kyle right now."

"You mean a booty call?"

"Whatever. My point is, I'm not moping around. I haven't moped around in over a year."

Marie seemed more convinced.

"I'm fine with it. Honestly. Now let's stop talking about some guy I dated two years ago, and let's start planning your wedding."

She finally relaxed, and all the concern faded from her eyes. "Let's."

***

I began planning the engagement party immediately because I only had a few days to pull it together. Fortunately, Matt allowed me to use the rooftop on his building for the party. It was beautiful up there, with a view of the entire city. And it was clean. I hung up some lights and rented tables and chairs. And for once, I ordered catering from someone else and didn't make the food myself. But I did make the cake.

Kyle came by my place for some action, and once we were done, I got back to work. I made the invitations and finished all the final touches. "You have a sexy man in your bed, and yet, you're ignoring him."

I rolled my eyes. "We had sex, didn't we?"

"But we usually have sex twice." He sat up in bed with the sheet over his waist.

"I'm giving you more time to recharge."

"Baby, I don't need more time." He pulled the sheet down and revealed himself.

I rolled my eyes again. "How can I say no to that?" I returned to addressing the envelopes.

He sighed then lay next to me at the foot of the bed. "What are you working on, anyway?"

"My best friend is getting married, and I'm throwing her an engagement party."

"Sounds boring."

"It'll be fun." I stacked the completed envelopes in a pile next to me.

"You bringing me as your date?"

"No," I blurted.

"You bringing someone else?"

"No. I'm going stag."

"That's pretty lame."

Hawke would probably bring a date but I didn't care. And I wasn't going to bring someone just to act like I was totally over him. I was over him, and I didn't need to prove it. I didn't care enough to play games. "It shows confidence. I don't need a man on my arm to feel secure."

He gave me that grin that attracted me to him to begin with. "That's sexy."

"Told you."

"But I think you should bring me along anyway."

"Because of the babes?" *Why else would Kyle want to tag along?*

His eyebrows furrowed in confusion. "No…for the free food. You're baking a cake for her, right?"

"Of course."

"That's what I'm interested in."

I continued making the invitations. "I'll bring you back a slice."

He turned his body so he was closer to me. The sheet no longer covered him. "Give me one good reason why you won't take me."

"Because I don't want to." He was being awfully pushy today. "Is that a good enough reason?"

"Oh…" He nodded his head in understanding. "Planning on picking up someone?" He had a teasing tone to his voice but disappointment was in his eyes.

I immediately thought of Hawke. "Definitely not."

"Then you should take me."

"Why are you being so pushy about this?" I set the invitations down and looked him in the eye.

"Because I like spending time with you." He held my gaze and didn't blink. "And your best friend is getting married. I'm sure that bums you out."

"What? Why would that bum me out?"

"Because you aren't getting married..."

I rolled my eyes. "I'm not like that. I'm truly happy for her and don't care that I'm not in the same situation. My day will come eventually, and whatever her status is, she'll be just as happy for me."

"Well, wouldn't it be better to have me for company instead of sitting alone?"

I stood up and grabbed his clothes. "You should go." I tossed his jeans at him.

"Whoa, what the hell?" He sat up and raised his arms in confusion.

"We agreed to a meaningless fling and now you're trying to change it. I told you I'm not looking for something more."

"Neither am I." He stood up and pulled on his boxers.

"Then why do you want to come so badly?"

"I don't know," he snapped. "Because we're friends. We can do other things instead of screwing."

"But I don't want to do other things." I made that clear, and I didn't feel bad for sounding so cold.

"What the hell happened to you?" he asked.

"What's that supposed to mean?"

"You're totally closed off like a concrete wall. I admit I'm not big on emotions and clinginess, but you're worse than any dude I've ever met. When was the last time you had a relationship?"

Hawke. "Two years ago."

"And you've been single since?"

"What's wrong with that?"

"It's just...that's a long time to be single."

"Maybe I like being single."

He shook his head. "No girl likes being single."

I threw his shirt at him. "Just go. This is getting too complicated."

"What happened to that guy two years ago?"

"What do you think?" I said sarcastically. "We're still together?"

"How did it end?"

I never thought about Hawke, so it was weird to talk about him. "He left me. He grabbed his things and took off."

"And that's it?" he asked. "No explanation?"

I didn't want to get into it. "No."

He sat on the bed again, his head bowed. "That's rough, Frankie."

"I'm over it," I said dismissively. "It was a long time ago."

"If you're over it, why are you so closed off?"

"Maybe I just haven't found the right guy. I'm very picky. It took me twenty-two years to find him, so I'm sure it'll take me the same amount of time to find the next one."

He held my gaze as he spoke. "Or maybe you just need to look a little harder." Silence echoed in the room but he said so much with his gaze. Then he grabbed his shirt and pulled it over his head.

Kyle and I had been fooling around for months. It started off empty and meaningless, but that was how I liked it. When Kyle left my apartment, I never wondered what he was doing. I didn't care enough to think about it. But now things had changed. Instead of just sex, it seemed like he wanted something more, like going to movies or out to ball games. "You should go."

"Yeah, I should." He pulled his jeans on then grabbed his phone from the nightstand. "Have fun at your party."

"I will."

He gave me a cold look before he walked out my front door then slammed it.

I sighed then returned to the invitations. The next person on the list was Hawke. His name and address were on the notes Marie gave me. I stared at his name then looked at his location. He had an apartment on Park Avenue. He must be doing really well. I wondered where he worked and if he was happy.

I wondered if he ever thought the same about me.

***

Axel walked inside wearing a designer suit and tie. He'd had a fortuitous career, and he reeked of new money. "Hey, sis."

"Look who it is." I came out of the kitchen and hugged him. We hardly ever touched each other, but I thought I'd make an exception. "Congratulations."

"Thank you. She cried when I did it." He brushed off his shoulder. "Because I'm insanely romantic…"

I rolled my eyes. "Who knew you'd ever take a wife."

He shrugged. "Caught me by surprise too. But she's the one, man."

"Man?"

"Sorry, sometimes I forget you're a girl."

I handed him a beer. "I guess my breasts aren't obvious enough."

"I wouldn't know. I never look." He sat on the couch and loosened his tie. "What's new with you?"

I sat beside him. "The invitations have been sent and everything is underway. It'll be a fun party."

"Awesome." He set his beer down and didn't drink it again.

I knew what was coming.

"Marie told me you're okay with Hawke being my best man."

Seriously, could we just move on?

"But I wanted to make sure before I actually asked him."

"You're making this into a bigger deal than it needs to be," I snapped. "Yes, we went out for a few months but we broke up. Couples break up all the time. He and I will get along just fine."

Axel stared at me with a look I didn't see very often. It was full of sadness—and pity. "He wasn't just a boyfriend to you. I was there, Frankie. Whatever you had…it was rare."

I used to think the same thing. But I didn't anymore. "But it's been two years, Axel. A lot has changed. I'm very happy with where I am in my life. I don't think about him anymore. I haven't thought about him in a long time." I never asked about Hawke since we broke up. I never even mentioned his name. And Marie and Axel never brought him up either. I knew they spent time with him, but they never mentioned it to me.

"Then why haven't you had a boyfriend?"

"None of your business," I snapped.

"Don't get defensive."

"I'm super picky. I don't settle. You know me."

"This is New York City. You should have found someone by now."

Did that mean Hawke had already found someone? Was he in a relationship? I pushed the thought away because it didn't matter. "Don't tell me where I should be in life. I'm very happy you and Marie are getting a happily ever after, but that doesn't mean there's something wrong with me just because I haven't found that yet."

He backpedaled. "You're right. I just don't want to go through with this if it's going to make you uncomfortable. He's my best friend but you're my sister. You're the priority."

When would people start believing that I couldn't care less about Hawke? "Ask him, Axel. He's been a good friend to you for a long time. He deserves to be your best man."

Hesitance was still in his eyes.

"Why don't you believe me? When have I ever given you the impression I wasn't over him?"

"You haven't. I just remember everything."

"It's in the past, Axel. The time Hawke and I had together was great, but it's been over for a long time. I've moved on and so has he. You're just going to have to accept that."

He sighed. "I guess so. It's just...you haven't talked since. Will it be weird?"

"Well, it's not going to be pleasant but it won't be terrible either. And don't worry about Hawke and me. It's your wedding day. He and I can put aside our differences for a day."

"There's a lot of stuff in between," he said. "Planning, parties, and all that shit."

"Well, we can get through that too. Stop being a drama queen."

He chuckled. "I just want to make sure everything is okay."

"Don't worry about us. Seriously."

"Okay." He finally loosened up. "I'm going to ask him. This is your last chance."

I held his gaze and didn't appear intimidated.

He stood up. "Okay. There's no turning back."

"Good. What happened between us is irrelevant. He's a good friend to you and has always been there for you. It wouldn't feel right if you asked someone else." While I wished I didn't have to see Hawke at all, my brother and Marie were more important. They deserved to have a special day with everyone they cared about. Nothing else mattered.

He patted my hand. "You're a good sister. I know I tease you a lot and say I hate you but...you're pretty cool."

"I am cool."

"Okay…now you're just conceited."

"No, I'm accepting your compliment. And it was a very nice compliment." I patted his hand in return.

He gave me a quick smile. "Thank you for everything you're doing for Marie. I really appreciate it."

"She's my best friend. She deserves only the best."

"She does."

"And thanks for not being an asshole to her."

He chuckled. "I'm an asshole…sometimes. But I'm pretty sure she likes it."

CHAPTER TWO

The Engagement Party

Francesca

Everything was perfect.

The white lights streaming across the sky lit up every table. Small candles glowed along with the centerpieces, and the New York Skyline gave the rooftop an unearthly glow. The three-tier cake I made sat on a table in the corner, and waiters moved around with bottles of champagne. The caterers had the food ready to be served.

I did a damn good job.

It was better than most weddings. It was over-the-top for an engagement party but it had to be perfect. This was for my best friend and brother, the two people most important to me. And I knew my parents would want the best for Axel if they were to experience it.

Yaya approached me and gave me a big hug. "Honey, it looks beautiful."

"Thanks, Yaya. It took me all day, but I made it happen."

"Just like your mother," Yaya said. "She was always good at these types of things. She was a social butterfly."

I wouldn't go to that extreme. I didn't enjoy making small talk with people I didn't know, but I didn't hate it either. "Thanks, Yaya. I know she would love it if she were here to see it."

"She would." She patted my back. "Axel is such a sweet boy, and he deserves the best."

He was nearly thirty years old, but she still saw him as a young child. "He is."

Other people started to file in as they arrived. Gifts were placed on the table in the corner, and people inserted cards into the large mailbox I decorated. My heart rate started to increase when I remembered I would come face-to-face with Hawke eventually. There was no way of getting around it, and everyone would watch our interaction.

The break up was devastating for me. I felt like I lost my parents all over again. Hawke made me whole like never before, and when he left, he broke me in half. It wasn't easy to get out of bed. It wasn't easy to eat. But I had two years to recover, and I needed to forget about that painful experience and hold my head high. I refused to let Hawke understand how much he hurt me. If he really cared, he wouldn't have left to begin with.

"Oh my god!" Marie gasped as she walked inside. "It's so beautiful!"

"I know." Now wasn't the time to be humble.

Marie hugged me and practically snapped my ribcage when she squeezed me. "You did such an amazing job."

"It had to be perfect for the bride."

"And the groom." Axel came next, wearing slacks and a collared shirt. "You did great, sis."

"Thanks."

To my surprise, he hugged me too. "I didn't know you had it in you."

"Yes, you did." I shoved him away playfully.

"Babe, doesn't it look awesome?" Marie stared at the lights then the centerpieces.

"It does, baby." He stared at her fondly before he turned back to me. "Thanks for making her happy."

"No problem," I said.

"I'm so getting head when we get home." He walked away then put his arm around her.

I tried not to gag.

Other people filed in, and I chatted with her other bridesmaids. I knew some of them from previous interactions but not really well. They worked with Marie at the magazine, so we didn't have much in common. But they seemed to be impressed with my work.

Family members and other friends came in and took their seats. Wine was poured and the laughter began.

Hawke still wasn't there.

Maybe he wasn't coming.

That would work out for me.

But he wouldn't miss Axel's engagement party no matter how much he wanted to avoid me. Was he dreading seeing me as much as I was dreading seeing him? Did he not care at all? What if he walked in with a date? What if he was married?

My stomach pooled with acid at the thought.

I was over him, but no matter how much time had passed, seeing him with a wife would hurt me deeply. My heart had slowly let him go, but that didn't mean it hadn't been devoted to him at one point in time. I always thought we would be together forever. If someone else was his forever, I wasn't sure how I would handle it.

"It's beautiful." His deep voice sounded exactly the same as it used to. I recognized that booming tone, coming all the way from his chest. The air shifted around him when he was near me, and his scent washed over me. I hadn't smelled it in years, but as soon as I registered it in my brain, memories of passionate nights washed over me. It was like I experienced it all over again in the blink of an eye.

My arms responded with goose bumps, and my heart hammered in my chest like someone gave me a shot of adrenaline. I felt cold and warm at the same time. My natural instinct was to run but my feet refused to let me move. I was over him, and I needed to prove that I was perfectly fine without him. "Thank you." My voice came out surprisingly steady, and I wanted to pat myself on the back.

I turned my gaze toward him, and the earlier strength I possessed disappeared. He wore black slacks and a gray collared shirt. A black vest was over his chest, highlighting all the muscles of his body. He somehow managed to pack on more muscle.

His chin was covered in a lining of hair from not shaving for a few days, but the look made him rugged and sexy. His eyes were just as blue as before, deep and captivating. I could fall into their depths all over again if I weren't careful. His brown hair was exactly the same as it used to be, slightly curly at the ends and a little messy. Had he run his fingers through it anxiously on the way here? Was he just as nervous as I was?

His eyes took me in, but they never left my face. He didn't look me up and down like the first time we met. His hands were in his pockets, and it was clear he didn't plan to greet me in any physical way—not even with a handshake.

Which was fine by me.

His eyes moved to the cake in the corner. "Can I assume that was your doing?"

"Yes." I glanced at the table then turned back to him. "I spent ten hours making it. It's absolutely perfect—for the perfect girl."

A tiny glimpse of affection moved into his eyes but it quickly disappeared. He continued to stand beside me, rigid but not uncomfortable. "It's nice to see you."

Did he really mean that? He was a smooth talker and could make anyone feel anything. He was aware of his talents. "It's nice to see you too."

"You look beautiful—like always."

That comment took it too far, and I didn't like it one bit. I knew this meeting would be difficult, but I didn't want to make it more painful than necessary. I did a good job hiding my reaction of disappointment. "Thank you. You do too."

"I look beautiful?" That cocky smile spread across his lips.

Was he seriously going to talk to me like nothing ever happened? The last time I saw him, he left me alone in his apartment. I fell to my knees and cried as he walked out of my life and never looked back. And that was after I gave him my journal, the most personal thing I possessed.

Maybe I wasn't as strong as I thought.

I managed to play along. "In so many words." I forced a smile that physically caused me pain then placed my hand on his shoulder. "Excuse me, I have more people to greet." I dropped my hand and walked around him. Once my face was hidden, I released the air from my lungs and finally felt my heart slow down.

Thank god I got that over with.

***

I sat beside Marie while Axel sat on the opposite side of her. Hawke was on Axel's other side. The tables were round, and I wasn't face-to-face with him, thankfully. But he was still too close for comfort.

"I guess you were right," Marie whispered to me.

"About what?" I drank my wine and realized I needed to pace myself. I already had three glasses.

"Hawke." She kept her voice low. "I saw you guys talking. It didn't seem weird at all."

"It wasn't." That was a huge lie, but I wouldn't admit the truth to her—not right now.

"I'm glad Axel and I were wrong. We were making a fuss over nothing."

"Like always." I clanked my glass against hers and took a long drink.

"Baby, let's dance." Axel leaned toward her and pressed kisses into her neck. It was clear he was a little buzzed—and very happy.

"There's no dance floor." She pushed him away gently.

"Right there." He pointed to the table near the cake. "Come on. I love this song."

She sighed like she was irritated, but there was an unmistakable smile on her lips.

Axel got up then pulled her to her feet. "I want to show you off to everyone."

"But everyone here has already seen me," she said as she let him pull her away.

"But now you're going to be my wife. I want everyone to know how lucky I am." He put his arm around her waist then guided her to the small area. Then he danced slowly with her, looking like a man very much in love. His eyes were glued to her, and he stared at her like he never wanted to stop. Marie was the only woman I'd ever seen him act like this with. She really was the one.

Hawke scooted over one seat so we were closer together.

Just leave me alone.

There was one empty chair between us but that wasn't enough space. I could smell his scent and I hated the way it made me feel. Memories kept rushing through my mind, the ones I tried to repress. "I'm really happy for them."

"I am too." I kept my eyes glued to them. It was better to watch my brother than to stare at Hawke's beautiful face. Those blue eyes had haunted me for a long time. It took me months to learn to sleep alone after he left. I wasn't weak or easy to break, but Hawke made a fool out of me and shattered me like colored glass.

"Marie makes him a better man. I've never seen that idiot so happy." He released a quiet chuckle.

"Marie is a better woman too." This conversation was too unnatural. How could we sit there and pretend we didn't remember the last time we saw each other? I said we were soul mates and he agreed. Or was he just saying that? I would never know because I refused to ask.

"How are you?" His eyes moved to my face.

I could feel them burn the side of my cheek. *I was doing much better before you walked through the door.* "Good. How are you?"

"I'm okay." He didn't elaborate further. "I heard your bakery is a success—congratulations."

He asked Axel about me? Or did Axel just say things? "Thank you. It's a dream come true." I didn't put much emotion into my words. It was too difficult to sound excited or remotely happy when he was this close to me. My stomach tightened in cramps, and my leg couldn't stop shaking under the table.

"I knew you would make it." His voice came out quiet, like he didn't want anyone else to hear.

I didn't know what to say to that. Our conversation wasn't natural like it used to be. When we first met, everything flowed like it was meant to. Now...everything was different. "It was hard work. But that just makes me appreciate it even more."

"That's a good way to look at it."

It would be rude if I didn't ask about his professional life, not when he asked about mine. "Where are you working now?"

"Well...that's a long story," he said with a sigh. "I worked at a broker for a year then I decided to open up my own investment company. It's been doing well."

That explained his apartment on Park Avenue. "Good. I'm glad things worked out."

"Thanks." He sipped his wine then turned his gaze on Marie and Axel.

Were we done now? I had enough chitchat for one night.

Matt walked through the door at the top of the stairs and searched the crowd. He must be looking for me.

Hawke turned his gaze back to me. "So, are you—"

"Matt, over here." *Enough of this torture.*

Matt found me then headed my way.

Hawke didn't repeat whatever he was trying to say.

Matt slid into the empty chair beside me. "You totally redid this place. It doesn't even look the same anymore." He wore jeans and a collared shirt. His hair was combed back, and his chest looked nice in his shirt.

I knew it was petty, but I hoped Hawke assumed Matt and I were together. I thought I was above that, but after seeing Hawke look so suave and completely indifferent to me, I was hurt. "It took some grunt work. You don't want to see the gunk underneath my fingernails."

"You better treat yourself to a mani." Matt winked at me.

"Actually, I should just rip them off because they're so dirty."

Matt cringed. "That would be creepy…no fingernails."

I chuckled. "It would be, huh?"

Matt seemed to notice Hawke staring at us. "Hi, I'm Matt." He extended his hand.

Hawke eyed it like he might not take it. But then he shook his hand. "Hawke. Nice to meet you."

"Are you a friend of Frankie's?" Matt asked.

"Something like that." Hawke took a drink of his wine and ended the conversation.

Matt turned back to me like that wasn't awkward. "Any cake left?"

"You really think I wouldn't save you a piece? Not after you arranged to let me use this rooftop?"

"Hey, we're even," he said quickly. "You helped me out with the banquet."

"In exchange for money," I said with a laugh. "That doesn't count as a favor."

"It does to me." Matt gave me an affectionate look before he saw Marie and Axel. "Is that the happy couple?"

"Yep."

"I recognize her from the bakery."

"Yeah, that's Marie. And that's my brother."

"I guess I see the similarities…" He squinted his eyes like he was trying to make out a small spot a hundred feet away.

"I don't think we look anything alike. But we have the same stubbornness."

"Was your mother a mule?" he teased.

"Actually, my dad was the stubborn one." I hadn't realized it until now.

"Well, I didn't mean to crash the party. I just got home so I thought I would check in."

"Thanks," I said. "I really appreciate all the strings you pulled."

"Anything for you, beautiful." He gave me one final look before he stood up and left the rooftop.

I didn't look at Hawke because I didn't care what his reaction was. Maybe he was jealous. Maybe he was angry.

Maybe he didn't give a damn.

"He seemed nice." Hawke sipped his wine again.

"He is."

"Friend of yours?" He spoke with indifference.

Was he trying to feel me out? Was he trying to figure out if Matt was my boyfriend? Or was I reading too much into it? If he cared about my love life, he would have made sure he was in it. "Yeah. He comes into the shop pretty often."

He didn't react, but his fingers loosened on the stem of the wineglass. "Does he own the building?"

"No, I don't think so. He just said he had connections."

"That was nice of him to help you."

"Well, I agreed to cater an event with six hundred people…and I'm still uncertain if I'm going to pull it off."

"You'll be fine." He said it without hesitation.

"Did you hear what I said?" I finally looked at him, and I wished I hadn't. His handsome face was hypnotizing. I assumed it would have no effect on me, but it did. "Six hundred. That's a shitload of people."

"But it's you," he said simply. "And you'll pull it off."

It irritated me that he spoke of me like he knew me. Two years was a long time, and I'd changed a lot. He had no right to assume I was the same person. I turned away again because I was disconcerted. The bitterness rose in my heart from being close to him, but then the attraction kindled whenever I looked at him. It was giving me whiplash.

"Do you like Manhattan?" Hawke just wouldn't leave me alone.

"It's everything I thought it would be." The traffic was a bitch and the bums were fearless, but the food was fantastic and the people were interesting.

"Give me more than that."

"I love it." I swore to Marie and Axel that I wouldn't have a problem with Hawke, but now I realized how premature my response was. But then again, I didn't expect him to talk to me. I thought we would say a quick and awkward hello and that would be the end of it. "Do you?"

"No complaints."

"Give me more than that."

That old smile stretched his lips. "I like the nighttime more than the daylight, because the city is just so beautiful from my window. I like ordering Chinese food at three in the morning on a Tuesday. I like finding new places to eat on the street I've been at for months. Is that enough?"

It was too much, actually. "Yes." I grabbed my drink and stood up. "I'm going to mingle. I'll see you around." I didn't give him a chance to say a word before I walked away and found a chair beside Yaya.

Yaya's eyes were glued to my brother. "So beautiful, aren't they?"

"They are." My body relaxed now that I was away from Hawke. "They'll have really cute kids."

"Awe…" She clutched her chest in emotion. "They'll be little angels."

"Not if they behave like Axel."

Yaya chuckled. "Axel has grown so much. Marie is so good for him. I'm glad he found her."

"And I'm glad she puts up with him."

"But he's so sweet to her now…it's so nice to see."

I drank my wine and nodded. Even though Hawke was on the other side of the rooftop, I could feel his stare. I didn't need to look to see if I was right. His sight burned into my skin and set it on fire.

"You doing okay?"

"More than okay. My brother is finally a grown up."

Yaya dropped her smile. "You know what I mean, dear."

"Everything is great with Hawke," I said without looking at her. "We're friendly."

"Good. I saw you two talking."

"Who says you can't go from lovers to friends?" *Everyone. Everyone said that.*

"That's great," she said. "I'm sure Marie was worried about it."

"She worries over a lot of things..."

***

The evening finally ended around one in the morning. People stumbled from the rooftop because of all the wine they had. A few people stayed behind to help clean up, and I was irritated when Hawke was one of them.

Ugh, just go away.

"Let's stay and help." Marie could barely stand on her feet. She kept wobbling, and sometime she would bend her ankle in a dangerous way because of her heels.

"Time for bed, baby." Axel wrapped his jacket around her then scooped her into his arms. He walked to me, carrying Marie like she was weightless. "I would offer to help but my lady is out of it."

"I wouldn't let you help anyway." I gave him a quick smile. "Go home and get some sleep."

"Thanks for everything, Frankie. Marie and I both appreciate it."

"Bye...Frankie." Marie's eyes were closed and her arms were around Axel's neck.

"I guess I'm not getting that blowjob after all." He cradled her closer to his chest and carried her from the rooftop.

I got back to work and cleaned up all the plates and utensils. My feet were dying in my heels so I kicked them off and immediately moaned when my feet were flat against the concrete.

The tablecloths were set in the corner, and the tables were broken down and placed against the wall. After people finished their tasks, they walked out and went home. Then I was stuck there with Hawke, unfortunately.

He stacked the chairs in the corner so the catering company could grab them in the morning. If I had to do this without him, it would have put me back two hours.

When he finished clearing the area, he came to my side. He didn't break a sweat over the work he did. It didn't seem like he did anything at all. "Is there anything else I can help with?"

"No. I got it." I put the cake back in the box and closed the lid. There wasn't much left but I knew Marie would want it tomorrow when she was hung over and miserable.

"That looks heavy."

"It's not." I scooped the cake into my arms. I got it up the stairs without him just fine. I could carry what was left downstairs.

"I really don't mind."

"And I really got it." I didn't want to snap at him but he was making it difficult.

"I just don't want you to get anything on your dress."

Like he really gave a damn. "Just get the door."

Instead of doing as I asked, he pulled it from my hands. "Still stubborn…"

His comment made me want to snap. But if I yelled at him, he would know I cared. And I couldn't let that happen. My natural instinct was to fight and snatch the cake away. But that would lead to a fight and the cake would probably be dropped. "Then I'll get the door…"

We walked down the stairs and headed out of the building. When we reached the sidewalk, I prepared to take the cake from him.

Instead, he waved down a cab.

"What are you doing?" I blurted.

"Are we supposed to walk?" He raised an eyebrow then got inside the car.

I growled under my breath then joined him in the back.

The driver asked for my address.

Hawke turned to me like he expected me to answer.

He was going to come all the way to my apartment? I kept my cool and said the address.

The cab drove through the city, and I kept my eyes glued out the window. I didn't want to look at him or make conversation. I just wanted to get away from him as fast as possible. At least I wouldn't see him for a few months after this. There were no other events that I knew about.

The cab driver stopped, and Hawke handed over the cash.

I got out of the car and grabbed the cake box the second Hawke was standing. "Thanks for the lift. Bye." I immediately turned away and walked inside my building. When I heard the sound of feet behind me on the tile of the lobby, I realized Hawke had followed me. "What the hell are you doing?"

"Walking you to your door." He had one hand in his pocket.

"Why?" I blurted.

"Well…you're a little drunk right now."

I felt the heat in my cheeks from the alcohol. "I can make it the rest of the way."

"I don't mind making sure you get there."

I wanted to punch him in the face. He was lucky I was holding the box. I knew I could sit there and argue, but that meant I'd have to interact with him longer. It would take less time to just let him get his way. "Whatever."

We took the elevator to my floor then stepped out. I quickly walked to my door and fished out my key. "Good night."

"Do you need help—"

"No." I walked inside. "See you around." I shut the door in his face and immediately locked it. I tossed the box on the kitchen counter then released the air I was holding in my lungs.

The night was such a disaster. I thought I could turn my cheek and pretend he didn't exist but I couldn't. He was everywhere, and the closer I was to him, the more I wanted to die.

His footsteps were finally heard as he walked down the hall. Like last time, I listened to them until they could no longer be heard. When the silence stretched, I was reminded of that horrific night.

And I died all over again.

Tuesday

Loneliness

Hawke

She hates me.

Francesca was pleasant enough. She said hello to me and greeted me with a smile. She made eye contact with me instead of pushing me away. When I spoke to her, she responded in a friendly way.

But it was all an act.

When she smiled, I could see the pull of her lips. She was exerting all her energy in trying to make her body do something it simply didn't want to do. It was like her entire being rejected my presence. When I spoke to her, she responded. But it was clear she didn't want to.

Whatever love she had for me was either gone or buried deep within. It was so far from the surface that it never saw the light of day. She didn't look at me the way she used to, like I was the only person who mattered.

It was like I didn't matter at all.

Could I blame her? I left her so suddenly and made the decision before I even spoke to her. I told her we were forever but I left anyway. She obviously didn't understand that I left for a good reason. How could I hurt someone I loved so much?

And still love.

No matter how much time had passed, that truth would never change. The short amount of time I spent with her was beautiful and pure. What we had was real. It was rare.

And I would never forget it.

But she had moved on.

It was better this way. If she despised me, then she didn't miss me. If she didn't care about me, that meant she had more important things to live for. She wasn't mourning me anymore. She had a new life—without me.

But I was still miserable.

***

"Yo." Axel walked into my office like he owned the place.

I was on the phone so I quickly ended the call. "I have a secretary out there for a reason."

"You know I have selective hearing." He drummed his fingers on my desk. "So, Chinese? Thai? Burgers?"

"I don't care." I didn't have much of an appetite.

"Chinese it is."

"You always pick Chinese."

"I know." He grabbed my jacket off the hanger and tossed it at me. "Let's go."

We headed to his favorite place just down the strip. The place was packed like always, so we had to wait ten minutes before we could get a table. It was in the center of the room, and everyone was talking like they were trying to be heard over a foghorn.

"I have to get the pot stickers," Axel said. "They're the best."

I glanced at the menu and decided to get my usual.

The waitress took our order and returned with our drinks. Then Axel droned on about the game from the other night. "I'm telling you, the Knicks are in the running this year."

"I hope they have a better season than the last one."

"They will," Axel said. "I'd put money on it."

I raised an eyebrow. "How much?"

"A dime."

I shook his hand. "You're on." A dime was a thousand dollars. I wasn't sure why we used gambling lingo when we didn't gamble that much. "The engagement party was fun."

"It was," he said. "But Marie didn't remember the end of it. When she woke up the next morning, she couldn't figure out how she got there."

"She had a lot of wine."

"You had a good time?"

Francesca came to my mind. "Yeah. You know me, I always love a good party."

Axel watched me with suspicious eyes. "I saw you and Frankie talking."

I was a master at hiding my emotions. Francesca was the only person who could see through my lies. "Yeah, it was nice."

"It was nice?" he asked incredulously. "It wasn't weird? Awkward?"

"No."

Axel rubbed his chin. "She said she couldn't care less about you. I guess she meant it."

Fuck, that hurt.

"Marie and I were worried about it, but I guess she was right. It was two years ago and both of you are over it."

"Yeah..." I took a drink of my iced tea.

"Frankie did a good job. When it comes to parties, she's a pro."

"Yeah. She always does the best when it comes to people she cares about." I remembered the way she slammed the door in my face. She couldn't get away from me fast enough. "That Matt guy is her boyfriend?" He was eye-fucking the shit out of her. And what was worse, he stared at her like he was in love with her. He hung on to every word she said and flirted like he was willing to do anything to get her.

It pissed me off.

"Matt?" Axel asked. "Who's that?"

"Some guy who let her use the rooftop."

Axel shook his head. "She doesn't have a boyfriend. That must be some guy she knows."

That made me feel better even though it shouldn't. What she did in her personal life was none of my business. I had no right to care or even ask questions about it. I left her, so I forfeited that right.

"Marie has some cute bridesmaids, huh?"

I didn't get a look at them. All I noticed was Francesca. She wore a champagne pink dress with matching shoes. Her bright green eyes constantly sparkled because of the overhead lights. Her long hair was done in big curls that reached down her chest. "Sure."

"But they are hideous compared to Marie. I got the good one."

I smiled for the first time. "Yeah, you did."

***

Two weeks had come and gone, and Francesca was the only thing on my mind. Over the past two years, I thought about her often. I always wondered what she was doing or if she was thinking about me. But now that I saw her, smelled her, I couldn't get her out of my head.

Every night I'd spent without her had been lonely. Girls came and went, their names never remembered. I went from several one-night stands to threesomes and foursomes. Nothing could satisfy what I'd lost.

I was unproductive at work because she was all I could think about. I browsed through spreadsheets but then recalled a memory of us together. I remembered the way she would lay on my chest while we slept together. I remembered how she would kiss me when we made love. I remembered the connection we felt, constantly binding us together.

I threw it all away.

Axel texted me around lunchtime. *Chinese again?*

I wasn't hungry. I hadn't been hungry in weeks. *I already have plans.*

Lame.

I didn't have any plans—until now.

***

I knew exactly where her bakery was. I'd walked past it countless times. Sometimes I walked by on purpose just to get a glimpse of her, but there were so many people in the shop that I couldn't see anything.

I was there the day The Muffin Girl opened, but Francesca didn't know I was there. I was in the building across the street, staying in a hotel room on the second floor. I watched through the window as she cut the ribbon. Axel and Yaya were there.

And I kept my distance.

When I arrived, I looked through the windows and saw an endless line of people. No matter what time of day I walked by, it was packed. They were either in love with Francesca or her baking.

Probably both.

Now that I was there, I didn't know what to do. Do I just stand there? Do I walk inside? Should I order something? Even if I did order something, I doubted Francesca would be at the register. She probably did all the bookkeeping or stayed in the kitchen making her creations.

I hadn't thought this through.

I walked inside and joined the crowd of people. The counters were lined with glass, and the baked goods were on display. There were pies, cookies, and muffins. Any time I looked at a muffin, all I could think about was her. I stood in line and scanned the place as I looked for that brown hair and those pretty green eyes. My gaze stopped when I noticed something on the wall.

In a glass frame was the pan I gave her. The engraving, *The Muffin Girl,* was still in the exact same spot. A date was written on a piece of paper next to it. I realized what it meant. It was the pan she used to make her first batch of muffins. She told me she would do that…but I couldn't believe she really did.

I felt like an asshole.

"Why are you here?" Her hostile voice burned my eardrums.

I turned to see her standing next to me, her black shirt caked with flour and sugar. Her hair was pulled back and revealed all of her exquisite features. She was thinner than she used to be, but she still had nice curves.

She put me on the spot, and I couldn't think of anything to say. I wasn't sure how she spotted me so easily. Maybe she had cameras. I didn't have a clue. "Just wanted to get something to eat. Or is that not okay?" I didn't mean to sound like a smartass but it slipped.

"There are a million other places to go in the city. Don't come here." Her eyes burned with fire, but not the good kind. When we used to fight, she said things she didn't mean. But now she meant every word.

"I didn't mean to upset you."

"Then don't come here. It's that simple." She turned to walk away.

"Francesca, wait."

She turned around, to my astonishment. "What?"

"Can I have a moment of your time?"

"No. You've already taken too much of my time as it is."

I knew what she really meant. "We're going to have to deal with each other. We may as well make it work."

"Deal with each other?" She had to raise her voice over the crowd. "No, we don't have to deal with each other. We just need to get through this wedding. Then you can disappear and so can I."

She really hated me. "We can keep yelling at each other in the middle of your shop or you can just sit down with me. What's it going to be?"

"I thought you came in here to get something to eat?" she challenged.

"I was going to until you denied me service."

Her eyes lit up again like she wanted to slap me. "Fine." She marched out the door and headed to the sidewalk. I was on her tail. "What do you want to talk about?"

I looked around. "Can we sit down somewhere? Or are we animals?"

"I don't have a lot of time." She crossed her arms over her chest. "I have plans for lunch."

With whom? "Just get some coffee with me. It won't take long."

She shifted her weight in irritation.

"There's a coffee shop right next door. And it's quiet."

"Then you should have gone there," she mumbled under her breath.

We ordered our drinks then sat at a table near the window. Light music played overhead, and the tables around us were vacant.

She looked at anything but me. Sometimes her gaze moved to the window, and sometimes she stared at the painting on the wall. When she exhausted those two things, she looked down into her coffee. Then she repeated the whole thing. Sitting this close to me was physically agonizing to her.

She wishes I were dead.

She checked the time on her phone and sighed. "You called this meeting. What do you want to talk about?"

"Us."

She sipped her coffee. "There's nothing to say, Hawke. Let's just play nice in front of Axel and Marie. No one has to know anything. We fooled everyone anyway."

"You didn't fool me."

Fear moved into her eyes but it quickly disappeared.

"I know this isn't ideal for you. This is difficult for both of us. But maybe if we talked about what happened, you wouldn't hate me so much."

She froze as the confusion spread across her face. "I don't hate you."

She doesn't?

"I'm indifferent to you."

My heart sank in my chest. *That was much worse.*

"I don't enjoy being around you but I don't mind it."

"It didn't seem that way when I spoke to you."

"Because you were talking to me," she snapped. "You wouldn't leave me alone."

I squeezed my coffee cup involuntarily.

"What did you expect to happen, Hawke? That we would just go back to being friends?"

"No." I wasn't sure what I expected.

"We weren't friends before, so why do we need to be friends now? Just say hi and bye and that's more than enough. We won't have any more problems if we keep it that way."

"But I don't want it to be that way."

She set her cup down. "What does that mean?"

I looked out the window before I turned back to her. "I just..." I didn't know what I wanted. "Axel and Marie are going to be in our lives forever. Instead of getting through the wedding, maybe we should learn to accept each other."

She raised an eyebrow. "Sounds a lot like being friends..."

"Well, why can't we be?"

She shook her head then bit her lip. "You're unbelievable."

"What?"

"You left me without looking back. You just walked out like you weren't leaving anything behind, and now you want to be friends? Am I the only one who thinks that's weird?"

"It's better than this, isn't it?"

"I…" She looked out the window then shut her mouth. Whatever she was going to say died in her throat. "Fine. Whatever."

"What does that mean?"

"Hawke, I couldn't care less about you. You're someone from the past, and I'm over what happened between us. I'm happy and have everything I've ever wanted. You mean so little to me that I can do this. If you really want to go out together and have a good time, fine. Let's do it."

I squeezed my coffee cup again as her words broke me. I knew I deserved them after the way I left her. How could I expect anything else? But that didn't minimize the pain.

She extended her hand across the table. "Friends?"

I eyed it but didn't take it. I thought about all the times those small hands were on me. They rested on my heart as she felt it beat. But now it was just a hand—a meaningless touch. My hand found hers and we shook. I thought I felt the distant spark, but I knew it was just on my end. She didn't feel anything. "Friends."

***

"Dude, can you believe that shot?" Axel asked as we entered his apartment building and walked up the stairs.

"It was just luck."

"No. It was all skill." He had the basketball tucked under his arm. He was sweaty from playing on the courts. I was too.

"How can it be skill if you were facing the opposite way of the hoop and throwing the ball over the back of your head?"

He shook his head. "Jealousy isn't a good color on you."

"And bragging isn't a good color on you."

Axel approached his door and unlocked it. "Keep it up, and Marie isn't going to let you eat her delicious cooking."

"Are you kidding me?" I asked. "She likes me more than you."

"No way. I give it to her good every night." Axel opened the door. "You couldn't handle my woman. She's crazy in the sack."

I walked in behind him. "I'll take your word for it."

Axel set the ball on the table near the door. "Baby, I'm home." He turned to me and winked. "I love saying that."

Marie came to the entryway wearing jeans and a t-shirt. "Axel, don't put the ball on the table. How many times do I have to tell you?"

He rolled his eyes. "I don't want it to get dirty."

She gave him an incredulous look. "You just played basketball with it. It's filthy."

"Fine, fine." Axel set the ball on the ground near his shoes. "No harm done."

"I'll have to scrub that table with Lysol…"

Axel approached her then gave her a quick kiss. "Missed you."

She melted right in front of my eyes. "Missed you too." She walked back into the living room.

Axel turned to me and winked. "That's the skill I was just talking about."

I tried not to laugh.

Axel and I walked into the living room and I stilled when I spotted Francesca sitting beside Marie on the couch. She wore jean shorts with a pink top. She hardly ever wore shorts because she was self-conscious about her legs. I didn't see why because they were absolutely gorgeous.

Wedding magazines were spread out around them, and they were cutting pictures out and laying them on the coffee table. There were pictures of flowers and wedding dresses. It looked like a kindergarten classroom.

When Francesca looked up, she noticed me. “Hey, Hawke.” She said it with a pleasant tone, and it didn’t sound like she was being fake.

“Hey, Francesca.” It didn’t feel right calling her that. I automatically wanted to call her by her nickname but I had no right to.

“You guys ready for dinner?” Marie asked. “I made spaghetti and meatballs.”

“Yes!” Axel clapped his hands in excitement. “Being married is awesome.”

“You aren’t married yet,” Francesca said sarcastically.

“Same difference,” Axel said. “We already live together.”

Marie gave him an affectionate smile before she got up. “I just need to set the table and everything will be ready.”

“Need help, baby?” Axel asked.

“Nope,” Marie said from the kitchen.

“You want a beer?” Axel asked.

“Sure,” I answered.

“Blue Moon or Dos Equis?”

"Doesn't matter."

"Coming right up." He walked into the kitchen and his voice carried into the living room. "Baby, you're looking fine today."

"Thanks," Marie said. It sounded like they were kissing because she said, "Not now, Axel. Your sister is in the other room."

"Like I give a damn," he snapped.

My beer was going to take a while.

Francesca put down the magazines. "How are you?" Her question seemed sincere. She looked me in the eye and everything.

"Good. You?"

"Great. Planning a wedding is fun. Now I know everything I want for mine."

The idea of her getting married made me sick. Acid built up in my stomach and it made me want to hurl. I did my best to hide my reaction and not vomit all over the hardwood floor. "Saves you time…"

She stood up and pulled her hair over one shoulder. "I'm glad you're here."

"You are?" I couldn't hide the surprise in my tone.

"Yeah." She slowly came closer to me and crossed her arms over her chest. The hostile look from earlier that week was gone. She didn't give me a look of fondness, but it wasn't full of hatred either. "I wanted to talk to you about last week. I thought about everything I said and…I apologize."

What was she apologizing for?

"I was really harsh and said a lot of mean things…that I didn't care about you. That's not true, Hawke. I'm sure you know that."

My heart fluttered.

"I guess seeing you again just threw me off balance. I thought I was going to be okay with it, but then I was around you and…everything came flooding back. I've had enough time to move on and come to terms with our break up but…I just wasn't ready for that. I was very ugly and mean… I'm sorry."

"You don't need to apologize. You had every right to be upset. You've never had a chance to tell me how you felt…"

"But it doesn't matter. That was in the past, and we've both moved on. There's no reason to hold on to hate when life is so short. While we weren't together very long, I really was happy. And I did love you."

My heart stopped beating.

"There's no reason why we can't be friends—real friends. If we really loved each other, we should be able to move on and be mature about it. I'm over you and you're over me. I guess it'll be weird in the beginning, but it'll go back to normal. If our best friends are married to each other, it'll make our lives easier to get along."

She was over me?

I knew she was but it hurt to hear her say it out loud. There was no possibility of misinterpretation. Right now, she was calm and understanding. She meant every word she said. She wasn't lying out of hurt or disappointment.

She was truly over me.

And she thought I was over her? Did she not understand why I left? I left because I loved her so much—not because I stopped. I stared at her emerald eyes as I thought of a response. Correcting her and telling her how I really felt wouldn't change anything. Even if she still loved me and wanted me, she couldn't have me. I was dangerous. I was a monster.

I would rip her to pieces.

This is all we could ever be. And wouldn't it be better to have her in my life once in a while than not to have her in it at all? Spending the last two years without her was torture. I'd never been so lonely in my life.

I would rather have some of her than none of her at all.

Tuesday

***

"Ugh, I hate playing Monopoly with her." Marie had twenty-five bucks and one railroad. She was pretty much done for. "She cheats. I swear."

Francesca coughed into her hand. "Sore loser…"

"Shut up." Marie grabbed a plastic house and threw it at her.

Francesca dodged and let the piece fly across the floor.

"Here." Axel gave her half his cash and his Boardwalk and Park Place. "Now you're back in the running, baby."

Marie smiled triumphantly.

I shook my head. "That's the lamest shit ever."

"So lame," Francesca added.

"What?" Axel asked innocently. "I'm not breaking any rules."

"Being a pussy is breaking every guy rule ever made," I said.

"I'm not a pussy," Axel said. "I'm just trying to help her."

"Fine." I grabbed all my cash and dropped it in Francesca's pile. Then I gave her all my properties, including three railroads. "I'd like to see you beat her now."

"Now that was some pussy shit right there," Axel said.

I shrugged. "I'm not breaking any rules, am I?"

Axel rolled his eyes then gave Marie everything else he had. "Kick her ass, baby."

"I'm on it," Marie said.

Francesca and Marie continued playing. After landing on each other's properties countless times and passing GO, Francesca dominated and ran Marie dry. Francesca threw all her money in the air. "I'm the chosen one."

I laughed until my stomach hurt.

Marie rolled her eyes and released an annoyed sigh. "Okay, Harry Potter."

"Only losers read Harry Potter," Axel said.

"You're just jealous you can't read at all," Francesca snapped.

"Francesca is banned from Monopoly," Marie said as she tossed everything in the box.

"That's not fair," Francesca said. "It's not my fault you suck."

"I don't suck," Marie said.

"Oh, yes, she does." Axel grinned like an idiot.

"Gross…" Francesca cringed.

Marie swatted his arm. "Don't say things like that in front of her."

"What?" Axel asked. "It's not like she doesn't know."

"But I don't think about it." Francesca stood up then grabbed her magazines. "I'm outta here." She grabbed her purse and checked her phone. She must have had a text message because she typed something quickly before she returned her phone to her purse.

It was ten in the evening. Who was she texting?

"I'll see you later." Francesca headed to the door.

"I'm going to head out too." I stood up. "Thank you for dinner, Marie."

"Any time," she said. "Get home safely."

Axel fist-bumped me. "Good game."

"Monopoly or basketball?"

"Both," he said with a shrug.

He lost both games so I didn't know what he was talking about. "See you later." I headed to the door and joined Francesca. I shut the door behind me and we headed down the hallway together.

"Sore losers, huh?" she asked.

"Yeah." It was the first time it felt the way it used to. Francesca and I were comfortable around each other. The chemistry was right like it'd always been. And that connection was still there—at least for me.

We exited the building and reached the sidewalk.

"Let me walk you home." It was late, and I wanted to make sure she got home okay. I would offer it to any girl, but she was special. I had to make sure she got there safely.

"No, it's okay," she said quickly. "I'll see you around." She gave a quick wave before she walked away.

I don't think so. I caught up to her. "I really don't mind. The city isn't safe at night."

"I can take care of myself, Hawke. You know that."

"It gives me peace of mind."

She stopped in her tracks and sighed. "I'm not going home, Hawke."

The meaning of her words hit me hard in the chest. It was like someone dropped an anvil on my head. The breath was knocked out of me. I felt cold—weak. Now I knew who she was texting this late at night. "I see…" I tried to hide the devastated look on my face but I had a feeling I couldn't. I knew she must be with other guys but…I tried not to think about it.

She avoided my gaze like she was uncomfortable. "Well...good night."

"Yeah." I wanted to offer to walk her anyway, but I didn't want to see the guy who opened the door. I didn't want to walk away knowing what was going to happen. Someone stabbed a knife into my chest and now I was bleeding everywhere.

Francesca turned around and headed up the sidewalk. She never glanced behind her to see if I was still watching her. The second I wasn't in her sight, she forgot about me.

Why did I have to be so fucked up? Why couldn't I just be normal? If I didn't have all these issues, she would still be mine. We might even be married by now. Maybe even have a kid on the way...

But I threw her away.

I lost her.

I fucked up.

I was fucked up.

CHAPTER FOUR

Hollow

Francesca

"Missed me?" Kyle took a drink from his beer on the nightstand. He was propped on the pillows with the sheets pulled up to his waist.

I shrugged. "Eh." I lay beside him with the sheets to my shoulder. My eyes were closed, and I was tired. I'd probably sleep there because I was too tired to go home.

"Eh?" Amusement was in his voice. "That's it?"

"I just saw you last week."

"A week is a long time, babe."

"Don't call me babe." I didn't like nicknames. They were too possessive.

"Grouchy... Did I not make you come?"

"No, you did."

"Then I don't know what your deal is." He took another drink. "I know you aren't on your period so that can't be it."

I kicked him playfully.

He lay back down beside me. "Something is off. I can feel it."

I didn't talk to Kyle about serious stuff. But I had no one else to talk to. Marie was the number one person I turned to but I couldn't tell her about this. It was a conflict of interest. "I'm just stressed out…"

"About?" He moved his hand to my hip.

"It's a long story."

"I've got all night." He squeezed my hip gently. "Now tell me."

I guess I had nothing to lose. "Remember that guy I told you about?"

"The one you were with two years ago?"

"Yeah," I said with a nod.

"What about him?"

"Well…he's back in my life."

His eyebrows scrunched in confusion.

I told him the entire story and how he's the best man in Axel's wedding. "Basically, I'm going to be around him all the time and there's nothing I can do about it."

"That sucks…"

"Yeah."

"What are you going to do?"

"I don't know. When I saw him for the first time, I was so angry with him. He kept talking to me, and I just wanted to be left alone. Then he came to my shop and that pissed me off even more. We sat down and talked, and I said a lot of mean things to him…that I didn't care if he lived or died."

Kyle cringed slightly. "Then what?"

"I realized how unfair I was being. Even though the break up was hard, he was good to me when we were together. He treated me right and made me really happy. And I loved him… I'll always love him."

Disappointment flashed in his eyes. "Why did you break up again?"

I didn't want to share Hawke's secrets even though Kyle didn't know him. "He had some personal issues. You know, he had a bad childhood and was never emotionally stable. He said he would hurt me so it was best if he just ended it."

"But he hurt you anyway."

"Yeah…"

"I don't know… I think that's pretty fucked up. He made you fall in love with him and then he just left. If he didn't see the relationship working from the very beginning, why did he waste your time?"

"Because he thought it would work."

"Sounds like a dick to me."

"He's not." I knew I shouldn't defend him. "He never tried to hurt me, not the way I tried hurting him when I said all those mean things. I knew he had issues so I shouldn't have gotten involved with him. I'm over him, and I've moved on. I don't want to hold a grudge and keep him at a distance. In the end, I do care about him. I don't want us to hate each other."

"You don't have to hate each other, but you don't have to hang out either."

"We don't hang out one-on-one. Our best friends are going to be married to each other. That makes it difficult."

"Man, that is complicated."

"See what I mean?" I asked. "It's less heartache for me to just let it go."

"It doesn't hurt to be around him?"

I shrugged. "I don't think about it. We had what we had, and it was beautiful…but it ended. I'll never regret what we had. But I'm not going to live in the past anymore."

He stared into my eyes without blinking. "If he wanted you back, would you go back to him?"

"No, that would never happen."

"Just answer the question."

"No, I wouldn't. I wouldn't go down that road again...not when I already know how it ends."

"So, I guess exes can be friends. Who knew?"

"It's not that uncommon. I know other people who do it. We'd had two years to get over it so it's different."

"So, you're okay with this?" He ran his fingers through my hair. "Because you seem pretty sad."

"I guess it makes me sad sometimes..."

"Why?"

How could I explain this in a way he would understand? My relationship with Hawke operated on a different wavelength. Axel and Marie were madly in love but even they wouldn't understand it. "Because I pictured a much different ending for both of us. Actually, we didn't have an ending. Even when we passed away and our bodies decayed, our souls traveled across the earth, tangled together."

Kyle had a blank look on his face like he didn't understand a word I said. "What does that mean, exactly?"

"We're soul mates."

His eyes narrowed in confusion. "You really believe that guy is your soul mate?" Skepticism was written all over his face, and he couldn't keep the condescension out of his voice.

Hawke and I couldn't work it out because he was too broken. His family had ripped him apart, severing his heart into pieces. Even the love I gave him couldn't fix all the wounds and holes. His mind was shattered, and he continued to believe he was a monster when he was nothing but a saint. But that didn't change the truth. That didn't change what we had—even if we could never be together. "Yes."

***

We went to several different florists in town and tried to decide which was cheaper. Marie was on a budget because she picked an expensive venue. Axel would let her do anything she wanted, but he had to put his foot down sometime.

"These hydrangeas look nice," she said.

"They could be a cute centerpiece arrangement."

"I don't know...they scream Easter."

"Just don't put any Easter eggs in the vases and you should be good."

She rolled her eyes and walked out of the shop. "That place was way too expensive."

"We could just make our own," I said. "You know, pick some flowers and put them in a pretty vase."

"Sounds like a lot of work..."

"Well, which do you want to save? Time or money?"

She released a sigh. "Weddings are stressful."

"You didn't know that already?" I asked like a smartass.

"I thought they were exaggerating."

"News flash," I said. "They weren't."

She walked into a hot dog shop. "I need something greasy and disgusting."

"Same here."

We ordered two hot dogs then sat down and stuffed our faces.

"How's it going with Kyle?"

"What do you mean?"

"It's a simple question," she said. "How's it going?"

"You know he's nothing serious. He's just a booty call."

"Well, he's been a booty call for a few months now," she said. "Nothing else is going on?"

"Nope."

"You know, that's how Axel and I started off. Now we're getting married."

Kyle wasn't my future husband. "It works for some people, not all."

"Can I at least meet him?"

"Why?" I asked. "He's not my boyfriend."

"How often do you see him?"

I shrugged. "It depends."

"On?"

"How stressed I am. Maybe one or two times a week."

"That's pretty often," she said. "What's he like?"

"He's nice," I said. "Perfect body. Pretty face. You know my type."

"If he's your type, why don't you give him a chance?"

"What makes you think he even wants a chance?" This felt like an interrogation.

"Who are you kidding, Frankie?" she asked. "Every guy you're with falls in love with you."

"So not true."

She put down her hot dog. "You really want to play this game?" She started to count with her fingers. "Cameron, John, Jason—"

"Okay, I get your point."

She smiled victoriously. "He's into you. I'm sure he is."

"Well, I'm not into him."

She picked at her fries. "You're never into anybody. The only person you've ever really liked is Hawke."

"Well, I'm picky. I'll find someone else eventually."

"You aren't going to find another Hawke," she said. "Let me save you some time."

"Believe me, he's not the kind of guy I'm looking for." When I settled down, it would be with a good guy that wasn't a flight risk. I couldn't carry someone's baggage anymore, not when it hurt me so much.

"It's weird seeing you guys hang out. It's like nothing ever happened."

"Two years is a long time, Marie. People move on. It's a part of life."

"I guess…but it's still weird." She finished her hot dog. "Man, that was good."

"I don't want to know what's in it, but it's delicious."

She wiped her mouth with a napkin then crumbled it into a ball. "Let's go on a double date?"

"What?" I blurted. "Hawke and I are never getting back together."

Her eyes narrowed on my face. "I meant Kyle."

"Oh…" That was stupid. "No. I don't see it going anywhere with him."

"Well, go on a date with him and give it a shot."

"If I liked him, I would know." *Damn, she was acting like my mom right now.*

"If you've been sleeping with him this long, he has potential."

"He's really good in bed," I said. "That's all I care about."

"How did you meet him anyway?"

"The gym."

"Romantic..."

I rolled my eyes. "I walked into the guys' changing room on accident and he was there...naked." My cheeks reddened at the memory.

Marie's jaw dropped. "Why didn't you tell me this story?"

"Because it's embarrassing." My face burned from the heat.

"Then what happened?" She leaned forward in her seat with wide eyes.

"I did something super stupid."

"What?" She slammed her hands down impatiently.

"I...I asked him out."

She covered her face and laughed until tears came out of her eyes. "Oh my god, Frankie."

I chuckled because it was kind of funny. "I wasn't thinking. I saw him...and his package...and I just went for it."

She wiped the tears from her eyes. "That's the most hilarious story I've ever heard. I'm telling it at your wedding."

My laughter immediately stopped. "Well, that would be awkward since I'm not going to marry this guy."

"Give him a chance, Frankie. Geez, you're uptight."

"I am not!"

"Look, it's my job to say things you don't want to hear. So here it goes; you haven't even tried to have a meaningful relationship since Hawke. You just look for quick fixes with hunky guys. That would be fine, but I know you aren't happy."

"Says who?"

"I can just tell," Marie said. "I'm not telling you to pledge forever with the next guy in your bed, but at least have an open mind to it."

I knew she was right even though I wouldn't admit it.

"The four of us should do something together. I promise I won't embarrass you."

"That's sad you have to make that promise." I glared at her as I spoke.

"Hey, you embarrass me all the time in front of Axel."

"He's my brother—it's different."

"Whatever." She threw a fry at me.

I threw the fry back at her. "Whatever to you."

She sipped her lemonade then a grin stretched on her lips. "So…how big is his package?"

"Oh my god. I'm going to pretend you didn't ask that."

"What?" she asked. "I'm just curious."

"It's very nice. That's all I'm going to say."

"Nicer than Hawke's?"

My smile immediately fell at the mention of Hawke. I didn't compare other guys to him. In fact, I refused to let myself think about him at all. Those memories were sacred to me. The nights we spent together were full of passion and love, nothing like what I had now. Nothing compared to that, and I refused to tarnish those memories with trash.

***

I was in the cake kitchen when there was a knock on the glass front doors. I put down my decorating tools and washed the buttercream frosting from my hands before I headed to the front.

It was 5:30 a.m. and the sun hadn't even risen. It was still dark outside, and the lights from the city glowed like everything was on fire. When I reached the door, a man was standing near the glass. He wore running shorts and a t-shirt. It was difficult to distinguish his features, but he had the body of a Roman soldier.

"We're closed." I pointed to the sign hanging in the window.

He stepped back slightly so his face was visible. "It's me." Hawke smiled as his headphones hung around his neck. The wire moved into his pocket where his phone lay.

"Oh." I didn't realize it was him. I unlocked the door and opened it. "Sorry, it's dark out there."

"It's okay." He walked inside. "I know I'm tall, dark, and dangerous." A teasing smile was on his lips.

I missed that smile. "And terrifying. If I saw you down a dark alley, I'd run."

"You should run toward me," he said. "Because I can protect you from truly terrifying things." His eyes honed in on my face before he turned and examined the bakery. "It's quiet."

"It's nice, isn't it?" I crossed my arms over my chest and stared at the empty chairs in the lobby. "But don't get used to it. In half an hour, it'll sound like the most popular club in town."

He chuckled. "Most businesses would kill to have your popularity."

"And I'm not complaining," I said quickly. "My ears are."

He examined the lobby and the different pictures on the wall. There was a collage of photos of me and my parents, Yaya, Axel, and one of Hawke. He and I were sitting in my kitchen, and we had cupcake batter all over our faces. Marie took the picture when we least expected it, so it was candid.

Hawke stared at it for nearly two minutes.

It was an awkward situation. I could have thrown away every memory I had with Hawke and started over, but I didn't want to forget what we had. To me, he wasn't just another boyfriend.

He was the one.

"I can take it down if it bothers you..."

He slowly turned to me, a distant look in his eyes. "It doesn't bother me at all."

"I mean...you named this place. You're important in its history."

He nodded slightly. "And that's a huge honor...The Muffin Girl."

I was glad he wasn't mad. "Well..." I trailed off because I couldn't think of anything else to say.

He stepped away from the pictures and examined the rest of the bakery. "It has an unusual architecture...but it gives it character."

"I wanted it to be unique."

"You accomplished that." He approached the counter and looked through the glass. "Can I get a tour?"

"Sure. It's nothing fancy."

"I'll be the judge of that."

I showed him the bread and pastry kitchen, where employees were already preparing for the day. Coffee was brewing and the aroma filled the kitchen. I showed him the walk-in freezer then led him to the cake kitchen.

"This is where you work?"

"Yep. I do all the wedding cakes." I stopped in front of the wall where I pinned all my pictures of previous cakes.

He stood beside me and looked at them. "Wow…you've done amazing work."

"Thanks…" I received compliments all the time, but it meant a lot coming from him.

"I like this one." He pointed to the image of a motorcycle club theme. There were toy motorcycles with a man and a woman. Leather vests with fringe covered their bodies.

I chuckled. "They fell in love in a bike gang."

"Now that's romantic…" His voice was full of sarcasm but he was smiling. "And badass."

"They're really sweet people," I said. "The nicest people I've ever met."

"Is this one for a wedding?" He pointed to the mermaid theme cake.

"No, it was for a birthday party."

"A three-tier cake for a birthday party?" he asked incredulously.

"You know how it goes…they're stupid rich."

I turned to him and finally realized I'd never asked why he was there. "So…what brings you here?" I didn't want to sound rude but I was curious.

"I was jogging by and thought I'd pay a visit."

"You jog this early in the morning?"

"When else am I going to do it?" he asked. "I box after work so I don't have time for cardio."

He boxed? "That makes sense."

"I live nearby—right on Park Avenue."

"I know," I blurted.

He turned to me with a raised eyebrow. "You know?"

"Because of the invitations," I said quickly. I didn't want him to think I was some kind of stalker.

He nodded in understanding. "I see."

"I'm happy that you're doing so well."

That old look came into his eyes, one that was full of affection and something else. "Thank you. I'm happy for you too. Every time I walk by this bakery, it puts me in a good mood."

"Because you want a muffin?" I teased.

"You caught me."

I opened a container and grabbed a new creation. "It's orange and cranberry."

"Ooh…" He grabbed it from my hand and took a bite. He chewed it slowly and wiped the crumbs from his lips. "Damn, that's good."

"Thanks." My cheeks reddened slightly.

"How are you not fat?" He finished it then sucked the stickiness from his fingers.

It reminded me of something I shouldn't think about. "I learned self-control a long time ago."

"Impressive." He wiped his hands on his running shorts. "Now that you showed me around your place, you want to see mine?"

"Your office?" I hadn't thought about it. I didn't even know where it was.

"I meant my apartment. It's just a few blocks over."

"Oh…" Being alone with him in his apartment made my hair stand on end but I wasn't sure why. It was clear he was over me and never wanted to be together again. The thought shouldn't have crossed my mind at all. "Sure. I guess."

"Unless you have another creation to make?"

I was just messing around in the kitchen. "No. I'm free."

"Cool." He pulled his headphones off and shoved them into his pocket. "It has a view of the park. It's pretty cool during the daytime. But it's really cool in the evenings."

"I'm sure it is."

***

We entered his building and approached the lobby. The sun was finally rising over the city and everyone was getting ready for work. Some people popped out of the elevator and speed-walked to their destination. Others filed down the stairs with a purpose.

"You have a nice building."

"Thanks." He got into the elevator then held the door open for me. Then he hit the button to the top floor.

The steel doors closed, and our reflections were visible in the pristine walls. The elevator rose slowly, and light music played overhead. Being alone with him in a confined space was a little uncomfortable. Seeing him in a t-shirt and shorts reminded me how nice his body was. I missed the way his chest felt against mine. When it was covered in sweat and warm, it chased the cold away.

The door opened, and we headed down the hallway. "It's nice being able to leave work whenever you want, huh?"

"It's definitely better than The Grind."

He chuckled. "I can imagine."

We rounded the corner and saw a woman leaning against the wall. She wore a black dress and heels. Her hair was a little messy and her make up was smeared. She looked exhausted like she had a long night.

Hawke suddenly slowed down his pace like her presence caught him off guard. His shoulders noticeably stiffened like he was uncomfortable.

Within a split second, I put the pieces together.

And I felt sick.

"There you are." The girl approached his door with a flustered look. "I've been calling you all morning." She crossed her arms over her chest then shot me a glare.

"What do you want?" Hawke asked coldly.

"I left my wallet."

Oh my god, kill me now.

Hawke didn't look at me. "Oh…I'll get it for you."

"It's on the night stand."

My heart shattered into a million pieces. I wanted to run away and hide. I didn't want to be there.

"Right…" Hawke got the door unlocked and stepped inside.

The woman stared at me like I was a piece of gum on the bottom of her shoe.

I kept my arms across my chest and hid the devastation on my face. Two years had come and gone, but seeing him with another woman hurt me as much as it would have the day he walked out. I knew he was with other people but to see it right in front of my face was…heartbreaking.

Hawke appeared with the wallet. "Here." He shoved it into her arms. It was clear he was just as uncomfortable as I was.

"Call me later." She turned on her heel and walked away.

Hawke didn't make eye contact with me. He remained rigid like he didn't know what to do. Silence stretched between us, and neither one of us knew what to say. He finally stepped into his apartment. "This is it…"

I entered behind him and immediately walked to the center of the room with my back turned to him so he wouldn't see my face. I tried to seem indifferent but I knew I was failing. No matter how much time had passed, seeing him with someone else was agonizing. "It's nice." I kept my voice steady.

His apartment contained floor-to-ceiling windows and had a breathtaking view of the park. Leather sofas were in the living room along with a fancy rug. A large TV took up the wall, and his kitchen was designed with granite countertops and stainless steel. "I'm jealous."

Hawke placed his headphones on the counter then walked further into the room. "I got a good deal on it. I knew the seller."

And I had a feeling I knew how.

"You want to see my office?"

I didn't mind seeing anything except his bedroom. All I would think about was all the girls who hit his sheets. There must have been hundreds by this point in time. I wanted to keep hiding my face but I was running out of time. "Sure."

He showed me the large room with an expansive desk. He had white bookshelves with textbooks as his primary décor. A large window was behind the desk and had another view of the park. "The view is distracting so I don't get much work done."

"I can imagine."

He showed me his bathroom next and the spare bedroom. But he never took me in his bedroom.

Thank god.

The sheets were probably still in disarray from the woman who spent the night with him. Strands of her hair were probably on the pillow. And it probably smelled of sex. "Well, I should get back to work." I headed back to the door and tried not to run.

"Yeah, I need to shower."

Had he not showered since that woman? Gross. "Well, I'll see you around." I didn't turn around and look at him. I wanted to haul ass and get the hell away from him as quickly as possible. That woman shouldn't bother me but she did. I needed to save face but I couldn't do that if he was looking at me.

"Francesca." His voice took a different tone, apologetic.

I didn't know what I was thinking, but I turned around. "Hmm?" I made eye contact with him but just for a brief second. His face looked torn, like he didn't want to say whatever he was about to say.

"I…" He struggled to find the words.

I knew he was trying to make an excuse for that girl. Her presence wasn't malicious, and he had no idea she was going to be there. He wanted to apologize for something he shouldn't apologize for.

"It's okay, Hawke." I turned away because I was going to get teary-eyed if I stayed any longer.

He lowered his gaze and looked at the ground. "I'm sorry…"

I kept walking. My heart ached and my feet carried me as quickly as possible. Old wounds were ripped apart. I had done the same thing to him the other night when I said I wasn't going home. He looked just as upset as I did now. But he didn't have to see Kyle in the flesh. "There's nothing to be sorry about."

***

When I walked into the weight room at the gym, Kyle was sitting on the bench. His dumbbells rested on his thighs and he stared at himself in the mirror.

"Yo." I walked up behind him wearing my work out gear.

He grinned when he saw me. "Look who it is." He whistled as he stared at me in my spandex. "You look like catwoman when you wear those." He wiggled his eyebrows in a sleazy way.

I ignored his cheesy line. "You wanna go on a date with me?"

He stilled like he wasn't sure if he heard me right. "You're asking me out?"

"Don't make a big deal out of it. My best friend wants to go on a double date. You down or what?" I leaned against the bench and put one hand on my hip.

"You're one smooth talker." His voice was full of sarcasm. "But since you're cute, I'll go out with you."

"Thanks. Saturday is good?"

"Any day is good." He winked at me.

"Would you stop doing that?"

"What?" he asked innocently.

"All the winking and eye-wiggling. You're hot without the bullshit."

"I think it turns you on but you don't want to admit it." He gave me a dramatic wink.

"I can call off the date, you know?"

"I'll pick you up anyway." He picked up one dumbbell and started doing curls. He stared at me the entire time he did it. "In the mood?"

I rolled my eyes. "I've never met someone so full of himself."

"Because a lot of people want to be full of me." He winked again.

I growled then stormed off.

"Hey, get back here." He put down the weights. "I was kidding."

I came back but I was on my guard.

He turned serious. "Why do you want to go on a date all of a sudden? You made it clear you were looking for some meaningless fling."

"Marie keeps pestering me about it, and…" I didn't want to go into details.

"Does this have something to do with Hawke?" He didn't seem irritated, not like he usually was.

"I saw him yesterday and some bimbo forgot her wallet at his apartment…it was awkward."

"What did you expect him to do?" Kyle asked. "He's single, right?"

"He can do whatever he wants." That didn't mean it didn't hurt.

"Because you've been fucking around with me for months."

I grew irritated. "I'm not mad at him, and he doesn't owe me a damn thing. But it still hurts to see him with someone else, whether it's meaningless or not." I shook my head. "Why did I expect you to understand?"

"Whoa…hold on." He raised both hands in surrender. "I'm not judging you. I'm just curious."

"Have you ever been in love, Kyle?"

He stared at me for a long time before he answered. "No."

"Then you wouldn't understand."

"You're wrong about that...but whatever." He racked his weights then approached me. "If you don't want to have a relationship with me, why are you asking me out?"

"Because Marie ordered me to, and seeing Hawke...just reminded me that I need to move on with my life. How will I find someone if I never give anyone a chance?"

He nodded. "I like Marie."

"She's bossy and pushy."

"I like bossy and pushy."

"She's marrying my brother," I snapped. "She's off limits."

He chuckled. "Not what I meant, sweetheart. I like that she tells you the shit you don't want to hear—that's all."

"So, you'll do the double date thing with me?"

"It doesn't sound like you even want to do it."

"Because I don't." I was always honest with the men in my life. I never wanted to lead them on or give them the wrong idea.

He shook his head. "So much for giving someone a chance."

"You already know how I am. We both know this isn't going to go anywhere. But maybe this can be a baby step for me."

"So it works out for everyone…" His voice was full of sarcasm but he was slightly amused.

"I'm sorry," I said. "You don't have to go. I know you aren't looking for something serious either."

"I wouldn't mind doing something outside of sex," he said. "You're really cool. I thought so the moment you walked into the locker room and stared at my junk like it was the biggest piece of candy you've ever seen."

I rolled my eyes and blushed at the same time. "Not my finest hour…"

"I thought it was sexy." He leaned toward me. "Can I wink now?"

I rolled my eyes again. "Fine. Just don't do it at dinner."

***

Kyle was at my door right on time. He wore a collared shirt and slacks, much fancier than his usual attire. He took in my dress, and his eyes appreciated the sight. "I like that."

"Thanks. You look nice too."

"I know." He had a smug grin on his face.

I walked out and shut the door behind me before he could wink or wiggle his eyebrows. "Marie and Axel are cool. You'll like them."

"I like everyone." He put his arm around my waist.

He didn't usually touch me outside the apartment, but I let the affection linger. "How was your day?"

"I woke up and played video games all day."

"At least you relaxed."

"Relaxed?" he asked with a laugh. "I was shooting people's heads off and throwing grenades. I wouldn't classify it as relaxing."

"Then how would you classify it?"

"Stimulating."

We headed down the sidewalk then reached the restaurant.

"So, Axel is your brother, right?" he asked.

"Yeah." I walked inside and searched the tables.

"So…what do I do?"

"What do you mean?" I spotted them at a table in the corner but I turned to Kyle before we walked over.

"He's your brother, so does that make this date serious? You're introducing me to your family."

"Oh." *Now I understood*. "No, it's not like that. Axel and I are friends as well as siblings. He won't read too much into it."

"You're sure?" he asked. "He's not a psychotic overprotective brother?"

"Nope. Now let's go because I'm starving."

We approached the table, and Marie immediately stared Kyle up and down. Then she gave me a quick smile that said everything her lips couldn't speak.

I ignored her meaning. "Hey. This is Kyle."

"It's a pleasure to meet you." He shook hands with Axel first.

"Likewise," Axel said politely. He sized him up with his eyes, looking at his clothes and his shiny watch.

"I'm so excited to meet you." Instead of shaking his hand, Marie hugged him like they were long lost friends. "I've been looking forward to this all night."

"Oh..." Kyle's lips stretched into a grin. "I'm glad someone's excited. Whenever Frankie sees me, she just seems bored."

"She's just rough around the edges." Marie laughed it off but she shot me a glare.

Kyle pulled out the chair for me before he sat down.

When I froze at his gesture, I realized it'd been a really long time since I went on a date. I almost didn't know how to act. It was like I forgot how to date. "Thanks..." I lowered myself into the chair.

Axel stared at Kyle without bothering to be discreet about it.

Marie picked up her menu then turned it so the guys couldn't see us leaning over the table and talking. "Damn, he's really cute."

"I know." There wasn't any doubt about that. When I saw him at the gym, I was immediately smitten.

"You did a great job finding him. He has really pretty eyes."

Axel cleared his throat. "I have really pretty eyes too."

Marie's face reddened in embarrassment then she lowered her menu like nothing happened.

Kyle kept grinning like an idiot.

I looked at my menu and tried to act like this wasn't incredibly awkward. "What are you getting?"

Kyle moved his hand to my thigh. "Not sure. What about you?"

I tensed when he showed me affection in public. It rubbed me the wrong way, and I couldn't explain why. We were on a date so that's what should happen but...something was off.

Axel glanced at Kyle's hand then sipped his water.

"Probably the spaghetti." I set the menu down.

"Maybe we can share a strand of pasta like that Disney movie." He squeezed my thigh under the table.

"Maybe…" *I needed wine.*

"So, Kyle." Axel set his water aside. "What do you do for a living?"

Kyle answered the question in stride. "I run a—"

"Do not interrogate him." I shot Axel a deadly look. "We're here to have fun, not examine his resume."

Axel glared at me. "I'm getting to know your boyfriend."

"He's not my boyfriend." I didn't mean to sound so harsh but it just came out.

"Ouch." Kyle squeezed my thigh again like he was teasing me.

The waitress came and took our order, thankfully. It was nice to have something to do instead of just stare awkwardly at each other. But once she was gone, the gloom returned.

"As you were saying," Axel said. "Before my bratty sister interrupted you."

"She is a brat," Kyle said with a laugh.

"I'll second that," Marie said with a raised hand.

I rolled my eyes in irritation.

"I own a law firm in Manhattan. It's on Sixth and Broadway." Kyle took a drink of his wine.

Axel obviously didn't expect that judging the surprised look on his face. "You own a firm?"

"Yes." Kyle remained humble about it.

"How old are you, if you don't mind me asking?" Axel asked.

I narrowed my eyes on him. "Interrogation..."

"Baby, it's fine," Kyle said.

I didn't like to be called that outside of the bedroom but I didn't correct him.

"I'm thirty," Kyle said. "My father was a lawyer, and he passed away a few years ago. His firm went to me and now I run it."

"Oh..." Axel nodded in understanding. "I'm sorry for your loss."

"He and I were really close so it was hard," Kyle said. "But working in his office makes it feel like he's still there sometimes..." His voice trailed away.

My heart ached for him so I rested my hand on his.

When he felt the affection, he smiled and squeezed my fingers.

Marie grinned as she watched our interaction. “So, this has been going on for a long time.” She leaned forward on the edge of her seat.

Kyle turned to me. “You talk about me, huh?” He wiggled his eyebrows. “I knew you were into me.”

“I tell her everything,” I said. “She’s my best friend.”

“How long?” Axel asked, his protective side coming out.

“About six months or so,” Kyle answered.

I wish he hadn’t said that.

“Six months?” Axel asked. “That’s a long time…” He turned to me with a disapproving look. “Why am I only meeting him now?”

“Because we aren’t serious,” I said. “Can we stop talking about Kyle and I now and just have fun?”

“You’re introducing me to your boyfriend,” Axel said. “I want to know more about him. It’s my job.”

I grabbed a piece of bread from the basket and threw it at him. It hit him right in the nose.

Marie covered her mouth and tried not to laugh.

“Don’t be annoying,” I said. “Now, let’s talk about something else.”

Axel wiped the crumbs off his face and pressed his lips tightly together. It was clear he was irritated but held his tongue because of Kyle.

"I heard you guys are getting married," Kyle said. "Congratulations."

"Thank you," Marie said. "We're really thrilled about it." She leaned toward Axel and kissed his cheek.

Axel softened up at her affection. "Yeah, I'm definitely marrying up. Marie has perfect legs and an even more perfect ass."

I ignored that last comment.

"Have you been to Frankie's shop?" Marie asked.

"I go in there pretty often," Kyle said. "Sometimes to see her…and sometimes for her treats." He gave me a flirtatious look.

I pressed my lips to his ear. "Don't be gross."

He moved his lips to my ear. "I'm being myself. I don't give a damn if people dislike me for it." Then he pulled away.

"How did you two meet?" Axel asked.

Marie immediately laughed then tried to hold it back. It came out as a quick snort that we all noticed.

Axel eyed her. "This should be good…"

Kyle turned to me and silently asked what I wanted to say.

"We met at the gym." I didn't elaborate further.

"You mean the locker room," Marie teased.

I kicked her under the table.

"The locker room?" Axel asked.

Axel deserved the perfect woman to spend his life with, and Marie was that person. But sometimes it was a pain in the ass that my best friend was with my brother. I couldn't just say anything around him. "I walked into the men's locker room on accident…and I bumped into Kyle."

"On accident my ass," Marie jabbed.

Kyle put his arm over the back of my chair. "I don't think it was an accident either."

"Well, it was," I said defensively.

"And then?" Axel raised an eyebrow.

Kyle took over. "Let's just say she liked what she saw and asked me out on the spot."

I didn't know why I bothered hiding things from Axel. Since Marie was my best friend, it was nearly impossible.

Marie laughed. "Best story ever."

"I really did go in the wrong room on accident." I didn't want people to think I was some weird creeper who didn't understand boundaries.

"How is that possible?" Axel asked. "You know how to read, and you've been in the locker room before."

"It was my first day at the gym, and I was a little lost," I said.

"But I helped her find her way." Kyle was enjoying this more than he should.

Marie clapped her hands in excitement. "I'm telling that story at your wedding."

I kicked her under the table.

"Ouch," she said under her breath.

"You tell people we're getting married?" Kyle asked.

"Hell no," I blurted. "Marie just wants me to get married so bad she thinks every guy I meet is my future husband."

"I wouldn't mind marrying you," Kyle said. "You definitely keep me entertained." His fingers rubbed the back of my neck.

Marie looked like her greatest dream had just come true.

Axel watched Kyle closely until the food came.

When the plates were set in front of us, I was grateful we had something to do other than talk. Tonight was supposed to be a fun and carefree double date, but it turned into a wedding planning session.

"How do you like yours?" Kyle asked.

"It's good. Yours?"

He stabbed his fork into one of my meatballs then ate it. "Delicious."

I took a piece of his chicken and ate it. "Hmm…pretty good."

"How about we split our food half and half?" Kyle grabbed his plate and prepared to switch them.

I was immediately taken back to my first date with Hawke. The night had gone in a similar way, and we swapped our food like we'd been together for years. Seeing Kyle do something so similar just made me nauseous. "No, I'm okay." I pulled my plate back toward me and kept my eyes downcast.

Marie gave me a questioning look.

I ignored her and kept eating.

Tuesday

Wrong Turn

Hawke

I was such a shithead.

Why the hell did Renee have to forget her wallet? Why did she have to stand by my door with day-old make up on her face and messy hair? It was so obvious she spent the night.

I didn't want Francesca to see that.

She was seeing some guy and that severed my heart into infinite pieces. Knowing she was with someone else…kissed someone else…made me sick. I had no right to feel that way. After all, I ended our relationship. I turned my back on her and left without a backward glance. We were madly in love and happy…but I threw it away.

I had no right to be upset about it.

The thing that hurt the most was her reaction. Francesca didn't care in the least. She walked into my apartment like nothing happened. Renee's presence didn't affect her at all. She examined my apartment and furniture and complimented the way it looked.

She really was over me.

I didn't want her to be hurt over Renee. I wasn't a sadist. But I would be lying if I said I didn't want her to care.

Because I cared.

***

After my evening boxing lesson, I met Axel for a drink. We got together throughout the week, playing basketball or drinking our problems away. I thought our relationship might change when he got engaged, and I was surprised it hadn't. He didn't spend all his time with Marie, which was unexpected.

If I had a fiancée, I'd be with her all the time.

"How was your workout?" Axel asked as he drank his beer.

"Fine." I was angrier than usual, so I was grateful I had a punching bag to take it out on. My coach asked if there was something on my mind, but I lied and said everything was just fine.

Axel started talking about the office and the portfolio he was working on. "Dude, you're smart for opening your business. I hate having a boss."

"Then do it."

"It's not so easy..." He shook his head and looked around the bar. "I wish I'd inherited something from my dad but I didn't get anything except his old tools and Chevy."

What? Was I missing something? "Sorry?"

"Oh." He shook his head like he realized his mistake. "Francesca's boyfriend inherited a law firm. Now he runs it and pretty much does whatever the hell he wants. He even..." Axel continued talking but his words came out as a blur.

She had a boyfriend?

So, that guy she was seeing wasn't casual?

She actually had a relationship with him?

Did she love him?

Did they talk about marriage?

"I know jealousy is an ugly color, but I'm totally jealous," Axel continued. "I'm all about working hard for things that you want but it would be nice to just be handed something for once, you know."

I didn't listen to a word he said. Someone stabbed a kitchen knife through my chest, and I was bleeding all over the place. This shouldn't bother me. I knew this would happen eventually. She was too damn perfect not to be chased after. I knew she would see other guys and eventually fall in love again but...I guess I didn't prepare myself for reality. "He's a lawyer?"

"Yeah," Axel answered. "I don't know what kind. I didn't get a chance to ask because Frankie didn't want me to 'interrogate' him." He rolled his eyes. "She's a drama queen, I swear."

"So, do you like him?" I hoped he was a loser that Axel hated. Then they would break up.

God, I'm such an asshole.

"Actually, I do." He shrugged. "It caught me by surprise."

Dammit.

"He's not uptight and serious. He jokes around a lot, particularly with Frankie. He doesn't let her get away with anything, and he calls her out on her shit. And he didn't seem threatened by me at all. It's like he couldn't care less about my opinion."

"Isn't that a bad thing?"

"No. I like a guy that doesn't care what anyone thinks. Less drama that way."

This was getting worse.

"And he's really successful and good-looking. I'm not going to complain when I know there are so many worse choices out there." He watched the TV in the corner of the bar.

I felt dead inside. I stared at the surface of the table and ran my fingers through my hair.

Axel turned back to me. "You okay, man?"

"Yeah, I'm fine." I didn't sound convincing whatsoever.

Axel continued to eye me. "I thought you were okay with Frankie? Whenever you guys are together, it's like you're friends again."

No, we just have a connection again. "I just have a headache."

Axel wasn't buying it. "Do you still have a thing for her?"

I'd always have a thing for her. "No."

He leaned back against the booth and didn't touch his beer again. His eyes were on me, cold and calculating. "Dude, I asked if you were okay with this and you said you were."

"I am okay with it," I snapped. "Can we talk about something else? Like sports? Music? Anything?"

He shook his head slightly. "What do you want me to do? I can't ask you to step down from being the best man."

This was getting out of hand. "Axel, I don't have a thing for Francesca. I'm totally and completely over her. I admit it's weird knowing she has a boyfriend but that's natural. It's always going to be weird when your ex is in a new relationship."

I held his gaze and hoped he would believe my bogus story.

Axel finally drank his beer again, which told me he wasn't skilled at reading people. "Okay. I'm glad I was wrong. It took me a long time to understand you two were never getting back together. I remember the way you used to be together. It just seemed like..."

We were forever. "Relationships come and go and the world keeps turning." I took a long drink of my beer in the hope it would wash the depression away.

"Why did you break up to begin with?"

Did we really need to take a trip down memory lane? "It was a long time ago..."

"But you never really told me why." Axel didn't know anything about my childhood, or the fact I had an uncontrollable temper that could lead to unforgiveable acts. He didn't understand I was a monster—and I would hurt Francesca.

"It just didn't work out." I watched the TV just so I wouldn't have to look at him. I wanted to leave and find somewhere to lick my wounds. Painful blows had been inflicted on my heart, and now it didn't beat the same.

It would never beat the same.

***

I needed to suck it up.

I was the one who left. She was on her knees in front of my door, but I still turned around and took off. She said we were soul mates, and I agreed with that statement.

But I still walked out on her.

There were times I wanted to beg her to take me back. There were times when I wanted to call her just to hear her voice. But then I remembered what I'd done to her in that bar all those years ago. I grabbed her by the arm and threw her across the floor. At the time, I thought I was grabbing Axel.

But that didn't change anything.

The hatred burned deep inside me, and that feeling led to anger and despair. I would always be a shadow of a man. I would always be dangerous. No matter what I did or what promises I made to myself, I would never be good enough for her.

This was how it had to be.

It didn't matter how much I loved her or what we had. It was gone anyway, buried deep in the past. Despite my jealousy and lingering possessiveness, I knew I had to turn the other way and ignore it. Francesca had moved on like she was supposed to.

This was what I wanted.

I knew she would find someone that would treat her right and make her happy. He would have a normal family and lack all the serious issues I possessed. He would love her and never let her go.

This was what I wanted.

So I should be happy for her. I shouldn't look at her like she was still mine. This day was going to come eventually, and I had to embrace it as much as possible. It didn't matter what we had between us, as earth-shattering as it was.

It simply wasn't possible.

When I went home that night, my shoulders were heavier than they'd ever been before. An invisible weight rested on them, and sometimes it was hard just to walk. An anvil lay against my chest, making it difficult to breathe.

I sat on the couch and looked out the window. The city was at my feet, and I sat on my iron throne. I accomplished everything I dreamed of, but it felt oddly empty. My life had never been complete…since she left.

The loneliness ate me alive most of the time. It was easy not to think about it when Francesca wasn't in my life. But now that she reappeared, her presence was a constant reminder of what I'd lost. She emitted a small beacon of light, something no one else could see but me. It shined bright despite its dullness, and I could see it in the darkest places. Sometimes it was difficult to resist the pull. I wanted to go to her and feel safe again, feel loved again.

But then I remembered she didn't feel that way anymore.

And she shouldn't.

I pulled out my phone and sent a message to one of my regulars. She was a model for Cosmo, and she had the figure of a swimsuit model. She was foreign and embarrassed of her poor English, so she didn't talk much—which I preferred. *Thinking of you.*

She responded immediately, like always. *Yeah? Be more specific.*

Come over here and I'll show you.

Tuesday

CHAPTER SIX

Plans

Francesca

Every day at The Muffin Girl was exactly the same. From morning until noon, it was chaotic, and there wasn't time to even glance at the clock. Orders poured in, customers filed inside for the flavor of the day coffee, and I worked on my creations in the back. I spent most of my time making wedding cakes, something I hadn't anticipated before I opened the shop. I assumed I would spend time baking new creations. I did do that, just not very often. But I couldn't trust anyone else to do the cakes right.

Liz walked by with flour smudged on her cheek. "Marie is here."

"Send her back." I was adding the frosting to the cake, making sure it was exactly perfect.

"Sure." Liz grabbed a set of cookie boxes before she headed back to the front.

"Liz?" I never took my eyes off the cake. "You got flour on your cheek."

"Oh." She wiped it off with her forearm. "Thanks." Then she disappeared to the front of the bakery.

Marie came to the back a moment later, wearing a tight gray dress and a necklace with teal beads around her throat. "Another day in paradise?"

I dipped the spatula in the bowl of water before I dabbed more frosting on it. "How many times do I have to tell you to come back here? You don't need to ask permission every time."

"What if you're hooking up with a guy?"

I stopped working on the bottom tier and turned to her with a quizzical expression. "In the back of the bakery?"

"Yeah." Marie kept an innocent look on her face.

"When it's open?" Did she think I was an enormous slut?

"Why not?" she asked seriously. "It's your shop. Besides, baked goods gets everyone in the mood."

Sometimes I couldn't tell if she was joking or not. "What's up, Marie?" I grabbed the piping bag and started making the ivory beads along the bottom layer of the wedding cake.

"I really liked Kyle the other night." A smile was in her voice.

"He's a real hoot." He was the cockiest guy I've ever met, apart from Hawke.

"And I can tell he really likes you too."

"He likes the fact I walked into the locker room and asked him out when he was naked."

"I think it's more than that…"

I set my tool down then removed my apron. "What time is it?"

"Oh, don't change the subject."

"What?" I asked. "We were talking about Kyle. That's not a subject." I grabbed my phone and eyed the time on the screen. "Damn, it's already one?"

"Time flies when you're in a fairytale."

I looked down at my shirt, which was covered with flour and frosting. "Yeah…I look like a princess."

Marie moved to a stool then glanced at me with excitement in her eyes. "Kyle is really something. Why did it take you so long to go on a date with him?"

I knew Marie only cared because she was my best friend. She always had my best interest at heart. But damn, her nosiness got on my nerves sometimes. "If he's so dreamy, why don't you go out with him?"

"Because I'm already marrying the dreamiest guy ever." She held up her ring finger, where the huge rock sat.

I cringed. "Axel is not dreamy. He's more like a nightmare."

Marie didn't push the argument. "I'm going shopping for my dress on Saturday. You want to come?"

"What kind of question is that?" I wanted to throw my spatula at her. "Of course I'll be there. I'll cry every time you put on a dress, and I'll down all the wine they have to offer."

"Great," she said. "I'm getting a designer gown so we'll start at Saks Fifth Avenue."

Marie was picky about clothes since she worked for a magazine, and I wasn't surprised she wanted her wedding dress to be the top-of-the-line. I'd always planned on wearing my mother's wedding dress on my big day. "Sounds great. I'll make the reservation."

"Best maid of honor ever."

"I know." I wasn't going to be humble about it. I was going to the moon and back for Marie, but I didn't mind in the least. I wanted the very best for her, and not just because she was marrying my brother.

"Have you talked to Kyle?"

"Not since we went out."

Marie pressed her lips tightly together like she wanted to say something.

I dared her with my eyes.

She made the right decision to back off. "So, you want to get lunch? I can tell you haven't eaten today. Well, you haven't eaten something besides frosting."

"I'd love to."

***

I just finished making homemade pizza when there was a knock on my door. I was currently rocking flannel pajama bottoms and a tank without a bra. Whenever no one was around, I let my true colors out. I was a messy slob, and I liked it that way.

I checked the peephole and hoped it was just Marie swinging by to discuss wedding plans, but it was Kyle.

Kyle had his arms across his chest. "Are you just going to stare? I know I'm beautiful, but it's rude to gawk."

I wanted to smack him upside the head.

I unlocked the door and cracked it. "Why don't you ever call before you stop by?"

"Why should I call?" He walked inside without waiting to be invited. "I would come by anyway even if you said you weren't up for it." He sniffed the air then headed into the kitchen. "What smells so good?"

I shut the door and released a growl. "If you'd called, I would have had time to put on some make up and change out of my pajamas." I followed him into the kitchen, crossing my arms over my chest to hide my hard nipples through the thin fabric.

He eyed the pizza on the stove. "Damn, this looks good."

"Thank you."

He turned to me as he leaned against the counter. His eyes looked me up and down, and the corner of his lip upturned in a smile. "You look perfect the way you are."

I knew he was just saying that. My hair was in a loose bun, and there was a hole in the crotch of my pants. "Uh-huh."

"You do." He slowly came toward me then moved his hands to my hips. That ghostly smile was still on his mouth, and his eyes lightened noticeably when he came near. "Honestly, I think you look better without make up."

"Liar."

"Baby, you know how I am. I don't say cheesy lines just to say them."

"Then you say them to get laid."

"And would I want to get laid if you really looked hideous?" He smiled in triumph when he knew he had me. He pressed his lips to the corner of my mouth before he pulled away. Then grabbed my breasts and gave them a gentle squeeze. "And I always prefer it when you're commando." He winked then turned back to the pizza. "Can I stay for dinner?"

Kyle was arrogant, but he had the right moves to make me melt. "Sure."

"Awesome." He grabbed a plate then sat down at the table. He immediately started eating before I joined him. "How was your day?"

"Good," I said. "Every day at the bakery goes by in a blur."

"Every time I walk in there, it's a damn zoo."

"Which is nice," I said. "The workday feels shorter."

"But you start work at five in the morning…" He cringed. "That's the worst thing ever."

"I don't mind. I wake up early anyway."

"Who the hell wakes up that early voluntarily?" He shoved the food into his mouth between his sentences.

"I still wake up at five on my days off."

"Weirdo..."

"I go to the gym, get my grocery shopping done, make breakfast..."

"Still a weirdo." He ate three slices before he rubbed his stomach. "You want to be my wife?"

I stopped in mid-bite. "What?"

"You can cook for me every day. Your food is always awesome."

"Why don't you ask me to be your private chef?" When I understood he was joking, I continued eating.

"Well, I want sex too. So, you'll have to be my wife."

"And what do I get out of this scenario?"

He eyed his lap then turned back to me with a smug grin on his face.

I wanted to wipe a slice across his face. "How was your day?"

"Good. My firm got a big case today."

"Oh?"

"The police found five terabytes of child pornography on this guy's laptop. Then he was caught paying for sex with a minor in Florida. The case moved from state to federal overnight. Pretty insane."

I didn't know anything about the legal system, and I didn't try to pretend that I did. "What's the difference?"

Kyle was never arrogant with his superior knowledge. "It goes through the federal courts, and it becomes a federal crime. The case gets a lot more exposure, and the sentence, if found guilty, is far more severe."

"Just because he committed the crime in a different state?"

"Technically," he said. "But with all that shit they found on his laptop, he's screwed anyway."

"You're prosecuting him?"

"Yep. We're putting the motherfucker away for a long time." Kyle didn't talk about work very often, but when he did, he was passionate about it. He took civil cases, among other things, but sometimes he landed high-profile situations like this one.

Kyle didn't work at the office very often. He was just a mere figurehead with a group of lawyers working underneath him. He spent a lot of time golfing, working out, and going on fancy trips. He definitely had the lifestyle most guys would dream of. "Will you be working on the case yourself?"

"Yeah, but I don't need to. There's so much evidence that we're going to nail him to the wall."

"I'm glad he won't be getting away with it."

"Me too." Kyle always seemed to be more passionate about cases that involved minors or sexual abuse than homicides. He never told me why.

But then again, I never asked. I tried to keep our relationship as straightforward as possible. We were just fuck-buddies that had great sex. Nothing more.

He looked out the window before he turned back to me. "I need a favor—and you owe me."

"That's not a good start..."

"My cousin is getting married this weekend in the Hamptons. I want you to be my date."

Even though I didn't react, my heart slammed in my chest. Perspiration immediately marked my brow and my hands felt clammy. I dropped the pizza slice because I lost my appetite. "What?"

"What, what?" he asked. "You know what a wedding is, right?"

"But why are you asking me to go with you?" We didn't do stuff like that.

"Because I need a date." He said it with condescension, like I was an idiot for not figuring it out.

I wasn't buying that. Kyle was a fine piece of man who didn't struggle to get dates. He could have whomever he wanted, whenever he wanted. "Take someone else. You know I'm terrible company."

"Right now you are," he said. "But I still want you to come with me."

The anxiety was starting to build. "We don't do that. We're just a fling." I never signed up for family functions.

"I just went out to dinner with your family and I didn't complain."

He couldn't be serious. "That's not the same thing and you know it. That was a double date—"

"With your brother."

"But he's engaged to my best friend—"

"Who's your sister-in-law," he said triumphantly. "Which makes her family. I did that for you, so you can do this for me."

I shook my head slightly. "Did you seriously just lawyer me?"

He grinned from ear-to-ear. "Don't try to argue with me. I promise you'll always lose."

"Will your mom be there?"

"Of course."

"And the rest of your family?"

"Yep."

"And you really want me to meet them."

He nodded. "I really do."

I knew I couldn't get out of this, not when he just had dinner with my brother. "Open bar?"

Kyle released a quiet chuckle. "Oh yeah. Plus, it's in the Hamptons so we'll be staying at my beach house."

"You have a beach house?"

"You didn't know that?"

"Uh, no."

"Well, now you do." He took his plate to the sink and washed it off before putting it in the dishwasher. "Wear something on the fancier side. As much as I love my family, they're pretty damn snooty."

"Great…"

He sat in the chair beside me then suddenly pulled me into his lap. His arms were thick and powerful, and they moved me with ease. The second my ass was in his lap, I felt his hard-on through his jeans. "Now that you smell like pizza, why don't we go into the bedroom?"

"Does that turn you on?"

"Oh yeah." He kissed the corner of my mouth. "Yum…pepperoni."

His words were so ridiculous that I laughed. "Yum…olives."

"Yes, baby. Talk dirty to me."

I laughed again and felt my stomach clench tightly from the effort. "You're just making me hungry again."

"For another slice?" he asked. "Or for me?"

"Can my answer be both?"

"Sure," he said. "But we know what the real answer is."

***

Marie and I walked into the wedding dress section of Saks Fifth Avenue.

"Can you believe it?" I asked. "You're actually picking out your wedding dress. The day is finally here."

"I know." Marie wanted to squeal. It was obvious in the way she couldn't stand still.

"You're going to look beautiful in everything you try on."

"God, I hope so."

I was excited for Marie. She was the coolest chick I knew, and she deserved so much happiness. And I knew she would make Axel happy for the rest of his life. I still didn't know what Axel did to win her over, but he obvious did something. "Let's check in."

After we told the receptionist we were there, we headed to a showroom where a pedestal was erected in front of mirrors. There was a changing room to the left, and on a table was a tray of champagne, glasses, and strawberries.

"Here are a few of our most popular dresses." The assistant placed everything in the changing room. "Let me know if you need anything else."

"Thank you." Marie practically ran into the changing room and shut the door.

I poured myself a glass of champagne and patiently waited for her to come out.

"Champagne?" A deep voice sounded behind me, and it was too familiar for me to not recognize it. Hawke stood near the table and eyed the empty glass. "When I get my custom suits, I don't even get a piece of gum."

Every time I saw him, I immediately focused on his eyes. They were deeper than the ocean, and they held more secrets than a diary. I remembered looking into them when we made love in the middle of the night. Sometimes random flashbacks played in my mind, and I did everything I could to fight them off. Despite all this time, I knew what we had was real. But that didn't mean I wanted to keep reliving it. "Maybe you should tip better."

Hawke smiled slightly and his eyes shined brighter. "Maybe." He took the seat beside me, wearing a navy blue suit with a black tie. A fancy watch was on his wrist, and his aviators were tucked into the front pocket.

"What brings you here? Need a dress?" It was still a little tense between us. All I could think about was that woman who left her wallet at his apartment. And after that thought left, all I could think about was the beautiful relationship we used to have. But with every passing meeting, it was getting a little easier. I didn't think about it so much.

A chuckle emerged from deep in his throat. "No. I have plenty at home."

"Yeah?" I asked. "You wear them around the house to make yourself feel pretty?"

"Very pretty." He went along with the joke with a smile on his lips. "Actually, Axel asked me to come."

I couldn't figure out why. "Because?"

He cleared his throat. "He wants me to tell him 'how damn fine Marie looks in her dress.'" He shrugged when he finished his sentence. "I guess it's my job as the best man."

I rolled my eyes because it sounded exactly like something Axel would do. "He actually gave you permission to check out his future wife?"

"I couldn't believe it either."

Marie came out of the changing room and lifted up the front of her gown as she stepped on the pedestal. It was tight around her waist but poufy everywhere else. She tilted her head to the side as she examined herself, and the lack of excitement in her eyes told us everything we needed to know. "This makes me look fat."

Hawke released an involuntary laugh because it was so absurd.

"I know it's your day and everything, but shut the hell up. You weigh a hundred and five pounds."

"I didn't say I was fat." She grabbed her gown and stepped off the pedestal. "I just said it made me look fat." She walked back into the dressing room.

Hawke leaned toward me and lowered his voice. "Isn't that the same thing?"

I shook my head. "Just ignore her."

He moved away again. "I think that's a good idea."

I sipped the champagne then grabbed a strawberry.

"This is pretty nice," Hawke said as he looked around. "No wonder why girls are so excited to get married."

"It's one of the perks. When my big day comes, I won't be doing it. But I won't regret that."

Hawke turned his eyes on me, and they changed slightly like the cogs in his mind were turning. His thoughts couldn't be read as easily as before, but it was clear when something was on his mind. "And why won't you be doing this?"

"I'm wearing my mother's dress."

His eyes immediately softened, and the emotion stretched across his face. He suddenly looked away, like he was putting as much distance between us as he could without actually moving. "That's nice..."

I sipped my wine just so I had something to do.

Marie came out again, this time in a mermaid dress.

"Ooh...I like that one." I watched her rise on the pedestal and examine herself in the mirror. "It really highlights your curves. And your ass looks great."

"Axel will love that." Marie positioned her hair in different ways like she was imagining how it would look with the dress.

Hawke leaned toward me. "I think she likes it..."

"I do too." I wanted to express every opinion that came into my mind, but I didn't want to sway her thoughts. Sometimes, it was easy to get sucked into your best friend's preference.

Marie continued to stare at herself without an overt reaction. But I knew her well, better than Axel, arguably. And I could tell she was picturing herself walking down the aisle, imagining how the rose petals sounded under her feet as she moved, and wondering how Axel looked as he watched her come closer.

I set my glass down then slowly came to her side. The dress fit her like it was made just for her. The tiny glitter embedded deep into the fabric was light and not overwhelming. The gown flared out past her knees and somehow made her look taller. "Marie…you look amazing."

She felt the fabric in her fingertips and released a deep sigh. "I think I'm in love."

I smiled and felt my eyes grow slightly moist. "I think I am too."

"You think Axel will like it?"

He'd like it if she wore a chicken suit. To him, she looked beautiful in anything. "Yes."

She clutched her hands to her chest. "I think this is it."

"Are you sure?" I asked. "You've only tried on two dresses."

"No, this is it." There was no hesitation in her eyes. Her heart was set.

"Then, congratulations."

She searched for the price tag until she found it. "I just hope it's not ridiculous. Axel said I couldn't go over ten thousand."

I couldn't believe she was willing to spend that much on a dress. But I held my tongue and didn't share my economical point of view.

When Marie found the price tag, she sucked in a breath and her eyes widened in sheer shock. "Ugh…shit."

"How much is it?" If it were just a few extra thousand, I wouldn't mind helping her. It was a gift to her and my brother.

"You don't even want to know…"

I yanked the price tag out of her hand. How expensive could it be? "Holy shit…"

"Told ya."

"This dress is twenty-two thousand?" Was it even legal to charge that much? "How do these people sleep at night?"

"I'm sure they sleep on a bed of money." Marie tried to make a joke to mask her pain. "Oh well… I'm sure I'll find something else." She slowly stepped off the pedestal and headed to her changing room at a snail's pace, clearly disheartened.

I wanted to get my best friend the dress she deserved but I simply didn't have that kind of money to spare.

Hawke came to my side. "What did she say?"

"She can't afford the dress so she's going to try a few others..."

Hawke put his hands in his pockets. "How much was it?"

"Enough to give anyone a heart attack." I returned to my seat and downed the entire glass of champagne.

Hawke remained outside Marie's door, his thoughts hidden behind his stoic exterior.

Marie came out in a new dress and returned the one she really wanted to the rack. I could already tell she hated the dress she had on, because when she stepped on the pedestal, she stepped on the bottom of the dress like she didn't give a damn about it.

I returned to her side and looked at the gown. It was pretty and fit her well, but it wasn't nearly as spectacular as the previous one. But I tried to make the best of it. "It's pretty..."

"Yeah...it's eight thousand. At least I can afford this one."

"You know, I'm sure we'll find a much better dress somewhere else. You don't have to get anything today."

Marie felt the tulle at the bottom then let it fall slowly back to her side. "It's kind of pretty..."

Maybe we should just call it a day so she could sleep on it. She was obviously too heartbroken to keep searching. "How about we go get a drink and come back another day?"

"A drink sounds wonderful." She bunched up her dress and returned to the dressing room.

When I turned around, Hawke was gone. I searched for him, but I didn't see him anywhere. Did he leave? Would he just go without saying anything? Maybe he had a phone call so he stepped out for a moment.

Marie came out in her casual clothes. "Now I feel hideous."

"Why?"

"I'm wearing jeans. I don't feel special in jeans."

I patted her back. "When we find the right dress, you can wear it every day and feel special."

"If we ever find the right dress…"

"Marie, it's been one day. Don't lose all hope."

"You're right," she said with a sigh. "I'm being a big bitch baby."

"A little…" I tried not to smile.

"Let's get out of here before I pull out my pocket knife and cut up a dress just to be spiteful…"

I grabbed the crook of her arm and began to pull her. "Yes, let's haul ass." We reached the front of the store and saw Hawke standing at the register. The clerk just returned his credit card to him then handed over a dress bag. “Have a good day, sir.”

“Thank you.” Hawke held the bag with both hands then walked toward us.

“What did you buy?” I asked. “They have suits here?”

“Oh god.” Marie slapped her forehead. “Hawke found something and I didn’t. How pathetic is that?”

Hawke made a ghostly smile before he unzipped the bag and displayed the brilliantly white wedding dress. The glitter caught the light, and the pristine fabric shined like it was made of crystal. “Axel wanted me to tell him how fine you looked in your dress. So, I have to make sure you get the right dress.” He held it out to her.

Marie’s jaw dropped, and she stiffened like her entire body shut down.

I was just as shocked. “What…?”

Marie covered her mouth. “Oh my god.”

“You seriously did that?” Now my mouth was gaping open.

“I can’t believe you bought my dress.” Marie threw her arms down. “Hawke, you didn’t have to do that. I can’t accept this. I just can’t.”

Hawke nodded to the sign sitting on the counter. *All Sales Are Final.* "I can't return it anyway. So please take it. You deserve to look beautiful on your special day. It's my way of saying thank you for making my friend so happy."

Marie covered her mouth again like she didn't know what else to do.

"Hawke…" I still couldn't process his generosity. "It was so expensive."

He shrugged in response.

"At least split it with me," Marie said. "My budget was ten thousand anyway."

"No." Hawke grabbed her hands and situated them around the bag. "It's a gift. I don't want anything."

Marie held the dress to her chest as her eyes watered. Her chest rose and fell heavily, and I knew the water works were underway.

Hawke dropped eye contact because he didn't know how to react.

Marie suddenly darted into his chest and almost knocked him over. "Thank you. Thank you so much." She squeezed his waist with the dress between them.

Hawke awkwardly returned the embrace, like he wasn't sure how to give her affection. He patted her on the shoulder and cleared his throat. "You're very welcome, Marie."

Even my eyes watered at Hawke's gesture. He didn't have to do that, and no one expected it of him. He did it out of the goodness of his heart. Two years ago, he left me because he claimed he was a monster. How could a monster do something so sweet and heartfelt? Why couldn't he just see himself for what he truly was?

Marie finally pulled away, the dress still clutched tightly in her hands. "You're my superhero, Hawke."

He shrugged again, clearly unsure how to respond.

"I have to call Axel and tell him how great his best man is..." She fished her phone out of her pocket then stepped outside to make the call.

That left Hawke and me alone, staring at each other and having a conversation without words.

"That was really sweet of you." I finally voiced what I was thinking.

"I saw her eyes light up when she put it on." He put his hands in his pockets. "After putting up with his shit for so long, she deserves something nice." He smiled at the end of his joke.

I smiled too. "She does."

He eyed his watch and cleared his throat. "Well, I need to be somewhere…"

I knew he was lying. When he walked past me, my hand moved to the crook of his arm.

It was the first time we touched in years.

He halted in his tracks and turned his head my way. His eyes took me in like they always did, absorbing my words, movements, and breathing all at the same time.

"You're a good person, Hawke. I hope you realize that someday."

He held my gaze without blinking. His blue eyes thawed from the ice that had frozen over. I saw the man I formerly knew, the vulnerable person under that rough exterior. Just for an instant, we were frozen in time, but a time different than reality. It was two years ago, and that connection between us burned like a raging forest fire. He couldn't hide from me, and I couldn't hide from him.

And then, instantly, it was gone.

Hawke stepped away, his arm out of my grasp. Once our touch ceased, the coldness took him all over again. His back grew rigid, and a hundred walls replaced the dozen walls he previously erected. He was shutting out the world. He was shutting out everyone.

Including me.

Tuesday

CHAPTER SEVEN

Drift

Hawke

Axel burst into my office door without knocking. My secretary didn't bother stopping him anymore. Nothing she said or did could get him to obey. He was like an out of control puppy that was too old to train. "Dude, what the hell?"

I closed out of my email. "Sorry?"

"Marie said you bought her wedding dress."

"Yeah. Your point?"

He dropped in the chair facing my desk. "My point? It was twenty-two thousand dollars. What the hell were you thinking?"

"That your fiancée had fallen in love with the dress and she should have it. You were the one who sent me out to tell you how hot she looked in it. I was just doing my job."

"But she would look hot in anything. She doesn't need an overpriced dress."

I shrugged. “She wanted it, man.”

“You didn’t have to do that.”

“I know, Axel. I wanted to.”

He scratched the back of his neck as he often did when he was uncomfortable. “At least let me pay you the ten thousand we were going to spend anyway. That’s fair. You shouldn’t pay for the whole thing.”

“It was a gift. Swallow your pride and just accept it.”

“It’s not about pride,” he argued. “I just don’t think that’s fair. Let me pay for half of it.”

“Why are you being a girl right now?” I spun a pen through my fingertips.

“I’m not.”

“Then let’s just move on. I wouldn’t have offered if I didn’t want to do it.”

Axel scratched the back of his neck again, speechless.

I was glad the argument had been settled. “So, I was thinking we would go to Vegas for your bachelor party. What do you think?”

Axel shrugged. “I don’t know…it’s just a bunch of gambling and strippers.”

“Isn’t that a good thing?” I raised an eyebrow.

“I’m not interested in the strippers.”

An unexpected smile stretched my face. "Wow…she really whipped you into shape, huh?"

"She didn't forbid me," he said defensively. "It just feels weird, you know? We already feel married. It'd be like I was cheating on her or something."

I wasn't going to push it on him if he didn't want it. I wasn't interested in seeing a bunch of strippers either. Every night of my life felt like a bachelor party. It was hollow and empty, and no matter how many times I washed my clothes, I smelled like booze and sex. "Do you have something else in mind?"

"How about a Yankee game?"

That was pretty damn lame. "We can do that any other time."

"Well, it's convenient for everyone. And cheap."

I would have to take the reins on this one. "I'll figure it out and let you know."

"No strippers, Hawke. I mean it."

"I understand." When Francesca and I were together, I didn't even glance at other women. In a universe where she was my fiancée, I wouldn't want to see strippers either. In fact, I thought it was pathetic.

***

Tuesday

I lay in bed with Rebecca beside me.

"What do you do for a living?" She trailed her fingers down my chest.

I took a final drink of my scotch and felt the ice cubes touch my mouth. She and I left the bar the second we made eye contact. There wasn't small talk then, and I didn't want to make small talk now. "I'm an investor."

"And what do investors do?"

I didn't feel like giving a lecture in finance. "It's just crunching numbers all day."

Her hair spread across my stomach, and her touch felt warm. "Is your real name Hawke?"

I got this question once in a while. "Yes."

"Do you—"

My phone started to ring.

While I would never admit it, anytime I heard my phone ring, I hoped it would be Francesca. I didn't know what I wanted her to say. I didn't know what I wanted her to do. All I knew was I needed to hear her voice.

But it wasn't her.

It was my mom.

Without excusing myself, I grabbed the phone and headed into the living room. I stood in front of the floor-to-ceiling window in just my briefs. Mom hardly called me anymore, and to my surprise, she didn't call when she was in trouble. I assumed she stopped calling because she didn't want me to come back. She wanted me to be free.

I answered. "Mom, are you alright?"

There was a long pause over the phone. "Hawke, why do you keep putting money in my account?"

I'd been making deposits since I started my investment company. Every two weeks, I cashed my check into my account. Then I put some in hers. "Because you have all the money you'll ever need. Move to an island somewhere. Just disappear. Be happy." Why did I keep hoping for a change when I knew it would never happen?

"Hawke, I'm fine."

"Does he still hurt you?" I squeezed the phone in my hand.

"No, Hawke. He doesn't."

Could I really believe her?

"Hawke, I don't need money. Stop putting it in my account."

I stared out the window.

"Hawke?"

I gritted my teeth before I spoke. "I'm here."

"I'm okay, Hawke. I don't need anything."

I was going to keep doing it anyway. "I'll talk to you later, Mom."

Mom knew the argument would go nowhere. “I love you, Hawke. You’re the greatest son any mother could ask for.”

I closed my eyes as I kept the emotion deep in my throat. “I love you too, Mom.”

CHAPTER EIGHT

Wedding Bells

Francesca

I stared out the window and watched the beach go by. The waves crashed against the shore, and people jogged with their dogs on leashes. Families had a beach day with their buckets and shovels in the sand.

"It's nice, huh?" Kyle kept one hand on the wheel.

"Very pretty. Where's your place?"

"It's a mile past the venue. We'll go there afterward."

"Sounds good to me." I was grateful we didn't have to make the drive back. It'd be nice to pass out after the wedding.

Kyle's hand reached for mine and held it on my thigh.

I let the touch linger.

"You look very beautiful." He glanced at me before returning his eyes to the road.

"Thanks." I wore a deep purple dress with a low cut in the front. Diamond earrings were in my lobes, the only nice pair I owned. "You look nice too."

He wore a black suit with a gray tie. He always looked good in a suit. Actually, he looked good in everything. He just cut his brown hair so it was a little shorter than usual, but sexy like always.

Kyle pulled onto the gravel path and drove until he reached the crimson white estate. A fountain was in the front, spraying water into the sky. A valet took our car when we arrived, and Kyle slipped him some money.

He moved his hand to the small of my back. "You doing okay?"

"Why wouldn't I be?"

"Well, this is a fancy party and my family will be here." He looked down at me, a shadow on his chin from not shaving for a few days.

"And why would that intimidate me?" Was I missing something?

"I forgot who I was talking to." He pulled me into his chest and gave me a quick kiss.

"That's right. I may be small but I am fierce."

"Very true." He kept me to his side as we walked inside and signed the guest book. Then we took our seats in the white chairs and waited for the ceremony to begin.

"Who's your cousin? The bride or groom?"

"Bride," he answered. "It's my dad's brother's daughter…if that isn't too complicated to follow."

"I got it."

Kyle moved his hand to my thigh, and he squeezed it gently.

I glanced around and noticed a few people were looking at us and trying to be discreet about it. Since the wedding was about to begin, I assumed that's why Kyle didn't greet his family. He only had eyes for me.

***

When the ceremony was over, we headed to the white tables and chairs on the perfectly manicured lawn. The estate was lit with twinkling white lights, and the air reeked of money. It was the fanciest gig I'd ever been to, but I didn't feel out of place.

"Who lives here?" I asked. "It's beautiful."

"My mother."

I tried not to gasp. "Your mom?"

"Yeah, I grew up here."

I eyed the mansion. "Here?"

"Yep." He smiled but didn't gloat.

"Dude, you must have gotten laid like crazy."

He chuckled quietly before it turned into a true laugh. "Well, yeah. But I think that had something to do with my rugged good looks."

"I'm sure it helped."

"And you've seen my package…a lot of people appreciate it." He winked at me before he placed his arm around my shoulders.

I rolled my eyes. "You're so arrogant, but yet, I keep sleeping with you."

"You know you can't live without me, baby." He kissed me on the cheek.

I didn't like nicknames outside the bedroom but I let it slide since he was in a good mood. Being at home clearly brightened his day.

No one had joined us at the table yet, but I suspected his mom and aunt would be seated with us. "Anything I should know about your family?" My appearance probably wasn't a big deal to them. Kyle must have a date on his arm to every event. I was just one of many.

"Nope. They're pretty cool. I mean, they raised me so they must be awesome."

My lips automatically upturned in a smile. I had to admit, I was a sucker for a momma's boy. "I'm sure they are."

Kyle's eyes left my face and landed on someone approaching us. "There's my Mom."

She was exactly how I pictured her. She had short blonde hair that was elegantly styled like Princess Diana, and she had striking blue eyes similar to Kyle's. She carried herself like a queen, but the arrogance usually associated with royalty was absent.

When she laid eyes on me, there was only a smile on her lips. No judgment or surprise was found in her reaction.

Kyle rose to his feet and helped me out of the chair. "Hey, Mom. What's happening?" He hugged her tightly then kissed her on the cheek. "Wow, you look sizzling. Trying to impress someone?"

She smiled, and her cheeks tinted red. "Just my son."

Kyle put his arm around my waist. "Mom, this is Francesca." He didn't introduce me as his girlfriend, and he didn't even mention I was his date.

Which was exactly what I was hoping for. "It's a pleasure to meet you, Mrs. Campbell." I extended my hand to shake hers.

Her eyes penetrated my face invasively. She examined every feature I possessed, her eyes lingering on the curve of my cheekbones and the emerald color of my eyes. She was trying to memorize me, place me in her mind so she'd never forget me. "The pleasure is all mine, dear." Instead of taking my hand, she embraced me. "It's so wonderful to finally meet you."

Finally meet me?

What did that mean?

Did Kyle talk about me?

I forced myself to respond. "You have a lovely home. I'm very excited to be here."

Mrs. Campbell pulled away. "That's very kind of you to say. Thank you." She didn't have an aristocratic air about her. In fact, she seemed humble, just like Kyle. "We've been living here since Kyle was born."

"It's beautiful."

"Thank you," she said again. "Please call me Julia."

"Sure."

Kyle pulled out his mother's chair before she sat down. Then we took the seats beside her. Other people filled the table, with glasses of wine in their hands. Waiters carried around appetizers. Crab cakes passed our table, and I felt my stomach rumble.

"Wasn't she beautiful?" Julia asked.

"She really was," Kyle said.

"I loved her bouquet," I said. "Those flowers were so pretty."

"Indeed," Julia said. "So, Kyle tells me you're a bit of a celebrity in Manhattan."

Huh? "He did?"

"That bakery of yours has been voted as the number one bakery in Manhattan two years in a row." She nodded in approval. "Very impressive."

What else did Kyle tell her? "Oh yeah. The Muffin Girl is my home. When I opened that shop, I thought I was going to lose my entire savings. Thankfully, it worked out."

"You're a very accomplished woman," Julia noted. "That takes serious courage."

Everyone said meeting their in-laws was a total nightmare, but this was a walk in the park. It seemed like she already liked me before she even met me. What exactly did Kyle say? I'd have to ask him next time we were alone. "Thank you. I had help along the way."

"She makes the best brownies ever," Kyle said. "Believe me, I've gained five pounds since we met."

"I'll have to try them myself sometime," Julia said.

"We'll bring some by next time we visit," Kyle said.

We will?

"What do you do for fun when you aren't baking?" Julia asked.

I didn't expect to get so much attention. "Right now, I don't have time for anything. My best friend is getting married, and I'm her maid of honor."

"Oh, that's wonderful," Julia said. "Weddings are so much fun."

"Are you making her cake?" Kyle asked.

"Of course," I said. "I wouldn't let anyone else do it."

Julia turned her eyes on Kyle. "How have you been, sweetheart?"

"Good," Kyle said. "Just working."

She gave him a look that said she didn't believe that.

Kyle rolled his eyes before he spoke. "Okay, I've been golfing a lot. But we recently picked up a big case and it's been the talk of the office."

"I heard about that." Julia didn't elaborate.

She must have some cut in the business. I couldn't think of any other reason why she'd be able to afford this place otherwise.

"I've been working out a lot," Kyle said. "Spending time with Frankie. You know, living the dream."

"That does sound nice," she said.

"What about you, Mom?" Kyle asked.

"Well…" Color moved into her cheeks. "I've been seeing someone."

"You?" Kyle asked in surprise. "Who's the lucky guy?"

"I met him at the courts," she said. "He's very nice. I think you would like him, Kyle."

"I'm sure I will," Kyle said. "After I make sure he's good enough for you."

Julia smiled like her son's affection made her the happiest woman in the world. "He owns a line of resorts in the Caribbean."

"He'll have to take me on a vacation to butter me up," Kyle said.

Julia chuckled. "He doesn't need to butter you up. He's a very nice man, and very respectable."

"There's only one way to test it," Kyle said. "I'll have to arm wrestle him. If he wins, he gets to date you."

"Arm wrestle?" I blurted.

"Yeah, he has to prove his strength to me," Kyle said.

Kyle was cute in a quirky way, but sometimes he said things that simply didn't make sense.

"You can challenge him when you meet him." Julia took a gentle sip of her wine.

I was a little timid around Kyle and his mom because I didn't know what Kyle said about me when I wasn't around. But she was very nice and warm, and it was clear the two of them had a great relationship that you wanted to participate in.

Kyle caught someone's eye across the lawn. "There Uncle Rob. I need to congratulate him. I'll be right back." He gave me a quick kiss on the cheek before he left me alone with his mother.

I should be afraid, but I wasn't.

Julia continued to stare at me in a friendly way. "Kyle told me about your parents. I was very sorry to hear that."

What didn't he say about me? "Thank you. It was a long time ago. I've made my peace with it."

She nodded. "I'm always here to talk if you need someone."

It was a nice offer, especially since we were practically strangers. "My Yaya raised me, and she's the best Yaya ever. I also have my brother Axel. He's a good guy."

"Kyle mentioned him. He said he liked him a lot."

That was a first. No boyfriend ever liked my brother, and vice versa.

"What does he do?"

"He's a financial advisor in Manhattan. He's the one marrying my best friend."

A genuine smile stretched her lips. "That's perfect. Congratulations."

"It's a dream come true. My best friend will be my sister-in-law."

"I'm lucky enough to have in-laws that don't drive me up the wall," she said with a light chuckle. "And I have the most wonderful son in the world."

Hearing her talk about Kyle like that made me smile. "Yeah, he's pretty great." He got under my skin sometimes but he really was an exceptional person. His carefree personality always put me at ease.

Julia was about to say something when Kyle returned to the table.

"I have a few people to introduce you to." Kyle extended his hand to me. "It's time to show you off, baby."

***

I met everyone in his family and made small talk. Surprisingly, they were easy to get along with. I never once felt interrogated. We spent most of the time laughing while downing our wine.

Kyle was by my side the entire time, and his hand was usually placed somewhere intimate. When the music played and everyone got on the dance floor, Kyle snatched my drink away. "Dance with me."

"I have to warn you…I'm pretty good."

"Yeah?" he asked. "I have a feeling I'm better." He pulled me onto the dance floor then immediately started to get down. Most of his dance moves were obscene, and frankly inappropriate. But they made me laugh so hard I got a cramp in my side.

We continued laughing and dancing together until a slow song played. I assumed that was the end so I headed back to the table.

Kyle grabbed me and pulled me back to his chest. He placed my hand on his shoulder then began to slow-dance with me, a ghost of a smile on his lips. "Where do you think you're going?"

"After all that dancing, I need a break."

"Consider this your break." His face was close to mine, and his cologne wafted into my nose. It hinted of masculine sweat and Hugo Boss. His hand was pressed against the small of my back as he slowly danced with me.

"I have a bone to pick with you."

"Yeah?" A playful smile was on his lips. "How do you want me to take you later tonight? On your hands and knees? Or on your back?"

My hair stood on end, and I felt distant heat course through my body. I swallowed the lump in my throat and let it pass. "No. Why do you talk about me to your mother?"

"Why wouldn't I?"

"Because we're just friends."

"We are?" he asked. "I've never once gotten that impression."

"Well, I'm not your girlfriend."

He shrugged. "That's debatable."

My eyes narrowed on his face, and I pressed my lips tightly together. "Kyle." I wanted him to be serious.

He suddenly dipped me and gave me a slow kiss. Everyone could see us but he didn't seem to care. When the kiss ended, he looked me in the eye. "Call yourself whatever you want. And I'll call you whatever I want."

***

At the end of the night, I was tired. I was ready to fall into Kyle's bed just down the road.

Maybe we could leave the windows open and listen to the waves crash against the shore.

Kyle placed my jacket over my shoulders. "I've got to keep my lady warm."

I pulled it around me and smiled. "It smells good too."

He put his arm around me as we approached the gate. "Let's just say goodbye to my mom before we go."

"Okay."

Kyle guided me inside, where his mother was taking care of the centerpieces that were left behind. "Mom, we're headed out."

"You are?" She set down the vase then hugged him. "It's always so nice to see you. I miss you."

"I miss you too. I'll come up more often."

"I'll hold you to that." She turned to the door and saw Uncle Rob trying to break down a table. "Kyle, could you give him a hand?"

"Yep," Kyle answered as he walked away. "I'm on it."

When he was gone, Julia turned to me. "It was so lovely having you here, Francesca. You're exactly as I imagined."

I had no idea what that meant. "I'm really glad I came. It was such a beautiful wedding."

"It really was, wasn't it?" she asked. She pulled me into her arms and gave me a warm hug. "I'm so excited you're here. I've been waiting so long." She squeezed me gently before she pulled away.

Waited so long? For what, exactly? "Kyle mentioned me a long time ago?" Maybe he brought me up when we first started fooling around six months ago. I hoped that wasn't the case because it made it seem like we were more serious than we really were.

"No, he mentioned you a few weeks ago."

"Oh." That wasn't adding up.

"I've been waiting for Kyle to bring someone home. Every time I asked, he said he didn't have anyone worth mentioning. And when he called me a few weeks ago and told me about you...I almost cried." She placed her hand over her heart. "And now that I've met you, I see just how perfect you are. My son is so happy. And now I'm happy."

***

We entered his beach house and headed to his room. I didn't say a single word to him. Despite how beautiful the house was, and the fact it was just steps from the beach, I didn't give him a single compliment.

I was pissed.

I tossed my bag on the floor then pulled out a shirt to wear to bed.

Kyle undressed and tossed his tie over the back of a chair. "Why are you so quiet?"

"Tired."

"Are you always angry when you're tired?" He knew me well enough to read me.

I changed before I got into bed. "Not really. But I am tonight."

"What's your deal?" He stripped down to his boxers before he got into bed beside me.

"You," I hissed. "You're my deal." I turned on my side and faced the opposite way of him.

"What the hell did I do?" He came behind me and grabbed my hip.

"Why did you introduce me to your mother? She thinks I'm her future daughter-in-law."

He sighed. "You know how mothers are. They assume every girl is their new daughter-in-law."

"Well, I don't blame her for assuming it," I snapped. "You've never introduced someone to her before. So why did you introduce me?"

"Maybe because I like you? Maybe because I can stand you longer than five minutes, unlike all the others? Shit, you're my best friend, and I can't bring you to a wedding?"

"Not when your mom thinks I'm your girlfriend."

"What does the label matter?"

"It matters to me." I finally turned over and glared at him. "Kyle, I told you from the beginning this was just a fling. It seems like you keep trying to turn it into something more. Why are you putting me in a situation I don't want to be in?"

He turned his eyes to the other side of the room. His eyes grew lidded and weary, like he was brainstorming a thousand thoughts at once. Then he turned back to me. "What kind of fling lasts six months?"

"I don't know. Is there a time limit to when it ends?"

"Have you slept with anyone else since we met?"

"No...but what's your point?"

"My point is, maybe this isn't a fling anymore. Did you ever think of that?"

"It's a fling," I said firmly. "I made that abundantly clear."

"If that were the case, you would have tossed me to the side months ago."

"Maybe you're just really good in bed."

He smiled against his will. "Obviously. But don't you think there's more than that?"

"No. And now your mother is all excited over nothing."

"Look, she was starting to wonder if I was gay. This gave her peace of mind."

I slammed my hand on the mattress. "Kyle. You gave her the wrong impression and you know it."

"So what? It's my problem, not yours."

I released a sigh that came out as a growl before I turned back over.

"Baby, don't be like that."

"I don't understand you sometimes."

"Look, my family always interrogates me about my love life. I brought you along so they would get off my back. Now that they've seen a real person, they'll lose interest in me."

"Or grow more interested."

"Frankie, just chill out."

I pulled my knees to my chest.

"Didn't you have a great time?"

"That's not the point..."

"No, it is the point." He turned me over then yanked my panties down my legs.

"I'm not in the mood right now."

"Well, I can't sleep when you're bitchy. So I need to fix it." Like always, Kyle seduced me with the right kisses and the right touches. He was good in bed, and knew exactly what he was doing. He'd been with me enough times to understand what I liked and what I hated. Things were simple with him, meaningless. Within seconds, my body was ready for him.

And then my anger disappeared.

Tuesday

CHAPTER NINE

Suit Up

Hawke

Axel and I walked inside the department store. We were there to try on different suits for the wedding. Axel was adamant about wearing white tuxes, and I knew Marie wasn't a fan of that.

I wasn't a fan of that either.

We headed to the dressing rooms in the rear, and a blonde and a brunette were talking quietly nearly a rack full of sports coats.

"Was the wedding fun?" Marie asked.

"Yeah, it was okay." Francesca had her arms across her chest, a classic sign of displeasure. There was something on her mind, something bothering her. I could read her like an open book, despite our long time apart.

Marie didn't catch on. "It must have been swanky since it was in the Hamptons."

"It was ridiculously swanky," Francesca said. "I didn't fit in at all."

"I'm sure you were—" Marie stopped in mid-sentence because Axel grabbed her and gave her a scorching kiss. His hands were on her waist and he crushed his mouth against hers like he hadn't seen her in years.

Francesca made a disgusted face before she turned away. "Anyway…" Her eyes fell on me, and there was a small explosion deep in her eyes. She clearly had no idea I was going to be there.

"Hi." No matter how many times we saw each other, it was still tense. We agreed to be friends and not talk about the past, but any time we were together, it was all we could think about. Space was between us, but the fire burned like it always had. I could deny it all I wanted but it wouldn't change anything. And while she may feel differently now, she still couldn't deny the heat. When it came to us, there was an innate attraction. Time and space couldn't diminish it. It was as absolute as gravity.

"Hi." She kept her arms across her chest. "How's it going?"

"Good." I glanced at the lovebirds, who were still smooching like the beginning of a porno. "But I've been better."

Francesca smiled in understanding. “I don’t get it. They live together. They see each other all the time.”

I completely understood it. I’d be doing the same thing to Francesca if she were still mine. But I agreed anyway. “Yeah.”

“How was your weekend?”

Terrible. Lonely. Unbearable. “Good. Yours?”

“Good.”

“So, you went to a wedding?” I suspected she went with Kyle. I hadn’t seen him yet, and I hoped I would never have to see him. My mind already pictured her with some imaginary guy. I didn’t want a real face for my nightmares.

“Yeah, it was in the Hamptons. It was really nice. Surprisingly, no one was stuck up.”

“Cool.” I crossed my arms over my chest.

Axel and Marie were still going at it.

Francesca sighed. “Should we throw something at them?”

“I can kick Axel in the knee.”

“I think we need to kick him in the groin,” Francesca said. “That would eliminate this from happening in the future.”

The corner of my lip upturned in a smile.

“Okay, enough.” Marie pushed Axel off. “Let’s pick out the suits.”

"Baby, I just missed you." He wrapped his arm around her and pulled her to his side.

"I missed you too. But we can talk about that later." They walked forward and examined the different displays.

Francesca came to my side. "Can you believe Axel used to be a jerk to her?"

I honestly couldn't. He'd been this way for so long that it was hard to remember. It was like the past never happened. "I think the old Axel is dead. This is Axel 2.0."

"I thought I liked this version...until it stuck its tongue down Marie's throat."

Her sarcasm always made me laugh, but I held it back. "Have you picked out your bridal dresses yet?"

"No. And I sincerely hope they aren't pink and fluffy."

"Marie has good taste."

"I hope so."

Marie picked out a gray three-piece suit. "This is nice. I like it."

"Why do we have to wear a vest?" Axel asked. "We're already wearing an undershirt, a shirt, a tie, and a jacket. Now we have to wear that too?"

"You wear them to work all the time," she argued. "So why is this any different?"

"Because I have to wear it to work. This is my wedding day. I can wear whatever the hell I want."

"Actually, no, you can't." Marie held up a finger.

"Come on," he said. "The white tuxes will look sick."

I would do anything for Axel, even look like a total loser on his wedding day. But I hoped Marie wouldn't let that happen.

"There's no way in hell you're wearing that." She shoved the suit into his chest. "Try this one."

"But it's gray," Axel argued.

"Gray looks great on you. It brings out your eyes."

"But I wear gray suits to work all the time."

Francesca and I exchanged a look that said, "This could go on for a while."

"Fine." Marie crossed her arms over her chest. "You want me to wear a purple dinosaur costume to the wedding?"

"It's not the same thing and you know it." He held the suit by his side.

"To me, it is." She poked him in the chest. "Now get in there and try it on."

Axel sighed like he was about to argue.

"Axel, let me help you out," Francesca said. "Just do what she says."

Axel narrowed his eyes. "But—"

"You'll live longer." I nodded to the dressing room.

When Axel realized it was three against one, he headed to the dressing room, dragging his feet the entire way.

After the door was closed, Marie turned around and faced us. "I love him. I really do. But...I just hate him. You know what I mean?"

Francesca nodded. "Unfortunately, I know exactly what you mean."

My eyes moved to her face, and I wondered what she was referring to.

***

"Hawke, come out." Marie's voice came through the door.

I buttoned the top of my jacket then stepped out. The suit fit me perfectly even though it wasn't custom made like all the others I owned. It was a deep charcoal gray, and it matched my brooding nature.

I stood in front of the mirror and put my hands in my pockets. Marie and Axel stood beside each other and looked me up and down.

"I love it," Marie said. "I think all the guys should wear it."

"Yeah," Axel said. "It really makes your butt look great."

I raised an eyebrow. "Uh, thanks." My eyes found Francesca in the reflection, and instead of checking out my ass, she was looking at my chest. Her eyes roamed over my body, and there was the same look of need I remembered from our past. When we made love, she would rub her hands up and down my chest, particularly over my heart. The touch wasn't sexual, but spiritual. The look in her eyes made me yearn for a past I could never relive. Everything was so simple with her. It was the only time in my life I'd ever been happy.

Being this close to her made it more difficult to be without her. When we didn't see each other or speak, it was much easier. But now that I was next to her, I couldn't control the feelings constantly flushing through my heart. My soul was naturally in tune to hers. It resonated with a distant hum whenever hers was near.

I could never get away from it.

Francesca finally spoke. "I like it. I think it'll look great on everyone."

"Me too," Marie said. "Well, that was easy."

"I hope getting our bridesmaid dresses is just as easy," Francesca said.

"Don't get your hopes up," Marie said with a laugh.

I headed back to the dressing room because I assumed we were finished.

Axel grabbed my arm before I walked inside. "So, do you do squats or what?"

"Sorry?" What the hell was he talking about?

"Your butt," Axel said. "What do you do?"

Francesca pressed her lips tightly together like she was trying not to laugh.

Marie rolled her eyes and pulled Axel off of me. "Babe, your butt is just as nice. Leave him alone."

"It is?" Axel asked. "I can't see it."

She patted his arm. "Trust me."

CHAPTER TEN

Girl Talk

Francesca

Marie and I grabbed a drink after work.

"So, Axel dropped the argument about the white tux?"

She sipped her cosmo. "Eventually. I'm not even sure where he got the idea. The last time someone wore a white tux was in the eighties."

"Axel has always been unusual…"

"I did a few things he liked and he hasn't brought it up since."

If she were dating any other guy, I would ask for details, but since it was my brother, I didn't want to know. I'd throw up in my mouth then have to swallow it. "Hopefully he lets it go."

"Those gray suits look so much better, and not just on Axel. Hawke looked amazing in it."

Hawke looked amazing in everything—and nothing. "I couldn't agree more."

"I still can't believe he bought that dress for me. He's a superhero."

"He's a sweetheart." Despite the cold and dark exterior he projected, he was the most compassionate person on the planet.

She stirred her drink before she took a sip. "You never told me why you broke up."

Whenever I got this question, I sidestepped it. "Yes, I did. It just didn't work out."

"What kind of reason is that?" she asked. "I didn't pester you about it when it happened because I knew you were out of your mind in agony. But you should be able to tell me now. Axel said Hawke won't tell him either."

I could never tell her the truth. "Marie, I would tell you in a heartbeat if I could. But I simply can't."

That caught her interest even more. "What does that mean?"

"Hawke had an issue but I'm not at liberty to discuss it."

"An issue?" Her eyes were wide. "What kind of issue?"

I gave her a confrontational look. "I can't tell you, Marie. It's his business, and I won't spill his secrets. I'm sorry."

"So, you guys didn't break up because you wanted to?"

I could tell her that much. "No."

She sipped her drink again. "Well, why can't you make it work now?"

"He still has the same issue."

Marie wasn't going to let this go. Her mind was working furiously behind her eyes. "What if—"

"Drop it. Hawke and I are never getting back together. End of story."

"You guys are really just friends?"

"As good of friends as we can possibly be." We would never be platonic. Anytime we were near each other, that old chemistry came to life. Our bodies naturally gravitated toward each other. It was out of our control.

Marie knew this argument was going nowhere. "So, you never finished telling me about the wedding."

This was safe territory. "I'm pissed off at Kyle right now."

"What did he do?" She rested her elbows on the table. The bar was loud with chattering voices, and I knew the men were eyeing her even if I couldn't see them. The rock on her finger acted as a natural bug repellent.

"When we get to the wedding, his mom knows exactly who I am. She's sweet and charming, and she's so warm toward me."

"Isn't that a good thing?"

"Then I found out that Kyle has never brought a girl to any family function. I'm the first. So she thinks Kyle and I are going to get married and crap." It was a nightmare.

Marie didn't seem surprised at all. "Well, you've been with him for six months."

"I haven't been with him. We've been fooling around for six months."

"Monogamously."

"We've never been exclusive."

"Well, I know you haven't been with a single person besides him in that time frame."

"Well, I'm sure he's been with lots of people." Kyle had a natural magnetism that pulled everyone in. Women constantly flirted with him at the bar, and I'd seen some make a pass at him at the gym.

"I highly doubt he's been with anyone."

"What?" I blurted automatically. "You don't even know him."

"I know he's head-over-heels madly in love with you."

My face fell, and the noise of the bar suddenly died out. Time slowed down as her words hit me somewhere deep inside. Marie kept a straight look on her face, not a hint of a smile in any of her features. "What?"

"Like you didn't know, Frankie."

"He's not in love with me." That couldn't be possible. Kyle was always joking around. There wasn't a serious bone in his body. There was no way he could have any deep feelings. We met in the men's locker room for crying out loud.

"He is," Marie said. "And you know he is."

This couldn't be true. "But he's not."

"Frankie, think about it. He's been stuck to your side for six months. You're always telling me how he wants to spend more time with you. And then he takes you to meet his family. How blind are you?"

Memories flashed across my mind. I remembered every time he wanted to sleep over, and when I tried to kick him out, he refused to leave. I remembered every time he asked me to dinner but I rejected him. When he came by my apartment for pizza, he made a joke that I should be his wife…or was it a joke? And then I met his family, and it was clear Kyle told them everything about me.

Marie's lips fell in a frown. "Sorry, girl."

I rubbed my temple as the truth hit me hard in the skull.

"I thought you knew."

"I wasn't paying attention…" Now I was in some serious trouble.

"Why is this a bad thing?" Marie asked. "Kyle is sexy, rich, and he has a great personality. And the biggest feature of all, he totally adores you. He puts up with your bullshit when most men would throw in the towel. He's a serious catch, Frankie."

"I know he's a catch."

"Then take the relationship seriously."

"But I can't." I couldn't make eye contact with her anymore.

"Why not?" she demanded. "Give me one good reason."

"I just don't feel that way about him. Of course, I like him and enjoy spending time with him, but that's it."

"How is that possible?"

"It's just is."

Marie wasn't buying it. "Don't get mad at me, okay?"

I knew what was coming.

"Does this have anything to do with Hawke?"

I closed my eyes as the pain washed over me. It took me a few seconds to open them again. "No."

Marie didn't believe me, not even for a second. "You say you're over him but you clearly aren't."

"I am over him."

"Bullshit."

"It's...complicated." No one understood this except Hawke.

"Then explain it to me."

I rubbed my temple again. "I'm over Hawke. It took me a really long time to finally move on and accept our relationship was really over. Marie, you were there."

"Yes, I remember," she said sadly.

"One day, I finally got out of bed on my own. I finally moved on and didn't look back. Finally, I was in a good place."

She hung on to every word.

"And I haven't look back since. I've been with other guys, and I don't think about him anymore. I'm happy...for the most part. But what I had with Hawke was...indescribable. Nothing will ever compare to what we had."

"You were only together for three months..."

"That doesn't matter. I know I sound crazy when I say this but...he's my soul mate."

Marie didn't laugh or make a joke, but she didn't seem convinced.

"I know you don't believe me and that's totally fine. But I know he was made for me, just like how I was made for him. Even now, there's a distant humming in my ear whenever he's near. There's a gravitational pull between us that constantly binds us together. No matter where I go or who I sleep with, it's there."

Marie took a deep breath. "Frankie…"

"And because of that attachment, it's hard for me to feel anything significant for someone else. Kyle is perfect in every way imaginable. If I'd met him first and never set eyes on Hawke, I'd be anxiously waiting for him to propose to me. But since I've already had my great love, I just can't love someone else."

Marie didn't blink as she watched me. Her drink was untouched, and her fingers rested on the table. She didn't even breathe. "If you feel like this…you really can't work it out with Hawke?"

"No." Nothing had changed. Just one look at Hawke told me everything was exactly the same. He still struggled with the same demons and he always would. He didn't believe in himself.

"But why?"

"We broke up for a reason, and that reason still exists."

"Well..." Marie tried to figure out a way around it. "If that reason was gone, whatever it was, would you be with him again?"

I'd fantasized about that possibility endless times. "No."

Marie's eyes darkened in surprise. "No?"

"I don't trust him anymore. He left me without a backward glance. I gave him everything and he still turned his back on me. I told him we were soul mates and he agreed, but that still wasn't enough reason for him to stay. I love him in a way no one else understands, but that isn't enough. He hurt me irrevocably. There's no guarantee he won't do it again."

She took several minutes to process everything I said. She eyed her glass but didn't take a drink. The world seemed to fade around her, and all she could do was replay my words endlessly in her mind. "That's so...intense."

"That's definitely a good way to describe it."

"So...if that's the case, why don't you attempt to fall in love again?"

"I can't."

"Have you tried?"

"Well...no."

"Maybe you should really try," she whispered. "Because you can't live the rest of your life like this. I want you to have what I have with Axel. You deserve to be happy."

Marriage and kids was something I couldn't picture—at least right now. "I think I just need more time before I'm in that place. Maybe one day I'll meet someone that will change everything. I want a husband who eats my cookies all the time, and I want kids to bake with on Sundays. I really do want all of that. But it's not so simple for me to find."

"What if Hawke was out of the picture? You didn't have to associate with him anymore?"

"I honestly don't think that would change anything. I'm still over him, even when I see him. Of course, my soul aches for him but I've got my heart under control."

"I don't know what I would do if I wanted Axel but could never have him."

"Don't think about it. It'll drive you crazy."

"How about you tell Kyle all of this and give the relationship a chance?"

"No."

"Why not?"

"Because I'm not in that place and he already is. I'm not going to put him through that. The right thing to do is let him go."

Marie's face fell in sadness. "But he's so good to you."

Kyle was thoughtful and passionate, and he was also fun and warm. He's affected my life so deeply without me even realizing it. He hid his feelings so well, but he didn't hide them well enough. He wanted me to himself even if I didn't feel the same way. He was selfless enough not to care. "But I'm not good to him."

Tuesday

CHAPTER ELEVEN

Heartbreak

Francesca

I was dreading this.

Breaks ups were easy. I said it was over and they accepted it without blinking an eye. Every other relationship I've had since Hawke had been meaningless flings, so the guys moved on without a backward glance.

But Kyle was different.

Through the course of our relationship, feelings had developed. That was my fault because I let it go on for so long. Six months was my longest fling, by far.

He came over after he finished his workout, and he walked in without knocking. "The hunkiest man in the world is here." He kicked his shoes off then joined me on the couch. "Whatcha reading?"

"Home Living." I found an interesting recipe for peanut butter cookies. I folded the corner down and tossed it aside for later.

Kyle put his arm over the back of the couch then kissed me. "Missed you today."

I didn't want to do this.

"I thought about your nice ass when I woke up this morning." He winked. "I gave myself a treat."

Why did he have to be so sexy and cute at the same time? "Kyle, there's something we need to talk about."

He rolled his head back with a sigh. "You're so serious all the time. Just chill for once."

"No, I need to say this."

"Fine, you don't have to come to the Hamptons again. I didn't realize you hated my family so much..."

"It's not that, Kyle. They were wonderful."

"Then what's your deal?"

"I'm trying to tell you but you keep interrupting me." I gave him a pointed look.

"Sorry," he said. "What's up?"

Now that I had the floor, I didn't want to talk. I didn't want to say a single word. His blue eyes were hypnotic, and I didn't want to see pain deep inside them. "I've been doing a lot of thinking and...I think we should end this arrangement."

He didn't react at all. He kept staring at me like he hadn't heard a word I said.

"It's just not working for me. But I think we should remain friends."

Silence.

He was giving me nothing to work with. Was he mad? Upset? Did he not care at all?

"No."

No, what? "Huh?"

"I don't accept that."

What did he just say? "Excuse me? You don't accept that?"

"Exactly," he said calmly. "I don't accept that."

My nostrils flared. "I'm sorry you don't accept that, but it's what's going to happen. Deal with it."

"Where the hell is this coming from, Frankie? Just two days ago we were fine."

"I did some thinking."

"And?" He raised an eyebrow. "You realized I'm an awesome guy who's done nothing but made you laugh and come?"

My eyes narrowed on his face.

"I know you have commitment issues, but that's not a sound reason. So, I don't accept that."

He was pushing me to the edge. "I can't be with someone who's in love with me. I'm sorry, but I can't do that to you."

Now he finally reacted. His calm composure disappeared, and panic moved into his eyes. "In love with you?" He forced a fake laugh that sounded nothing like himself. "Me? You think I'm in love with you?"

"Are you telling me you aren't?"

"Of course not." He laughed again and looked away. "That's what this is all about? Then you have nothing to worry about, Frankie."

I wasn't as in tune with him as I was with Hawke, but I still knew him pretty well. "Kyle." My voice took on a gentle tone, wanting to be sensitive to the topic. "For what it's worth, you fooled me. Marie is the one who pointed it out."

Now his carefree façade was completely gone. A somber and sad man replaced him. "I guess I'm surprised you didn't figure it out sooner." He moved his forearms to his knees and rested them there. His fingers interlocked together. He stared at the hardwood floor beneath his feet.

I automatically rested my elbow on his thigh and wrapped my arm around his. "I can't keep doing this knowing that's how you feel. It would be wrong."

"Why?" he whispered. "We've been fine up to this point."

"Because I can't hurt you, Kyle." I didn't want to. I may not love him, but I really cared about him. We had a lot of good times together. I'd had my heart broken before, and I never wanted someone else to go through that.

"If you leave, that will hurt me."

"But it'll hurt worse down the road."

He turned toward me, locking his eyes with mine. "Frankie, why won't you let me in?"

My eyes moved to the floor.

"You say you don't love me, but I know if you gave me a chance, you would. For this entire relationship, you've had your walls up. How do you expect to feel something for anyone if that's how you go about it? Give me a chance. A real one."

I shook my head. "I'm sorry, Kyle."

He tilted his head slightly as he regarded me. "Please don't tell me it's because of him."

"It's not...but it is."

He released a disappointed sigh. "You said you would never go back to him."

"I still wouldn't."

"And you guys have been broken up for two years."

"I know."

"Then why do you keep living in the past, Frankie? Let it go and move on."

"It's not like that," I said. "I'm over him. I just…he's my soul mate. I've told you that before."

Kyle didn't have a response to that. He rubbed his palms together, fidgeting in place. "After all this time, you still believe that?"

"I know that."

"But if you can't be with him, what does it matter?"

"I just can't love someone else. Maybe one day I can, but today, I can't."

He leaned closer to me. "What if I'm okay with that?"

I didn't enjoy this at all. I didn't enjoy seeing him fight for me. "You deserve someone so much better than me, Kyle. You're the perfect guy. You could have any girl you want."

"But I only want you." He turned toward me and grabbed my hand. "I've been around—a lot. I've dated every kind of girl you can think of. No one has ever caught my interest and held it the way you have. I love the fact you're such a beautiful woman but you act like such a tomboy. I love the fact you don't wear make up to work and put your hair in a loose braid. I love the fact you don't care what anyone thinks so you are always yourself. There's no one else like you. I would much rather have the girl I really want—even if she doesn't feel the same way."

It was getting hard to keep my resolve. "You still deserve better, Kyle."

"What if I don't want better?" he asked. "Don't throw this away." He squeezed my hand.

"I'm sorry." I couldn't look him in the eye anymore. It was becoming too painful. As I sat there and ended our relationship, I realized how attached I'd grown to him. This was much harder than I'd anticipated.

"Are you telling me you want to be alone forever?" he asked. "Always jumping from guy to guy? You don't want a husband and a family someday?"

"I do want that. Truly."

"Then have it with me."

"But I'm not ready for that. I need more time to move on."

"I can give you all the time you need." He pressed his forehead to mine.

If I didn't pull away now, I would get suckered in. "Kyle, the bottom line is I don't feel the same way. If I did, I would reconsider this. But I don't."

"But you might—"

"I don't." I hated being so cold. But if I didn't keep a firm hand, Kyle would convince me to stay. Then I would keep dragging him through the mud, using him night after night. "And who knows if I ever will."

Kyle finally released my hand, giving up. His eyes lost their light, and there was no longer a fight in him. He knew there was nothing he could do to change my mind. I was very stubborn, but this was a rare moment when it wasn't the issue. "There's something I want to say before I go."

I swallowed the lump in my throat. "Okay…"

"If you ever change your mind, will you call me?"

I didn't see that as a possibility. And if I did change my mind, it might take years for me to get to that point.

"I don't care how much time has passed. If you decide you're finally in a place for something serious, I want to be the first person you call."

He never once told me he loved me, but now it was obvious how strong his feelings were. All his cards were on the table, and his desperation filled the air. He was always so suave and cool. But now he wasn't playing any games or hiding any emotion.

"Frankie?" he pressed.

I cleared my throat. "I will."

CHAPTER TWELVE

Believe

Hawke

Axel sat across from me in the bar but he didn't touch his beer. His fingers were typing away on his phone.

I wasn't much of a talker anyway, so I drank my beer and enjoyed the silence. Sometimes, when I was alone, my thoughts drifted to Francesca. She went to a wedding last weekend, and I suspected she went with that guy she was seeing. Did she meet his family?

I shouldn't be thinking about it.

It didn't matter.

She was happy.

That's what I wanted.

Axel sighed and kept typing.

The noise caught my attention. "Writing a novel?"

"I'm trying to get that fine piece of ass down here."

"Your fiancée?" I would never talk about Francesca that way, not because it was disrespectful, but because I wouldn't want any man ever thinking about her fine piece of ass.

"Yeah. She just got off work, and I want her to join us." Axel never went anywhere without her. He was obsessed to the point of insanity. He used to complain about clingy chicks, but he was the clingiest dude I'd ever known.

"Maybe she has other plans."

"She doesn't."

I wondered if she got sick of him. Sometimes, I couldn't get Axel to play ball with me because he wanted to stay home with her.

Axel finally smiled and put his phone down. "She's coming."

I was indifferent to her presence. I liked Marie and thought she was a good woman for Axel, but my true fondness stemmed from her friendship with Francesca. She was there for Francesca every single day, including the difficult time of our break up. I would always respect her for that. "Cool."

"She's wearing this black pencil skirt that makes her legs look unbelievable."

Am I supposed to care? "Nervous about getting married yet?"

"Nervous?" He said the word like it was preposterous. "Why would I have asked her if I didn't want to?"

"I didn't say you didn't want to. I just asked if you were nervous."

"No, I'm not nervous." He took a long drink of his beer. "I mean, we're pretty much married anyway. Nothing will be different."

I didn't agree with that.

"Besides, I love her." He shrugged off the words. "I don't want to be with anyone else."

I understood that kind of devotion. I'd felt that way toward Francesca. Actually, I still felt that way. Different women visited my bed but they were just warm bodies. I never remembered their names or faces. They were insignificant, something to pass the time. "I'm happy for you."

"Now every guy in the world will know I'm the one fucking her every night, not them." He adjusted his watch and checked the time.

I remembered how possessive I'd been of Francesca.

Still was.

Marie walked inside and headed to our table. She looked slender in her pencil skirt and tight-fitting blouse. Her long blonde hair was in open curls.

Axel whistled as he rose from his seat. “Hot momma.”

Marie rolled her eyes like his words didn’t impress her, but the smile on her face made it clear she loved the attention. She moved into his chest and kissed him.

Axel gripped her tightly like he usually did, craning his head down so he could kiss her. She was nearly a foot shorter than him even when she wore heels. “Missed my baby,” he said into her mouth.

“I missed you too.” She gave a final kiss before she moved away.

Axel pulled out the chair for her. “What can I get you?”

“A glass of wine.”

“Coming right up.” He kissed her on the forehead before he walked away.

My first thought was to make fun of him for being so whipped, but I held my tongue. I knew my comments only came from jealousy. I had that once before and I threw it away.

Like an idiot.

Marie dropped her smile and vehemently glared at me.

The temperature in the room elevated a few degrees, and I could feel the hostility radiating from her like the hot sun on a summer day. "Bad day?"

Her eyes were dark as coal. "I'm not your biggest fan right now."

What? I just bought her a twenty thousand dollar wedding dress and she was mad at me? "Sorry?"

She glanced at Axel and made sure he was still at the bar before she turned to me. "I don't know what happened between you and Frankie all those years ago because she refuses to tell me, but it's clear the problem is with you, not her."

Marie never once questioned me about my relationship with Francesca. Axel did a few times, but when he realized he wasn't getting anything out of me, he threw in the towel. This confrontation was unexpected, and a little late.

"Hawke, just fix whatever the problem is and be with her."

Where is this coming from? "Did she say something to you?"

"No."

Now I was more confused. "Then why are you saying this to me?"

Her voice raised a few levels. "Because she had a great guy but she threw him away."

What?

"Kyle was smart, sweet, and handsome. He kissed the ground beneath her feet and did everything to make that girl happy. But no matter how hard he worked to bring them closer together, she wouldn't budge. When Frankie found out he was in love with her, she dumped him. *Dumped him*."

Would it make me an ass if I said I was happy about that? "I'm still not following."

Marie's claws were about to scratch my face. "I guess I'll spell it out for you. Frankie told me you're her soul mate, and even though she's over you, she can never fall in love again. Her one true love came and went, so how can she possibly love someone else? Her emotional capacity is completely stunted because of what you did to her. She's out of her mind about it. I don't want her to end up alone because of whatever happened between you. I want her to move on with Kyle and have ten damn babies or have ten damn babies with you. So, get over yourself and get her back. It's obvious you're still the only man she really wants."

Axel came back to the table with the glass of wine. "White is okay, baby?"

Marie smiled like we were discussing rainbows and unicorns. "It's perfect. Thank you." She kissed him on the cheek.

He smiled like an idiot hopelessly in love. "So what were you guys talking about?"

"Nothing." Marie took a long drink.

I eyed my glass. "Not a thing."

***

The Muffin Girl was packed like every other afternoon. I sat at the small table on the patio and continued to look inside. The workers worked like bees behind the counter, serving the dozens of people in line. One half of the shop was reserved for meals, while the other side was for baked goods only. The place was chaotically organized, but that's what made it such an interesting shop. People loved it.

They loved her.

When I finally found the courage to walk inside, I headed to the front and peered in the back. People walked back and forth as they gathered more supplies from the rear. Eventually, I spotted Francesca. She wore a black shirt with the store logo on the front. It was covered in flour and sugar like always. Somehow, she looked more adorable when she was messy.

"Can I help you?" A girl behind the counter eyed me with interest, liking the designer suit I wore along with the expensive watch on my wrist.

Hope was in her eyes, like she wished I were there just to talk to her.

"Is Francesca busy? I'm a friend of hers."

Her hope deflated like a popped balloon. "She's always busy. But you can walk back there and talk to her if you want." The girl walked away and got back to work.

I took the invitation and walked to the rear of the shop. I'd been back there before so I knew where I was going. Shelves were full of bags of flour and sugar, and the door to the massive walk-in refrigerator was on the opposite wall.

As I came closer, I got a better look at her. Francesca was working on a wedding cake, and it looked nearly done. The top had two toppers, both of seahorses, and seashells decorated the different tiers.

I didn't want to scare her, so I stopped a few feet away and watched her work. Flour was smeared on her nose, and she probably didn't know it was there. She held the frosting bag in one hand and examined the texture of the cake, searching for something only her experienced mind could see. When she found a single imperfection, she made the adjustment with her tool. Then she stood back and checked her work.

"Hey."

She spun around the second she heard my voice. Fear was on her face, like she didn't want it to be me. But at the same time, a small amount of joy was deep inside, like she always hoped I'd be standing there when she turned around. "Hi…" She set her frosting bag down then wiped her palms on her jeans. "Didn't hear you come in."

"Sorry, one of your girls told me to come back here."

"It's okay," she said quickly.

I eyed the cake. "It looks nice."

"Yeah…it took me twelve hours but it's another masterpiece."

"I'm sure the bride will appreciate it."

"I hope so. It's why I do this every day."

I put my hands in my pockets and tried not to stare at her too intensely. I tended to do that without thinking. "Did you plan on doing wedding cakes when you started this place?"

"No," she answered. "But I haven't found a cake decorator with enough experience. Arguably, wedding cakes are the most important aspect of the bakery. If we ruin one bride's day, we'll never recover."

"Talk about pressure." I gave her a slight smile.

"You joke about it but it's a serious thing." She moved to the sink and washed her hands of the filth under her fingernails. "So, what brings you here? Other than to gawk at my cake."

Talking to her was so easy, and sometimes, I forgot how far apart we were. "I talked to Axel the other day...he said you broke up with your boyfriend." Actually, that was a lie. Marie was the one who told me, but I didn't want to throw her under the bus.

"Oh..." Francesca nodded slightly, clearly uncomfortable with the topic. I was the last person she wanted to discuss this with. She tucked her dark hair behind her ear, and when she moved her shoulder, her long braid moved to the front. "Yeah, it just didn't work out."

And I knew why. "Are you okay?" Honestly, I didn't know why I was there. I didn't know why I was asking her any of this. All I knew was she was in pain—over me. Marie's words forced me to reconsider everything. I still loved Francesca and always would. I wanted her in my life again. I hated living without her. It was unbearable.

But would I hurt her?

Had I changed?

Or was everything exactly the same?

"Yeah, I'm fine." She avoided eye contact, regaining her bearings. "It wasn't working, and we thought it was best if we went our separate ways."

Why was she lying to me? "I'm glad you're okay. Just thought I would check."

"Well...thanks." She tucked her hair behind her ear again.

"So, are you done with that cake?"

"Yeah. Now it's ready for delivery."

I nodded, my hands in my pockets. "If you're free, want to get lunch?" The words flew out of my mouth.

"Uh...now?"

"Unless you're busy." I kept a suave look on my face.

She fidgeted slightly under my stare. "Sure."

She said yes?

She looked down at her dirty shirt. "As long as we go somewhere casual."

I chuckled. "How about pizza?"

"That works."

***

We sat across from each other in the booth, and we were both tense. It wasn't because we were uncomfortable being around one another. In fact, it was the opposite. The pull was felt between us. Some invisible force was yanking me to her. When I got close enough, I felt the burn on my skin. But I wanted to get burned—as long as I got to be near her.

She eyed the menu. "I think I'm going to get plain cheese."

"It's a classic for a reason."

When the waiter came over, we both ordered and handed our menus over. Then we were left alone again, just our sodas on the red and white tablecloth. The flour was still on her nose.

"You have a little powder on your nose." I didn't want to embarrass her, but I didn't want her to look in the mirror later and feel worse.

"Oh." She quickly wiped it on her forearm. "Thanks. Flour splotches are a hazard with the job."

"It makes it more noble."

She smiled slightly then immediately dropped it.

I didn't know why I asked her, and now that she was here, I didn't know what to do with her. Seeing her from a distance, always in the company of others, drained me. I just wanted to be in her presence, even like this.

It made me feel better.

She held my gaze, her lips pressed tightly together.

I continued to look at her, taking comfort in her green eyes. I used to stare into them endlessly, and when she was asleep, I used to anxiously wait for them to open.

She broke the contact when it became too much. “How’s your mom?”

I lowered my gaze.

“Sorry…she had to come up eventually, right?”

“The question doesn’t bother me.” Francesca could ask me anything she wanted. She had that right—always would. “She’s okay. When we talk, she says everything is fine. He doesn’t hit her anymore. But I don’t believe that.”

She held her hands together on the table.

“I’ve been depositing money into her private account for a long time now. I want her to run away. She has enough money to start over anywhere she wants. But she won’t.”

She bowed her head in sadness. “I’m sorry, Hawke.”

“I know.”

We stared at each other for several minutes again, a silent conversation happening between us. I would give anything to be normal, to not have this problem. I could be with the one woman I actually loved. But I was forced to keep my distance from her, to suffer in silence.

"Axel told me he liked Kyle."

"That's a surprise," she said. "Axel doesn't like anybody."

"I know…so he must have been pretty great."

"He was." She fidgeted whenever she talked about him. "What about you?"

"What?" I asked. "Does Axel like me? I'm not sure sometimes."

She laughed, and her green eyes brightened. "You know what I meant."

I shrugged. "Nothing has changed with me, Francesca." That was enough to answer her question. I had meaningless one-night stands and woke up alone. My life was constantly the coldest month of the year. I hadn't felt alive…in forever.

"No one special in the past two years?"

"No." I was hurt she would even ask that. "Anyone else besides Kyle?"

"A few here and there…but nothing serious."

The waiter brought the pizza slices and placed them between us. It disrupted the tense moment, which was good for both of us.

Francesca looked out the window while she ate her food, keeping her thoughts hidden from me.

I ate quietly, my eyes fixed on her.

Neither one of us said another word for the rest of the meal. Just being in each other's presence was enough to quiet our aching hearts. Five feet separated us, but there was so much more distance between us.

It stretched forever.

***

The last punch broke the bag.

It ripped from the chain and fell to the ground, making a loud thud as it crashed to the concrete floor.

My knuckles were sore from the constant pressure, and sweat marked my forehead. I breathed hard, but I wished I were out of breath. I stepped back and shook my arms, getting the blood flowing again.

Zander, my trainer, grabbed the bag from the ground. "It's busted."

"I'll pay for it." I unwrapped my wrists and felt the circulation increase.

"Something on your mind, Hawke? You seem particularly pissed off."

Just at myself. "No."

Zander gave me an incredulous look but didn't voice his doubt. "You can always talk to me, kid."

Kid? I'm almost thirty. "I know."

"Wash up and we'll pick this up tomorrow."

Without another word, I headed into the locker room and got under the running water. I began my training to dissipate my anger. I thought if I trained hard enough, my temper would fade away.

But it didn't make a difference.

***

When I got out of the shower, I spotted Rebecca going through my nightstand. "Do you mind?"

She flinched when she'd been caught.

"What the fuck is wrong with you?" I was a private person, and I didn't appreciate being searched like a criminal. I slammed the drawer shut and gave her a venomous glare. "Get dressed and get the hell out."

"I'm sorry, Hawke. I was just looking for ChapStick."

"Then you should have asked."

"It was an honest mistake." She didn't get dressed and continued to sit on my bed wearing one of my t-shirts. In her hands was my journal.

Now I was pissed. "Honest mistake?" I snatched it from her violently. "Leave before I throw you out."

"Look, I'm sorry. Just calm down."

I grabbed her clothes from the ground and threw them at her. "Go. Now."

She stood up and slowly pulled her clothes on, taking as long as possible.

I pulled on my running shorts and a t-shirt, purposely not looking at her because I was afraid I would rip her throat out.

"What happened to her?"

I turned her way, my guard up.

"Francesca."

My temple thudded from the blood traveling through my body, and my hands formed fists. "None of your damn business."

Rebecca searched my face and found the answer to a question she never asked. "You love her."

That's when I snapped. I gripped her by the arm and dragged her out of my apartment.

"Hawke, I was just curious—"

"Don't call me again." I shoved her across the threshold.

"Let me explain—"

I slammed the door in her face then locked it.

My journal was personal. It detailed every aspect of my life. After I read Francesca's, I decided to make my own to deal with my pain and suffering. I'd been doing it for years with no sign of recovery.

But I kept writing.

CHAPTER THIRTEEN

Remission

Francesca

"You like it, right?"

I stood in front of the mirror in the floor length gown. It was deep green and skin-tight, bringing out the natural color of my eyes. With my dark brown hair, I felt like a fancy park ranger. "It's nice."

"Be honest." Marie gave me the stink-eye.

"It's very pretty."

"Come on, Frankie." She threw her arms down. "Tell me the truth."

"You want the truth?" I asked.

"Yes." She crossed her arms over her chest.

"It's your day and you shouldn't give a damn whether I like it or not. That's the truth."

Marie rolled her eyes. "I want you to be comfortable."

"Marie, I would wear a Godzilla costume if that's what you wanted. Now pick whatever the hell you want and I'll walk the runway with a smile on my face."

She finally smiled. "You're the best maid of honor ever."

"Yeah, I know," I said like a smartass.

"Alright. Then let's get it."

***

After dress shopping, we went to the deli where Marie got a salad that looked like a head of lettuce.

I eyed it with disapproval. "I know you're on a diet but...you need to eat real food."

"Get off my back," she said defensively. "Axel is already on my ass at home."

At least she was eating with him.

"Anything new with you?" she asked. "I feel like all we talk about is me."

"Because we do."

She shot me a playful glare.

"Well...Hawke and I got lunch the other day."

She stopped stabbing the lettuce with her fork and turned her full focus on me. "Seriously?"

"Yeah, he came by the bakery and asked if I was hungry."

"Shut. Up."

"What's the big deal?" I admit it was a little unusual but we'd been seeing each other pretty often anyway.

"He asked you out on a date. That's a pretty big deal."

"It wasn't a date."

"Sounds like it."

"Marie, believe me. I would know if I were on a date or not." I sipped my soda then took a bite of my meatball sandwich.

"What happened?" she asked excitedly. "What did you talk about?"

"He asked me about Kyle…and if I was okay." That question surprised me the most. I didn't expect him to ask me about my romantic relationships—ever. It was too awkward for both of us.

Her jaw practically touched the table.

"What?"

"He asked about your ex-boyfriend?" She was practically squealing. "He's so trying to get you back."

"I don't think that's what's going on." I knew him a lot better than she did.

"Then explain to me what's going on." She gave me a sarcastic look, like she expected me to prove her right.

"I think he found out about the break up and wanted to see if I was okay, like he said. And I think he asked me out to lunch because he's going through a hard time and just needs to be near me…it soothes him. It's hard to explain. I think he's a little lost right now and doesn't know what to do."

"Lost?" she asked. "Lost from what?"

"Just in general."

"Or, he knows you're officially single and wants to swoop in."

"No." That wasn't it.

"Why are you against that possibility?" she asked.

"Because I know him. Nothing has changed. I think knowing I was in a relationship with another guy bothered him. Once I was single again, he got to feel like I was his…even for just a few minutes. And that made him feel better."

Now Marie looked confused. "You aren't making any sense—at all."

"I know…but trust me."

"You're wrong and I know you are." She said it triumphantly, like she knew something I didn't.

"Why are you so sure of that?"

"Just am." She kept eating her lettuce but there was a smile on her face.

"Marie?"

"What?"

"What aren't you telling me?"

"Nothing." She wouldn't make eye contact with me.

"Girl, I'm about to pull your hair out."

"It's nothing," she said. "Just drop it and keep eating that ridiculously big sandwich."

"You want to split it?"

She sighed in sadness. "I wish."

I knew Marie was up to something, but I also knew she wouldn't talk unless she wanted to. I would just have to wait until her mouth unhinged on its own.

***

I was sitting in my apartment watching TV when something weird happened.

A small noise sounded in my ear, but it was so quiet that I wasn't sure if I heard it at all. The air in the room changed. It became dense, increasing in temperature and humidity. A sudden static filled the air, putting me on alert. For some inexplicable reason, I no longer felt alone.

I grabbed the remote and turned off the TV, listening for a sound that never came. My eyes moved to the door, suspecting someone was on the other side. A sensation formed deep inside me, and it kept telling me someone was on my doorstep.

I couldn't explain it.

I wasn't even sure what was going on.

I slowly approached the door, making my feet as quiet as possible. My breathing was slow and steady, and there wasn't an ounce of fear in my body. When I reached the door I stopped.

I knew who was on the other side.

Hawke was on the other side of the door, standing there without making a sound.

I wasn't crazy.

I just knew.

I pressed my eye to the peephole just to make sure.

And I was right. He stood there with his hands in the pockets of his running shorts. The t-shirt he wore fit his chest and shoulders nicely. He looked directly at me like he knew I was there even though I didn't make a sound.

I opened the door without thinking. Words left me and I didn't know what to say. He would ask how I knew he was there, and I wouldn't have an answer. We stared at each other wordlessly.

Hawke's eyes didn't give anything away. They were closed off and guarded, like usual. His chin was covered in hair like he hadn't shaved in days. His hands remained in his pocket, and it didn't seem like he intended to say anything.

I kept the door open but didn't cross the threshold.

"I want to sleep with you—a one-night thing." He held my gaze as he said it. There wasn't a demanding look in his eyes, but it was clear he wanted it.

I knew what he meant. It was nothing physical or lustful. His words were literal.

But should I?

I'd worked so hard to get over him.

It took me an entire year just to get out of bed in the morning.

My heart would always beat for him, but that didn't mean I should be stupid.

But I wanted him to come in. I wanted to be with him.

I knew I shouldn't. It wasn't a good idea. What if it led us down the road that would lead us nowhere?

Or what if I regretted saying no?

"Just one night."

He nodded his understanding before he stepped inside. His hands were by his sides and he didn't make a move to grab me. Wordlessly, we went into my bedroom.

The mattress was the same one I used to sleep on with Hawke. The bedspread was still yellow, and the furniture was the same too. Hawke noticed it, judging the way he glanced at everything.

I turned off the light then got into bed. Hawke didn't remove his shirt or his shorts, and slid in beside me. It was early for my bedtime. I usually went to sleep at ten, but it was only nine.

Hawke lay beside me but didn't touch me.

I turned on my side and faced the window, away from him. I waited for the feel of his large hands, the way his body felt pressed to mine. He hadn't touched me in so long that I couldn't remember how it felt.

Then he pressed his chest against my back, the heat automatically picking up the second we made contact. His hand moved around my waist, slowly coming to the front of my stomach. He took his time, like he was trying to appreciate every moment of it. Then he pressed his face into my neck, taking a deep breath as he inhaled my scent.

It felt better than sex.

It was so good it hurt.

My body ached from the pain and the pleasure.

I took a deep breath and felt my chest convulse. He hadn't held me like this in years. We used to do it every night, and I tried to forget how great it felt so I could carry on without him.

It was home.

I tried not to cry because that would ruin the moment. The pain I pushed down far inside was emerging from deep in my throat, and I couldn't let it escape. I had to be strong and accept the moment for what it was.

Hawke breathed deeply against me, his breaths abnormally quick. His fingers spanned completely across my stomach, feeling the bare skin under my shirt. His hips were pressed against me, but the bulge I expected to feel was absent. His arm squeezed around me before he pulled me further into him, wanting us to be as close as possible.

It was heaven.

But it was hell.

Our souls finally stopped aching now that they were together. The throbbing and bleeding stopped just for an instant in time. But when he left the following morning, the pain would start all over again.

While I controlled my breathing and stopped myself from crying, my eyes continued to water. A tear came loose from my eyelashes and rolled down my cheek toward my lip.

Hawke pressed his lips directly against my skin, making me feel alive for the first time in two years. "I needed this."

"I needed it too."

***

We woke up to the sound of my alarm.

When my eyes opened, I realized I was on top of him. I slept on his chest just the way I used to. It was the warmest and comfiest spot on the bed. My hair lay across him, and his hand was fist deep in the strands. His chest rose and fell at a steady rate despite the obnoxious sound of the alarm.

My fairytale was over.

I moved off his body and tried not to scream. The one thing in life that gave me comfort was going to leave again, walk out and return to keeping his distance from me all over again.

Why did he have to leave me to begin with?

"You get up at five in the morning?" he asked as he rubbed the sleep from his eyes.

"Yeah. Sorry."

"Maybe we should have slept at my place."

"You can keep sleeping if you want. Just lock up before you leave."

"No, it's okay." He kicked the covers back and sat at the edge of the bed. After he blinked his eyes a few times, he looked at me. He had a sleepy look in his eyes, but he somehow made it look sexy. His hair was messy from my pillow, but even that looked good.

"Hawke?"

"Hmm?" He held my gaze, and the same disappointment burned in his eyes. He didn't regret coming over last night, but he regretted the fact he had to leave.

"What did Marie say to you? Or what did you say to her?" I knew Hawke wouldn't lie to me, even if he thought it would spare me pain. Marie, on the other hand, would lie out of her ass if she thought it was in my best interest.

"She told me the real reason you broke up with Kyle." He didn't sugarcoat it. "He fell in love with you but you didn't feel the same way, and you told him you never would...because of me." There was no victory or joy in his voice.

I couldn't figure out any possible reason why Marie would do that. Why would she spill my secrets like that? And to Hawke of all people? I didn't know they had a one-on-one relationship.

Hawke answered my unspoken question. "She told me off for breaking your heart, and she told me I needed to fix whatever issue I had if I ever want to make our relationship work...because you said we're soul mates."

My cheeks reddened slightly in embarrassment.

"I still feel the same way." His thigh touched mine as we sat on the bed next to each other.

I tried not to look relieved. If he looked back on our relationship and said we were just two idiots in love, it would have broken my heart. The fact he still believed what I did made me feel less alone. "Why did you come over last night?"

"I missed you—more than usual."

I waited for something more.

"I've been in a lot of pain lately...your presence heals it."

I knew what he was talking about.

He rubbed his palms together slowly, like he was thinking through the next sentence in his mind. Then he rose to his feet. "I should go. I know you have work."

Hawke's departure was the best thing for me right now. I didn't want to get attached and hope last night would lead to something more. We could never go down that road again, not because I thought Hawke would ever lay a hand on me, but because he would rip my heart out again sometime in the future. This painful distance was all we could handle.

And it was all we could ever handle.

***

My stomach burned from where he touched me.

I could still smell his scent on me.

It felt like a dream because it was so magical. I never wanted to wake up and let the vision slip into the recesses of my mind. But I knew I needed to let it go. If not, it would consume me.

I placed a new batch of cinnamon rolls in the glass counter and looked up to see a familiar face.

Kyle was standing there, a forced smile on his face.

I didn't expect to see him again. "Hey."

"Hi." Instead of making a smartass comment, he looked awkward, like he wasn't sure if his presence would piss me off or not.

I wiped my hands on my napkin then came around the counter. There was a crowd behind them as people waited in line to order. When I approached him, I saw the pain deep in his eyes. He was trying to hide it, but he was doing a miserable job. Without thinking twice about it, I hugged him.

He returned the embrace immediately, like it was the real reason he came all the way down there. He squeezed me to his chest and rested his chin on my head. "I'm sorry if this isn't okay…"

"It is." I pulled away then crossed my arms over my chest. The hug was purely friendly, and I didn't want to lead him on.

"I just...wanted to see how you were doing."

"I'm okay." I knew I was taking the break up better than he was. Just last night, I slept with Hawke. My body wanted to break down because it felt so good. "You?"

He shrugged. "I've been better. Actually, I'm worse than I thought I would be. I've never done this before. You know, gone through a break up."

My heart went out to him. "It sucks. I'm not going to sugarcoat it for you."

"Yeah, I'm figuring that out." He released a faint chuckle, and that former smile was reappearing. "What have you been doing?"

"Working and helping Marie plan the wedding."

"Sounds like two full-time jobs."

"More like three."

He laughed again. When his eyes settled on me, the fondness shined from deep within. "Let's get lunch. I miss you."

I missed him too. I may not have fallen in love with him, but he became one of my closest friends. It was weird not seeing him anymore, not spending the night with him anymore. But I knew that had trouble written all over it. "I don't think that's a good idea…" I wasn't risking my heart by spending time with him, but he was. And I couldn't do that to him.

He sighed like he feared that might be my answer. "I get it."

"But I'm glad you stopped by."

"Yeah…it's nice seeing you." His smile dropped and the depression replaced it. "I guess I'll see you around, Frankie."

"Take care, Kyle."

He gave a slight nod before he parted the crowd and walked out.

***

"I've got a problem with you." I pointed my finger in Marie's face the second I met her on the sidewalk.

"Me? What?" She projected that innocent-not-so-innocent look that I could see right through.

"You told Hawke about Kyle." We were standing in front of The Plaza, and Axel and Hawke would join us in a second.

The blood left her face. "He told you?"

"Of course he did. Why wouldn't he?"

"That little bitch." She pressed her lips together in disapproval.

"He's not a little bitch." I waved my words away. "But that's not the point. Why did you tell him?"

She threw her arms down like she'd been keeping something bottled up inside. "Frankie, who says stuff like that? 'He's my soul mate but we can never be together. I was with a perfect guy for six months but I couldn't fall in love with him because I've already had my great love.' I mean, are we in a Shakespeare play right now?" She put her hands on her hips and regarded me coldly. "Frankie, that was the most intense conversation I've ever had. I was pissed off that Hawke did this to you so I told him off."

"I figured that out..."

"And I don't regret it. He deserves to be put in his place once in a while."

I crossed my arms over my chest.

"When did he tell you?"

"The other night."

"What did you guys do?"

Should I tell her? "He spent the night."

Her jaw unhinged and practically fell on the concrete. "Say what?"

"We didn't sleep together," I said quickly. "We just slept, if you catch my drift."

"He went over there just to sleep with you?" she asked incredulously.

I knew we didn't make sense to normal people. "Yeah, I knew he was outside my door—"

"What do you mean you knew? Didn't he knock?"

That was another supernatural thing that made me sound crazy. "No, I just knew he was there. He came inside and we went to sleep. That's it."

"No kissy-kissy? No touchy-touchy?"

"We snuggled together."

She shifted her weight and shook her head slightly. "You guys are the weirdest people in the world. Frankie, I don't mean that in a joking way. I literally don't get it."

"I don't blame you…"

"What does this mean? Are you guys getting back together?"

"It doesn't mean anything," I said with a sad tone. "We just wanted to be together, just for the night. It made us both feel better."

She cocked her head to the side and opened her mouth like she was going to say something. "You know what? Never mind."

It was a good thing this conversation was being dropped.

But Marie revisited it. "So, you're not getting back together?"

"Ever."

"Like, *ever*?"

"Ever."

"I just don't get it. How can two people who love each other so much not make it work?"

I wish I could give her the answer. Hawke didn't trust himself and never would. When his temper flared, he was out of control. He didn't think he could stop himself from becoming a monster, just like his father. I knew that would never happen, but Hawke refused to believe me. And even if he did, it wouldn't matter now. He hurt me more than any punch he could land. He broke me into a million pieces, and those fragments were still scattered on the wind. He would never be able to find them all and piece them back together.

***

"Oh my god, I love it." Marie spun in circles in the ballroom as she looked up at the crystal chandelier. "Isn't it beautiful? Axel, don't you just love it?"

Axel looked around the room, his hands in his pockets. "Sure."

Marie stopped in her tracks. "What don't you like about it?"

"I didn't say I didn't like it."

"But you don't *sound* like you like it."

Hawke turned to me, a distant smile upturning the corner of his lip. "This could take awhile."

"No kidding." I stood beside him but kept my arms across my chest, making sure they didn't reach for Hawke by their own discretion.

"Do you like it?"

"Like them fighting?" I asked.

A hearty chuckle came from deep in his throat. "No, do you like The Plaza?"

"Oh. Yeah, it's nice."

Hawke picked up on my tone. "Not your thing?"

"I don't like being inside. I'd rather be at the beach or a vineyard, something under the sky."

He nodded. "That's more you."

"I'd love to get married on a hillside. You know, with daisies in the grass and a valley in the distance…" It's always what I imagined.

Hawke turned away, his face a stoic mask.

When I pictured my future, I saw a husband. He didn't have a face but he was there. I just hoped that dream came true someday. This infinite torture with Hawke would drive anyone insane.

"That sounds nice."

I purposely turned my gaze to the piano in the corner. It was black, and the wood was sleek.

Marie and Axel were still arguing in the middle of the room.

"If you don't like it, just tell me." Marie put her hands on her hips.

"Baby, I said it was fine."

"Well, I don't want just *fine*. I want you to love it."

Axel ran his fingers through his hair in irritation. "Honestly, I'm not going to love any place you pick. I don't give a damn where we get married. All I care about is you showing up in a dress that makes your tits look incredible, alright?"

Hawke chuckled under his breath. "He's smooth…"

I rolled my eyes. "And disgusting."

"Come on," he said quietly. "You don't think they're a little bit cute?"

"I don't know…he's my brother."

"Even so."

"You think they're cute?" I asked incredulously. Cute wasn't in Hawke's vocabulary very often.

"I don't think a lot of things are cute, but they're one of the few." He ran his hand down his chest to smooth out his tie. He was wearing his suit like he just got off work before we met there. At six three, he was already a powerhouse, but when he rocked his Hugo Boss suits, he looked even more impressive.

No matter how much time had passed, my knees would always feel weak around him. When I first saw him, all I felt was a physical attraction. He was gorgeous and any girl would agree with me. But when I got to know him, I saw so much more beneath that muscled exterior. And I think that's why he was even more beautiful. "Where are you going for the bachelor party?"

"The Rainbow Room."

"In the city?" I figured they would go to Vegas or do something cliché.

"Axel doesn't want to do anything crazy. I figured a night of drinking and gambling in an upscale place would be fine."

"No strippers?" Axel was definitely a stripper kind of guy.

"He said he didn't want any."

"Wow..." He really is a new man.

Hawke chuckled. "He's over the moon for Marie. And I don't think that's a bad thing."

"No, definitely not."

"What are you guys doing?"

"Uh...going to Chippendales."

"What's that?"

"The male strip show..."

Hawke tried not to laugh. "Well, I guess Marie isn't as hung up on Axel as he is on her."

"It's not the same thing. Honestly, when those guys are rocking their G-strings, it's funny rather than sexy."

"If I rocked a G-string, it wouldn't be funny at all."

I swallowed the lump in my throat. "No, it wouldn't."

Hawke eyed his watch then returned his hand to his pocket. "The other night was nice..."

We hadn't talked about it since he left. "Yeah..."

"I haven't slept that well in years."

"Neither have I."

Hawke moved closer to me, his gaze still set on Axel and Marie. When he was right next to me, his fingers brushed against mine. His knuckles were calloused and dry, like he punched dry wall on a regular basis.

The touch was so innocent, but it sent chills down my spine. My entire body flushed with heat, and my throat went dry. My tongue felt too big for my mouth, and my lungs automatically contracted to release a shaky breath. Just the simple touch floored me, like a branch soaked in kerosene along with a lit match.

When I turned my face toward him, his gaze was on me. He watched me intently, searching for something in my eyes. His look massaged me everywhere, penetrating my darkest crevasses.

He came closer to me, breaking through my shield. I could hear his breaths, and within a moment, I could smell the distant hint of mint. His cologne washed over me, and I was reminded of our night together, cuddling in each other's arms. My fingers suddenly burned from being so close to the fire raging in his soul.

I wanted to break the connection because it was so strong. My body couldn't handle the proximity, the intimacy. But I didn't step back or turn away. I held my ground because I wanted it. I wanted something I could never have, and Hawke felt the same way. We would rather be tortured by each other's presence than feel the cold of each other's absence.

He finally pulled his fingers away from mine, taking the heat with him. Then he leaned away, like he didn't trust himself that close to my lips. He cleared his throat and looked away.

Marie and Axel returned to us. "This is the place." She clapped her hands and hopped up and down.

I missed their entire argument because I was so absorbed in Hawke. "Great." I had to force my enthusiasm because I was in such a different place.

"Awesome," Hawke said. "It's a beautiful place."

Axel didn't give a damn about the venue, but when he watched Marie hop up and down in excitement, he smiled. He wasn't the selfish man I used to know. Now, he lived his life for a single person.

And it showed.

***

We went to my apartment and watched the game. I whipped up some finger food and set them on platters on my coffee table. Fortunately, I had a case of beer in the fridge. It actually belonged to Kyle, but I knew he wasn't going to need it.

Axel had his arm around Marie while he held a beer on his thigh.

I sat on the couch with Hawke, but there was at least three feet in between us. Just the other night, he slept over, but it didn't seem like it ever happened.

"Dude, Manning better make this." Axel didn't blink as he watched the TV. "If he doesn't, I'm never buying a Papa Murphy's pizza again."

"You never eat it anyway," Marie said with an irritated look.

"True," Hawke said. "We always go to Luigi's."

"That's not the point," Axel said. "It's just the principle of the matter."

"To say you aren't going to do something that you weren't going to do anyway?" Marie grabbed his beer and took a long drink. "Talk about making a difference..."

Axel watched her seal her mouth around the head of the bottle. "You're going to be sucking something else later..."

I tried not to gag.

And to my horror, Marie smiled when she pulled the bottle away. "You're letting me get married at The Plaza. It's the least I can do."

"Whatever," Axel said. "Don't act like you don't love it."

"Okay..." My stomach just did a tumble. "I know you guys are in love and everything but enough."

"Sorry." Marie crossed her arms over her chest. "Sometimes I forget you guys are siblings."

"Because I'm unbelievably sexy and she's plain?" Axel asked.

"The other way around, actually," Marie teased.

Axel smiled then gave her a quick tickle. "You're going to get spanked for that."

"Ooh..." Marie curled into his side.

I turned to Hawke. "Got any Pepto-Bismol?"

He chuckled under his breath. "I wish."

Axel grabbed two egg rolls I made from scratch and shoved them into his mouth. "Damn, these are good." His mouth was so stuffed his words were incoherent.

Since I grew up with him, I could decipher his code. "Thank you."

"Marie's cooking is better though." After he chewed the hunk of food in his mouth, he swallowed.

I knew that wasn't true, no offense to Marie. And she knew it too. But the fact Axel said it was still sweet. "You're right."

We continued to watch the game, and when it was over, I was restless for them to leave. Sitting close to Hawke made me hot under the collar. The way our hands touched earlier made my heart beat at an unhealthy pace. It was impossible to be so near each other and not be aware of every movement and every breath. I was struggling to remain in control. I desperately wanted him to touch me, to hold me. The need was inexplicable.

Finally, Axel stood up. "Baby, ready to go?"

"Yeah, I'm tired." Marie joined his side. "We had a long day."

"But at least we know where we're getting married." His arm moved around her waist. "That's a good step."

"Very," Marie agreed. "We'll see you guys later." She discreetly glanced at Hawke, silently telling me she knew something was going on but she wouldn't call me out on it—at least in the presence of Axel and Hawke.

"Good night." I wondered if Hawke would leave with them, but he remained in his seat.

"Basketball tomorrow?" Hawke asked.

Axel turned to Marie. "Is it cool if I play ball after work?"

Hawke turned to me and fought an oncoming grin. "Fucking pussy…"

Axel snapped his head in our direction. "What did you say?"

"Nothing." Hawke kept an unreadable expression.

Now I was trying not to laugh.

"Axel, you don't have to ask me if you can play ball," Marie said.

"I know," Axel said. "I just didn't know if we had dinner plans or something."

"We don't," Marie said. "So, he'll see you tomorrow, Hawke."

Hawke nodded. "Cool."

Marie and Axel walked out hand-in-hand.

The second the door was closed, the air filled with static. It rang in my eardrums and caused the sound of the TV to fade to the background. My palms were suddenly seared with heat. They burned even though there were no flames.

Hawke's body tensed slightly underneath his suit. The tension rose, and the supernatural connection between us formed. I could feel his heartbeat without touching him. I could smell the sweat that started to form on his chest.

I squeezed my thighs together.

We couldn't be alone in the same room together without this happening, without the gravitational pull that our bodies constantly emitted for each other.

Hawke grabbed the remote from the coffee table and hit the OFF button. The TV immediately went black.

A lump formed in my throat and I tried to swallow it, but my mouth had suddenly gone dry.

Hawke turned to me, and when our eyes locked, the walls came down. The resistance had disappeared. At least neither one of us wanted to fight it anymore. At the same instant he grabbed my hip and pulled me on top of him, I crawled into his lap and straddled his hips.

His arm wrapped completely around my waist and he dug the other into my hair. He pressed his face into my neck and took a deep breath, smelling me. My arms hooked around his neck and my thighs squeezed his hips. The touch gave each of us so much relief, but so much angst at the same time. When our bodies were pressed together this way, time slowed down. The world bowed to us so we could cling to each other in desperation.

Tuesday

CHAPTER FOURTEEN

Resistance

Hawke

What the fuck was I doing?

I couldn't stay away from her, not anymore. My heart was bleeding and she was the only one who could stop the wound. I'd never wanted something so much in my entire life. Anytime she was in my arms, all the pain disappeared.

Would I ever hurt her?

Could I hurt something I loved so damn much?

At times like this, the answer was no. I would never lay a hand on her. The idea of her being in any kind of pain sent me over the edge. I couldn't handle it. I'd rather die than cause her pain.

But what if I was angry around her? What if she became an innocent bystander?

What if I turned into my father?

I'd seen the wreckage his drunken rage had caused. My mother was a helpless victim that couldn't get away. If she ran, he would follow her. And the beating would be much worse. I drank like anyone else, but I'd never been drunk in my life.

I was afraid of what would happen if I ever did.

For the past two years, I'd spent every day drinking and fucking. Every night when I went to bed, I dreamt of the one woman I actually gave a damn about. I wasn't just insanely infatuated with the softness of her hair or the curve of her kissable lips. I was madly in love with her soul—because it was mine.

Why couldn't I have the one thing I wanted? Hadn't I suffered enough? Francesca was the only thing that could make me whole. I'd never love anyone else for as long as I lived. Even now, I wished every girl in my bed was her.

A knock on my door shattered my thoughts.

I wasn't expecting company, so I wasn't sure who it was. In my heart, I hoped it would be Francesca. But if she were here, I would know. Somehow, I would know.

I opened the door and saw Danielle on the other side. She wore a trench coat with heels. I didn't need her to open the jacket to understand she only wore lingerie underneath.

"You look like you've had a long day." She tilted her head to the side, trying to be sexy.

"I may have."

"Let me make it better." She took one step inside, coming in without being invited.

I'd fucked Danielle before and it was always fun. She was kinky in ways most girls weren't. I did a lot of nasty shit that most guys only dream of.

But now I couldn't do it. "Not tonight. Actually, this is it."

She tilted her head again, but this time in confusion. "Wait…what?"

I needed to stay away from Francesca. I didn't trust myself. But I really thought I could do right by her. If I were ever angry around her, I would leave. That would solve any future problem. If I just removed myself from the situation, I would never have to worry about hurting her. "I'm with someone."

"Again…what?"

Two years ago, leaving Francesca was the best decision. I'd seen too many similarities between my father and I, and after the way I savagely threw her across the floor in that bar, I didn't deserve her.

But now I did.

"I belong to someone. I can't do this."

Danielle moved her hands to her hips. "You have a girlfriend?"

"No." It was so much more than that. "I'm sorry for wasting your time, Danielle. I'm unavailable. I know you'll find someone that appreciates you more than I did."

Her pride was clearly wounded by the pissed look on her face. "Whatever, Hawke. Don't come crying to me when you miss this—all of this."

There was only one woman I missed. "Good night."

She flipped her hair over her shoulder before she sauntered off, moving her hips with an attitude.

I shut the door and walked back into my empty apartment. I had no idea what I was doing, but it didn't seem like I was in charge of my life anymore. Something else was making all the decision for me—my soul.

***

I waited outside the bakery at five o' clock. I knew Francesca got off work at that time, and I was hoping to run into her without making it seem like I planned it on purpose.

I knew she felt the way I did. That much was obvious by the way she clung to me for dear life. She dumped a nice guy because he simply wasn't me. But I remembered how much I hurt her. That wasn't something someone could forgive so easily.

Would she forgive me?

At five o' clock, she made her move. She walked out of the bakery in a black t-shirt covered with flour.

I walked with my hands in my pockets and purposely headed her way. Right when I crossed paths with her, she spotted me. She stopped her in her tracks and looked up at me, that same look of fear and joy she always gave me. "Hey."

"Hi…" She immediately played with her hair, like she was self-conscious about the flour that was caked all over her.

Little did she know I wanted to lick it all off. "Just got off work?"

"Yeah. It was a long day. What about you?" The further into the conversation we went, the less tense she seemed. Sometimes, she was on edge around me, but I suspected it was because she was constantly guarding her heart.

"A lot of paperwork. I'm not a big fan of it."

"Isn't that all you do?"

I shrugged. "In a nutshell, I guess. But there's more to it than that." Francesca never really discussed my company. We hadn't had much time alone together so it never came up. She had no idea how wealthy I was or how hard I worked to open my business. I had more money than I could ever need, and I wanted to give it all to her.

"I'll take your word for it." She adjusted the strap of her purse and shifted her weight.

"Want to come over for dinner?" I hadn't planned on asking her that, but now that she was in front of me, the words slipped out. I missed spending time with her, just she and I.

Her green eyes lightened noticeably, giving her away. She wanted to stay away from me, but she didn't have the strength to keep up her resistance.

Neither did I.

"I should shower." She looked down at her dirty shirt.

"You can shower at my place." Shit, my mouth was out of control.

"And put on the same dirty clothes?" she asked with an awkward laugh.

"You can wear some of my stuff."

She took a deep breath like the idea of being surrounded with my smell was the biggest comfort in the world. I understood the sensation. Anytime she was close to me, I was on crack. It felt so good at the time even though it felt shitty later when the high was gone. "Okay."

I knew that would be her answer even though she didn't want that to be her answer. "Then let's go. I'm making salmon and greens."

"It's nice to have someone cook for me for once."

And it was nice to have dinner with someone for once.

***

Knowing she was buck-naked in my shower made my cock rock-hard. It hadn't been this stiff since the last time I'd been with her. She turned me on like crazy, even when she was covered in powder and sugar.

I prepared dinner in the kitchen while I listened to the water run in the shower. I imagined the droplets sliding down her gorgeous figure. She was always self-conscious about her thighs. She said they were too big.

But I thought they were perfect.

When the water turned off, my dick finally stopped throbbing. But I had a feeling it would swell up to the size of a balloon once she came out in my clothes. I grilled the salmon on the stove and then prepared the greens in a separate pan. I ate like a health freak all the time. It was the only way I could retain my muscle and not gain fat.

When she came out, dinner was ready.

She wore one of my Yankees t-shirts along with a pair of running shorts that were rolled a dozen times at her waist. That was the only way she could get them to fit. Her hair was slightly damp and her face was free of make up.

Fuck, I wanted her.

"It smells really good."

"Thanks." I sat down at the table and she sat across from me.

She pulled her hair over one shoulder and ate quietly, her eyes glued to her food.

I ate slowly and watched her the entire time.

"Do you cook often?"

"Every night. I don't like eating out."

"That's healthy."

"I'm not a fan of all the oil and grease they put into everything. At least at home, I know what I'm getting."

"I do the same thing."

I chewed a few pieces of broccoli. "Decorate a wedding cake today?"

"Actually, no," she said. "But I made a ton of bear claws."

"That sounds delicious."

"They were," she said with a smile. "I sampled them. You know…to make sure they were good."

"I bet."

She finished her food before I did. "That was really good. I'm impressed."

"I'd like to take all the credit, but I think Google deserves some of it." I took our empty plates and placed them in the sink.

"You cooked so shouldn't I clean?" It was a fallback to our old relationship. When she stayed at my place for the week while her floors were getting redone, she did all the cooking, and I did all the cleaning. Remembering the past made me sad. All I could think about was the way she fell to the floor when I walked out of that apartment for the last time.

"No." I didn't give her an explanation why, and she was smart enough not to ask.

"What's for dessert?" She changed her tone to lighten the mood.

You. "I don't have a sweet tooth."

"I remember differently…"

"I only have a sweet tooth when it comes to you." I could invite her into the living room to watch TV but that's not what I wanted to do. I had a feeling she didn't either.

I pulled her chair out then lifted her to my chest. One arm was cradled under her knees while the other supported her back. Her arm immediately circled my neck like she was expecting it.

I carried her into my bedroom and set her on the mattress. Then I pulled off my shirt and jeans until I was just in my boxers.

Francesca sat at the edge of the bed.

I pulled the sheets back then got in, lying back on the pillow.

She didn't move.

I sat up and watched her, trying to gauge her thoughts.

She looked at the sheets then felt the fabric with her fingertips. Her eyes were half-lidded, somewhere faraway.

Then it hit me. "They didn't mean anything to me."

Francesca turned her eyes on me.

I grabbed her arm and gently pulled her to me. "Don't think about it. We both know you're the only one who really matters. So don't compare yourself." When I lay on her bed, I thought about Kyle and the fact he probably fucked her on that mattress. But then I remembered she dumped him because he could never compete with me.

And none of them could compete with her.

I pulled her flush against my body and hooked her leg over my hip. It was 7:30 and neither one of us were planning on sleeping. But I wanted to lay with her and just look at her. I wanted to stare at those beautiful green eyes that sent chills down my spine. I wanted to feel the hum of our bodies as they lay so close to each other.

This healed me.

Francesca moved a hand to my chest, and her fingers grazed over the skin. Her lips were slightly parted, and her teeth were showing.

I wanted her—badly. But I preferred this. She wasn't just another woman to me. She was *the* woman. And just being with her was enough for me. I didn't think about fucking her or burying myself inside her to mask the pain. I only thought about kissing her, massaging those lips with my mouth. I only thought about loving her in the way she deserved.

"What are we doing?" she whispered.

"I don't know. But I like it."

"I like it too."

My hand moved into her hair and I pulled it from her face. The moment felt like a dream, a reality where she was mine. Sometimes, I wondered where we would be if I hadn't left. Would we be married? Would we have a child together? I never wanted to have kids, but it didn't sound so bad with her.

For the rest of the night, we just stared at each other. Sometimes, she would close her eyes and doze off, but even then I would continue staring. Her fingers would move across my chest, and eventually they lay over my heart. We spent the night falling in and out of consciousness. I wanted to sleep because she chased my nightmares away, but I also wanted to stay awake just so I could watch her.

I wanted to treasure her.

***

After an hour of playing basketball, we washed up and headed to the deli.

"I'm surprised your wife gave you permission to go out." I loved teasing him about this. Just a few years ago, I distinctly remember him telling me he would never get married. Now, he was whipped.

"Shut the hell up." He grabbed his tray of food then took a seat at the table.

I did the same.

"And she's not my wife—yet. But she will be soon." An involuntary smile stretched his lips.

I wanted to make another joke but I held it back.

"You like The Plaza?"

"Sure." It was just another hotel to me.

"That's how I feel about it too. Not sure why Marie is so obsessed with it. I honestly think she just likes the idea of it more than the actual place. Personally, I've always pictured myself getting married outside somewhere."

"Why don't you tell her that?"

He shrugged. "It's her day. She can whatever the hell she wants."

"Pushover..."

"Look, she's my lady. If she wanted to get married at Funworks, I wouldn't have said anything."

"Well, somebody should," I said with a laugh.

Axel ate half his sandwich in a few bites. "So, who'd you share your bed with last night?"

It'd always been a little awkward talking about girls after Francesca and I split up. We never went into detail about it, but Axel asked me questions now and then. And he wasn't stupid. He knew I went back to my old ways the second I moved here. "No one." That was a lie. Francesca was in my bed, but I didn't think that would be the best answer.

"That's odd."

I'd been going over my situation with Francesca endlessly. I went back and forth in my decision, but I knew what I really wanted. With every passing day, it would only become more difficult. And if I wanted this, I had to do this right. "Axel, we need to talk about something..."

"Yeah?" He raised an eyebrow as he threw a chip in his mouth. "You got Chlamydia?"

"I'm gonna pretend you didn't ask me that."

"It's a legitimate question. You must have something right now. One time, I had a crabs scare."

I glanced at my food and lost my appetite. "Nothing like that."

"Phew. Then what's up?"

"It's about Frankie."

His entire expression changed. He went from laid-back to on edge. He watched me with a guarded look, his suspicion evident in the burn of his eyes and the fine line of his lips. "What about her?"

"I've been doing a lot of thinking and...I want her back."

He leaned back in his chair, growing angrier with every passing second. "This better be a fucking joke."

"It's not."

He leaned over the table, getting close to me. "Let me get this straight. You dump her two years ago after you tell her you're her fucking soul mate, and now that you're seeing her again, you want to give it another try?" Axel wasn't particularly close with Francesca but he was incredibly protective of her. He claimed it was because she didn't have a father, but I knew it was because he loved her, whether he would admit it or not.

"It's more complicated than that."

"No, you just want what you can't have. Frankie gets a nice boyfriend and then you get jealous—"

"She broke up with him weeks ago."

Axel's jaw was still hanging. "Why are you telling me all of this, Hawke? I'm still pissed at you for what you did to her. And I still don't know why you did it."

"It's not because I stopped loving her."

"Shut up, Romeo."

"And I'm telling you this for a reason."

The vein in his temple was starting to pulse. "I have a feeling I'm not going to like it."

"I just want your support in this. I'm going to tell her how I feel. And I know it would mean a lot to her if you were on board with it. She acts like your opinion doesn't matter to her but I know it does."

"You didn't give a damn about my support last time. Why is this any different?"

"Because I know I fucked up. I admit that."

He watched me with scrutiny.

"And I deserve to be doubted. I deserve your reservations."

He crossed his arms over his chest.

"But I do love her, Axel. I always have."

"I think it's a terrible idea..."

"I'm not asking for your permission, Axel. I just wanted to give you a head's up. I'm going to tell her how I feel, and I already know how she feels. But it would make things a lot easier if you supported both of us. Because this is what we want."

"You're speaking for her, but you have no idea what she'll say."

"I do know what she'll say."

Axel shook his head slightly. "You weren't there, Hawke. You didn't see how bad she was."

I dropped my gaze because the pain burned a hole in my skin. I couldn't meet his stare because I didn't deserve to. "I know I hurt her. I had my reasons."

"Which you still won't admit."

"Believe me, I thought I was doing the right thing."

"And what's different now?"

I couldn't answer that without giving anything away. "Everything."

He sighed and rested his elbows on the table.

"Axel, come on."

The pissed look was still in his eyes. "Look, if she does take you back, I'll support her decision. But I really, really hope she doesn't. While I love you like a brother, I don't think it's right that you can drop her then pick her up again whenever you feel like. My sister deserves better than that."

I couldn't agree more.

"So, good luck. But I hope you crash and burn."

Tuesday

CHAPTER FIFTEEN

Confessions

Francesca

"Getting nervous?" The wedding was only two months away. Maybe that seemed like a long time, but in reality it wasn't.

Marie sat beside me on the couch. Magazines covered my coffee table, and we were marking them up like a white board. She still hadn't picked the flowers for the wedding, and we were trying to find the perfect centerpieces. Fortunately, everything else had been taken care of. This was the last thing remaining. "Why would I be nervous?"

I tilted my head and gave her a fiery look.

She turned away with guilt in her eyes.

"I know Axel is my brother but you can tell me these things. I won't think less of you. Remember, I like you more than him."

Marie chuckled. "Yeah, that's true."

"So, spill it."

"I guess I'm a little nervous..." She closed the magazine and bent it in her hands.

"What about, exactly?"

"I don't know... Sometimes, I wonder if this is the real him, you know? What if he goes back to his old ways when he gets bored with me?"

"That's never going to happen, Marie. Believe me, a man in love never gets bored."

"I hope you're right."

I rested my hand on her wrist. "I am."

"It seems like he genuinely loves me—"

"Seems like it?" I asked with a laugh. "That guy is a dog and you're his bone. Even when he doesn't want to play with you, he doesn't want anyone else to play with you. You have absolutely nothing to worry about."

"I know...but I remember the way he hurt me."

"It's in the past."

"I don't usually think about it, but now that I'm marrying him, it comes into my mind every now and then." She kept bending the magazine. "Will he be a good father? Will he cheat on me someday? Will he leave me for someone else right under my nose?"

"Yes, no, and no."

"How can you be sure?"

I released a deep sigh. "You can't be sure, actually. No one is ever sure. But Axel is as close to a guarantee as you're going to get. Every time you feel insecure, just remember who Axel is. He's sweet, caring, and very loyal. Even if he didn't feel the same way anymore, he wouldn't have an affair. That's just not him."

"You're right..."

"Do you feel better now?"

She stopped bending the magazine and released a deep breath. "Yeah, I think so. Maid of honor to the rescue."

I flexed my bicep. "With super strength and super cooking abilities."

"What a fattening superpower."

I laughed then opened another magazine.

"So...anything happen with Hawke?" She turned the pages and kept her eyes down. She tried to act like she wasn't interested, but her tone of voice gave her away.

"I spent the night a few days ago."

"What?" She dropped the magazine on the floor.

"I didn't sleep with him." I had to make that clear. I didn't want anyone to think I was his fuck buddy.

"But you slept with him? How many times has it been now? Three?"

"Something like that..."

"And you think this is normal?"

"No...we'll stop."

Marie gave me a look that said she didn't believe that.

"We just got carried away. Sometimes, it's hard to resist each other. But I'm going to put an end to it. It makes me feel so good at the time, but I feel like shit afterward. I want him even more, but I can never have him."

"You guys are twisted," she said. "Do you at least kiss?"

"No."

She looked like an owl because her eyes were so big. "That's the weirdest thing I've ever heard."

"You can be intimate without sex."

"But...I guess I just don't get it."

Nobody does.

Marie grabbed the magazine from the floor. "Anyway...the hydrangeas look nice. Maybe some white ones would look good."

"Yeah." I eyed the picture in her hand but kept thinking about Hawke.

Just then, a knock sounded on my door.

Marie immediately stiffened. "Gee, I wonder who that could be."

"It's probably Axel looking for you."

"I highly doubt it."

I left the couch and slowly walked to the entryway. I had a strong suspicion it was Hawke, but I wanted to be wrong. We'd been spending way too much time together, and we weren't doing activities that were considered friendly. There was nothing physical involved but we definitely weren't innocent.

I didn't bother checking the peephole before I opened the door.

And, sure enough, it was him.

He wasn't wearing a suit like he usual. He wore dark jeans and a gray t-shirt. Somehow, his shoulders and chest were more pronounced in the casual attire. His jeans hung low on his hips, and he was desirable in every way imaginable. But I pushed the thought away because it wasn't safe to think that way.

"Hi." His hands were by his sides, and his arms looked enormous in the short-sleeved shirt he wore.

"Hi." Our greetings were always a little strained. It didn't seem like we knew exactly what to do when we saw each other. But after a few minutes, you couldn't keep us apart.

"How are you?"

"Good. You?"

He didn't cross the threshold. "Okay." He moved his hands to his pockets as he blocked my doorway.

Now what? I would ask what he wanted but I had a feeling I already knew.

"I was hoping we could talk. Are you free right now?"

I glanced over my shoulder. "Actually, Marie—"

"Was just leaving." She appeared by my side with her magazines shoved into her bag. "I need to make dinner. Axel gets cranky when a hot meal isn't on the table." She walked past me. "Hi, Hawke." Then she disappeared down the hallway.

Hawke kept his eyes on me.

"Well, I guess I'm free now. Want to come in?"

"Actually, have you eaten?"

"No."

"Want to grab a bite?"

Spending time with him wasn't a good idea. We'd already seen each other enough. This wasn't good for either of us, but I would tell him that after dinner. I felt rude dropping it on him now.

***

We grabbed pretzels from a stand in Central Park then walked down the path. It wasn't the kind of dinner I expected, but when Hawke suggested it, I loved the idea.

"So much for being a health freak," I said as I finished my pretzel. "There are a hundred places you could have picked that would be better for you."

He'd already finished his a few minutes earlier. "Eh. Live a little, you know?"

"I do know." I crossed my arms over my chest because the chill was getting to me. Central Park was a beautiful place, one of the rare spots where you could actually find trees. While I loved the city with the secret restaurants where you had to know someone to get in, and the old buildings that were too important to destroy but not enough to renovate, and the interesting people, trees and grass were appreciated. It reminded me of home.

Hawke continued to walk beside me, and it didn't seem like he had any intention of saying whatever he wanted to say. Maybe he was going to say the same thing I was thinking. Since we were so alike, that was probably the case. And that gave me relief. Hawke and I started down a road that we could never tread. While it was unfair to both of us, that was the truth. We had to cut each other off before we made a mistake. Once this wedding was over, we could avoid each other a lot more easily.

"So, what did you want to talk about?"

He eyed a bench on our left then took a seat.

I did the same even though I preferred to walk. Anytime we were sitting near each other, I somehow ended up on his lap.

He rested his forearms on his thighs as he looked across the path. It didn't seem like he was going to say anything at all, or he was thinking of the right words to use.

I patiently waited, knowing Hawke wasn't the type of person to be rushed.

He finally turned to me, a different look in his eye. "I messed up—really bad. When I think about what I did two years ago, I hate myself. I grabbed you and threw you like a stuffed doll… Thank god you weren't hurt."

Why was he bringing this up after all this time? "Hawke, it was an accident. You didn't even know it was me. Cut yourself some slack. No one thinks less of you for what happened that night."

"I do."

"Well, let it go."

"And I'm sorry for leaving. I thought I was doing the right thing and…now I realize I was completely wrong."

I no longer noticed the cold air or the way it felt against my bare skin. My lungs stopped working and remained static. Even if I wanted to move, I couldn't.

"Since the engagement party, I've gone back and forth about us. There are days when I think it could work. But then there are nights when I remember what kind of monster I am."

I still didn't breathe.

"But I'm absolutely miserable without you. The past two years have been a dense fog. I can't remember most of it. All I know is, I thought about you every single day since we've been apart. My feelings have never changed—not once. And now that we're together again, my heart is finally starting to beat. My body is thawing. Hope is writhing inside me. I'm tired of keeping you at a distance. I'm tired of aching for you. I'm tired…of being without you."

I need to breathe.

"I worked it out in my head and…I think I can make this work. I think I can be the man you need. If I ever lose my temper or get out of control, I'll just leave. I'll never hurt you, Francesca. I know I'm like my father but...I'm not him."

My lungs finally caved in and took a deep breath of air. I heard the words he spoke but I couldn't believe them. Every day since he left me, I waited for that speech. Every day, I hoped he would realize his worth and come back to me.

And now he had.

He watched my reaction, seeing the coat of moisture on the surface of my eyes. "Muffin, be mine."

My immediate response was yes.

Yes.

The other half of my soul was sitting beside me, and he no longer wanted to keep his distance. It was all I'd ever wanted. I pictured myself walking down the aisle toward him. I imagined our son looking just like him. I saw all of it in the blink of an eye.

He scooted closer to me on the bench, his hands reaching for mine.

But I pulled them away.

Hawke froze and stared at me.

"I..." I couldn't believe what I was going to say, but I knew it was the right thing to do—for me. "You know how I feel about you, Hawke. That's never changed."

He listened to me.

"And it's hard to stay away from you when every part of my body craves you. You're still in my dreams. You're still in my thoughts."

He took a deep breath like he was scared.

And Hawke was never scared.

"I know you would never hurt me, Hawke. I've known that from the beginning. Never once was there any doubt about the kind of man you were. You don't harm people. You protect them. You're innately good, someone I'm immensely proud of. You fight for what you believe in. You're a warrior. I'm so glad that you finally realize that about yourself, that you're your own man. But that's not the issue."

He finally broke my gaze and stared at the concrete.

"You have no idea how much you hurt me..."

He closed his eyes like he was in pain.

I'd never had a chance to tell him just how bad it was. He never knew how dark my skies became. Maybe he moved to a new city and started over, but I never did. I had to live in the same house where I made love to him. I had to tell Yaya Hawke and I were through. I had to drive by his apartment in the hope I would see his truck. "I was on my knees and you still walked away. Instead of working it out with me, you ran. You were going through a hard time, and I understand that. But we should have gone through it together, not apart."

He didn't make a move.

"I want to give this another chance because I know you're worth it. But...I'm afraid you'll repeat the same mistakes the second there's a bump in the road. I'm afraid you'll lose faith in yourself when things aren't easy. I'm afraid...you'll rip me apart again."

"I won't."

"And I want to believe you. But it took me two years to get over you, and I don't think I can do it again. Obviously, I will always love you. But if I get sucked in again...I'm afraid I won't be able to get out. I can't go through that kind of pain four times... I can only handle three."

Hawke cringed when he understood the meaning of my words.

"Somehow, losing you was worse than losing both of my parents. It wasn't because you were my first love or a boy I really liked. It was because you're my soul mate, the person meant for me. You told me we were forever. But...you still left." My voice died in my throat because I couldn't speak anymore.

Hawke said nothing for a long time, and the silence stretched on for so long it didn't seem like he would say anything at all.

I rested my hands in my lap and felt my heart break all over again.

"Muffin."

The nickname went straight to my heart.

"You're right. What I did was unforgiveable."

I watched him and tried not to breathe loudly.

"I regret it—more than anything." He turned his eyes back to me, and they were full of desperation, an emotion Hawke hardly ever showed. "I wish I'd turned around. I wish I'd called. I wish…for a lot of things. But I can't change what happened. All I can do is live for the future. Muffin, you're my future. You're my world. I will spend the rest of my life trying to make this up to you."

I wanted to believe him—and a part of me did.

"What we have is too good to ignore. I'll never love any other woman but you. You're it for me, Muffin. You're the one and the only. And I know you feel the same way. So, please, give me another chance. I promise I won't hurt you again."

"You promised we were forever…"

"And I haven't broken that promise. I'm still here."

"But you weren't there when I needed you most." I wasn't the type of person to hold a grudge or live in the past. Life was too short for pettiness. But this was different. I couldn't trust him not to hurt me again.

"And I'm sorry for that. But I'm here now. Give me a chance. We can take things slow. I will earn your trust again."

"You can't earn it back when it's broken."

Hawke's eyes changed. Instead of being infinitely deep and mirrored, they darkened. A drop of moisture covered each eye, and his breathing changed. The strong and silent man I knew was breaking right before my eyes. The white part of his eyes began to redden. He grabbed my hand, and the quick pulse in his wrist proved his panic. "Please. I can't live without you, Francesca. Please don't turn me away. Don't give up on me."

I took another deep breath, and that's when the tears came. I didn't bother fighting them back because they were unstoppable. My chest heaved with pain, and even though it crushed my soul, I pulled my hand away. "I'm sorry." This was the hardest thing I've ever done, turning away my one true love. But I couldn't go through that pain again.

I couldn't take an entire bottle of painkillers and hope it claimed my life—not again.

Hawke didn't reach for me again. In fact, he looked away, turning his face so far I couldn't see his features.

Silence.

I kept crying, wishing he would hold me. And I kept crying because I hated myself for the way I just hurt him. He told me he needed me, but that wasn't enough.

Then I heard him sniff loudly.

My eyes stared at the back of his head, fear gripping my heart.

He rose to his feet and walked away, heading the opposite way I was facing. His footsteps sounded on the concrete, and they became quieter as more distance was put between us.

I couldn't move.

I could hardly breathe.

I stayed on the park bench until I stopped crying. But I only managed to keep my tears back until I returned to my apartment. When I was in bed with the covers pulled over my head, I started all over again.

Tuesday

CHAPTER SIXTEEN

To Be Alone

Francesca

A week came and went.

A very long and hollow week.

Hawke and I didn't cross paths, and that wasn't surprising since we were avoiding each other. It's not that I didn't want to see him, I just thought it was too soon after that heartbreaking conversation.

I hoped this wouldn't affect Marie and Axel, especially since their wedding was just over the horizon. I was going to keep this knowledge to myself so they wouldn't know anything about it. If anything, it would just stress them out. Their best man and maid of honor couldn't be in the same room together. Talk about a mood killer…

I worked more than usual, staying at the bakery and working on creations instead of going home alone. All I could think about was that conversation with Hawke.

I kept going back and forth in my mind. Maybe I should just give him another chance. I was still in love with him, so I should be with him. But then I remembered all the pain he caused me and how easy it was for him to leave. So, I steeled my resolve and pushed on.

But I missed him like crazy.

***

After I showered and got ready for bed, my phone vibrated on the nightstand.

The second it made a sound, I hoped it was Hawke.

When I looked at the screen, I saw Kyle's name.

I miss you.

Just when I thought I couldn't feel worse, I did. Should I write back? Should I just ignore him? I couldn't say the same words back because that would just give him false hope. While it was cold, saying nothing was probably the best decision.

Can I call you?

I sighed when I read the message. If he had something to say, I couldn't ignore him. *Yeah.*

My phone lit up immediately. "Hello?"

"Hey." He took a deep breath and forced his voice to come out friendly. "You weren't sleeping, were you?"

"No...but I'm lying in bed."

"Alone?" Hope was in his voice. "Sorry, don't answer that. I'm an idiot."

"No, you aren't, Kyle. And yes, I'm alone.

A sigh of relief came through the phone. "I know I sound like a huge pussy right now, texting you and calling you..."

"I don't think that."

"Well, I do. It's pathetic. I swear, I've never been like this before. I'm not clingy and needy. But I'm acting like a chick right now."

"I don't think that either. You're going through a hard time. That's understandable."

He paused for thirty seconds. "It's just weird not talking to you anymore. I used to see you all the time, and now you're gone. It's like I lost my best friend..."

"I know the feeling..."

"You were in my life for six months. I don't know about you, but that's a long time. I've never had a single girl around that long before. You're the only one who doesn't annoy me."

"Thanks for the compliment," I said with a chuckle.

"I miss you, Frankie. Do you miss me?"

Now we were in dangerous territory. "I think we should stick to appropriate topics. Otherwise, you're just going to make this harder on both of us."

"You're right."

"How's work?"

"That case is going to trial. We'll win."

"I know you will." I turned on my side with the phone pressed to my ear. "How's your mom?"

"Good. I haven't talked to her much."

"She doesn't know about me?" Maybe I shouldn't have asked that.

"Nope. I'm dreading telling her. Not to make things worse but...she's was totally smitten with you."

"I really liked her too."

"Everyone likes my mom," he said with a chuckle. "And she likes everyone."

"What else is new with you?"

"I need to find a new gym but can't decide."

"You don't have to change gyms because of me, Kyle."

"I know. It's not that I don't want to see you. It's just...you look so fine in those leggings. If you're on the treadmill, I'm just going to stand behind you and watch your ass shake the entire time."

I laughed at his brutal honesty. "You're lucky I know you aren't creepy."

"Perverted is a better word."

"I'll wear baggy pants from now on."

He cringed over the phone. "Yuck, don't do that. You aren't helping anybody."

I chuckled again, and it was the first time that week I actually felt good.

"So, what's new with you?"

I just got my heart stomped on. "Marie picked out a venue for the wedding."

"I asked what was new with you, not your friend."

The only interesting thing going on in my life was Hawke. "The shop is doing well. I just made cranberry bear claws. They're a hit."

"I bet they are. I'll have to come by and try them out."

I wanted to see Kyle. Actually, I wanted to ask him out for a drink. I missed talking to him. Our conversation always flowed like water.

"So…how's Hawke?"

I wasn't sure why he asked about him if he didn't want to know. "We're…not really talking right now."

"And why is that?"

I didn't want to hurt Kyle even more but I didn't want to lie either. He already knew how I felt about him. "We'd been spending a lot of time together, and I thought it was getting too intimate. When I decided to tell him how I felt, he asked me to take him back. He said he wants another chance."

Kyle was absolutely silent.

A minute passed.

"That's great." He cleared his throat. "That's what you wanted, right?"

Yes, in a complicated way. "I told him no."

"What?" he blurted. "Why did you say no? You love the guy, right?"

"Of course." There wasn't a doubt about that. "But I don't trust him. He'll hurt me again like last time. I couldn't handle that."

"Well, I wouldn't hurt you." The sincerity in his voice rang true like a distant bell.

"I know."

"So, let me get this straight. You dump this amazing, sexy, and successful guy that's hooked around your finger, and you turn down your 'soul mate' when he asks you to take him back. Frankie, what the hell do you want?"

It was a good question. "I don't know…but it's not either one of those."

CHAPTER SEVENTEEN

The Burn

Hawke

Everything hurt.

Everything.

I've been hurt a lot in my life, physically and emotionally, but hearing Francesca tell me that…broke me.

We were done.

I fucked it up too bad.

She didn't trust me.

I pushed her away.

And I only had myself to blame.

I wasn't the type of guy who cried. It simply wasn't in my nature. Even when I was a child it didn't happen. Either, I was emotionally stunted or I simply had been hurt beyond repair.

But I cried.

I turned away from Francesca and left without looking back. My sight was disrupted by the droplets, and my nose burned with every breath I took. My chest cracked from the pressure of my broken heart.

I hated myself. I left Francesca to protect her, but all I accomplished was ruining us both. Now I couldn't get her back. Now I couldn't fix it. I lost the one girl I loved. She was the only person who knew my secret. She was the only person who understood me, and despite all my flaws, accepted me.

But I fucking threw her away.

I didn't go to work the following day. That's how hard I was taking the rejection. I stayed in bed and waited for the phone to ring. I hoped Francesca would change her mind and call me.

But I knew she wouldn't.

The following day, I got back on my feet and tried to carry on. Francesca was always on my mind, and I was easily distracted during the day. In the back of my mind, I'd always thought I'd have the power to be with her again if I chose to. But knowing that option was gone shook the ground beneath my feet. The day I left was the day I said goodbye to her. She hadn't been mine ever since.

I blew it.

Every day passed like a meaningless blur. I couldn't tell you what I did or what I ate. My mind was working at lower capacity because the rest of my body had shut down. I used to work out to relieve stress but even that didn't interest me.

Axel texted me a few times and asked me to get lunch with him.

I always told him I was busy.

He probably knew what happened between his sister and I. Francesca would tell Marie, who would tell Axel. He was probably smiling right now, thrilled that Francesca made the right decision.

But I really loved her.

***

There was a knock on my door.

I sat on the couch and debated answering it. If it were Francesca, I would be there in a heartbeat. But a week had come and gone and I hadn't heard from her, so it was unlikely to be her now.

They knocked again. "Hawke, I know you're home. Put the lotion away and open the damn door." Axel banged his fist against the wood.

If he knew I was there, then he wouldn't leave until I gave him the attention he wanted. I opened the door then walked back to the couch, not even trying to be a decent host. "What's up?"

"I haven't heard from you all week. You disappeared from the map." He sat beside me on the couch and faced the TV.

"I've been busy."

He made a disgusted face. "With my sister?"

Unsure what he meant, I turned to him. "What?"

"My sister. Is she in the bedroom or something?"

Why would he think that? "No."

"But I'm guessing she's been here a lot?"

Did he really not know anything? Or was he just playing dumb to get me to talk? "She hasn't been here at all, Axel."

Axel finally understood my meaning. "You decided not to tell her how you felt?"

Was he being serious? "I did tell her."

"And?"

"What do you think?" I snapped. "If she took me back, I'd be grinning right now." I put my feet on the coffee table and stared at the TV.

"She said no?"

"Don't act like you don't know anything."

"I really don't..."

"You expect me to believe that?" I snapped. "Francesca told Marie what happened, and I'm sure she told you."

He remained serious, and his eyebrows didn't furrow like they usually did when he was lying. "She didn't say anything to me, Hawke. And I never told Marie what you told me."

"Why not?"

"Because I knew that goddess would run off and tell Francesca everything. I assumed that conversation was between us."

If he didn't know anything, that would mean Francesca hadn't told Marie. She was keeping the knowledge to herself but I wasn't sure why. Maybe I would ask her one day…if we ever spoke again. "Well, I told you what happened. She didn't want me."

Axel didn't gloat or look even slightly pleased. "Did she say why?"

"She loves me and always will, but she doesn't trust me. I hurt her when I left and…she couldn't handle going through that again. Honestly, I don't blame her. But, she and I are different than other people. I thought she would give me another chance."

Axel scratched the back of his neck. "I can't believe it…"

"You got what you wanted."

"I…" He rested his forearms on his knees. "I don't get it. She leaves that guy because she wants you, but when you want to start up your relationship, she says no? I don't understand."

"It's complicated..."

"I'm really surprised."

I crossed my arms over my chest. "I don't know what to do, Axel. I've never been so low." I rested my neck on the back of the chair and looked up at the ceiling. "She's it for me." I didn't like having deep conversations with anyone besides Francesca, especially not Axel. It was just too weird. But I didn't have a filter at the moment and just blurted out everything. "She's the one. She's the only girl I give a damn about. But I fucked it up so bad that she can't be with me."

Axel leaned back in the chair and held his silence.

I wish I could turn back time and change the past. I wish I'd turned around and walked back inside that apartment. Instead of leaving, I should have picked her up and never let her go.

"I think I can help you."

What did he just say? I lifted my head up and regarded him.

"But you're going to have to tell me why you left the first time."

That wasn't something I was willing to do.

"I'm not trying to be nosy," he said with a raised hand. "But I can't figure this out unless I know all the facts."

"Why do you want to help me anyway? You told me to crash and burn."

"I know what I said." He didn't meet my gaze as he spoke. "But if I did something stupid and Marie left me…I would do absolutely anything to get her back. It seems like you really love my sister despite what happened in the past, and I know she's obsessed with you. But I need to know what happened, Hawke."

I debated telling him for a long time. It was my darkest secret in the world, but if I could trust anyone to keep it to himself, it was Axel. "You can't tell Marie."

"Promise."

"I mean it, Axel. If you betray me, we're done."

"I already gave you my word."

I cleared my throat before I told him the entire story, from the very beginning so it would make sense. I told him about my abusive childhood and the way my mother protected me. Then I told him about the relationship I had with my mom once I moved out and how I was constantly saving her from my father's blows. Then I told him about the night I left—and why I left.

Axel took everything in without saying a word. He moved his hand to his forehead and pulled it all the way down his face, squeezing the bridge of his nose before he lowered his hand to his chin. "Holy shit."

I didn't feel better sharing that secret with another living person. In fact, it just reminded me of all the demons that still haunted me.

"Fuck, I don't even know what to say."

"You don't have to say anything. Don't pity me or look at me differently. That's the worst thing you could do."

He nodded.

"Now that you know, what difference does it make?"

"It makes a huge difference, actually. I thought you left her because you got tired of her or because she made a small mistake and you held it against her forever. I didn't realize...that was the reason."

"I would never leave her unless I had to."

"Hawke, you would never hurt my sister. How could you possibly think that?"

"Because I already did. Remember?"

He sighed. "It was clearly an accident."

"Don't make excuses for me," I said coldly.

"I'm not."

I averted my gaze. "I don't want to talk about this anymore."

Axel dropped the subject.

"Now, how can you help me?"

He rubbed his chin. "You want my advice?"

"Advice for what?"

"How to change her mind."

"I'm not going to change her mind. Francesca doesn't change her mind about anything. If she decides something, she sticks to it, practically out of principle."

"Just don't give up on her, Hawke. Convince her why she should give you another chance."

That wasn't so easy.

"Look, she's already in love with you. She claims you're her soul mate. All the hard work is already done. Now, you just need to stand your ground and tell her she doesn't have a choice. You're hers and she's yours. Period."

I eyed him closely, surprised by the suggestion.

"It's what I would do with Marie."

"Yeah?"

"Yeah."

Francesca seemed set in her ways. When she told me it wouldn't work, it was clear she already made this decision sometime in the past. The idea of living without her, never having a real chance with her, broke my soul. I couldn't live out the rest of my life this way, never being with the one person I actually loved.

Axel was right.

I couldn't give up.

CHAPTER EIGHTEEN

Round Two

Francesca

After a long day at work, I lounged around in my apartment. I lay on the couch and hardly moved, and even when my stomach rumbled, I didn't get up. When I was depressed, I hardly ate anything.

My stomach growled just when someone knocked on the door.

Please be a pizza guy.

I wore my flannel pajamas with the hole in the crotch, and I had my bunny slippers on my feet as I headed to the door. It was probably Marie with a bottle of wine and a stack of wedding magazines.

I opened the door and blurted, "I'm sick of picking out flowers."

Hawke stood on the other side, carrying two grocery bags. "Good thing I don't have any flowers then."

My jaw dropped, and I tried to mask my surprise. "Uh...hi." Why did I have to look like shit right now? My hair was in a messy bun, and I wasn't wearing any make up. My tank top had a chocolate stain on it from the liquid chocolate I sucked right out of the bottle.

Why is this happening to me?

"Hey." Hawke was suave, like always. He acted like he didn't notice how terrible I looked. "Can I come in?"

"Why?" The words sounded rude, even to me. "I mean...what's going on?" Last time I saw Hawke, he left me on that park bench. The conversation was more painful than the break up itself. And now he was on my doorstep like nothing happened.

"I wanted to make you dinner. You liked my salmon so much."

"Uh..." Why couldn't I say something that sounded remotely intelligent?

He eyed the door then me. "I'll let myself in..." He walked past me and headed to the kitchen.

***

I pumped dry shampoo into my greasy hair then plastered on make up as quickly as possible. I exchanged the old and stained pajamas for yoga pants and a pink camisole.

When I came back into the kitchen, Hawke was almost done with dinner. "I'm making cilantro lime tacos."

"Sounds good." I wasn't even sure what that was.

He turned off the stove without looking at me. "You didn't have to change. You looked great before."

Goddamn liar.

He set the table then poured two glasses of wine. Then he sat down and waited for me to join him.

I took the seat then eyed him across from me.

"Do you need anything else?"

Why was he waiting on me when it was my kitchen? "I'm fine. Thanks."

Hawke ate his food quietly, not staring at me like he usually did.

I thought I would lose my appetite with his presence but I was still starving. I ate my food quickly and silently. It really was good. Everything Hawke made seemed to be delicious.

Hawke sipped his wine when he was finished with his meal. He looked out the window to the city beyond.

"That was really good."

"Thanks," he said. "And thank you, Google."

I was still processing the fact he was there, sitting across from me at my kitchen table. "Hawke, what are you doing here?"

He gathered the dirty plates and carried them to the sink. His back was turned to me and it was pretty clear he wasn't going to answer my question. After he was done with the dishes, he sat on my couch.

Now I was even more confused.

I joined him in the living room and immediately crossed my arms over my chest. "Hawke, what's going on?"

"What do you mean?" He eyed me from his side of the couch. "I just wanted to have dinner with you. Is that okay?"

"Of course. I just…I guess I'm confused."

"What's there to be confused about? Even if we aren't together, we can't stay away from each other. So, we may as well just give in." He turned to the TV and kept his distance from me. He grabbed the remote and changed the channel. "South Park is on. You like that show, right?"

I nodded.

"Then South Park it is." He settled into the chair and didn't make a move toward me.

Whenever I was close to him, I felt that natural pull. But tonight, I didn't feel anything at all.

The confusion of the situation was throwing me off balance, and being so close to him made it difficult for me to think. So I just sat there and watched TV.

And so did he.

***

I grabbed my dumbbells and stood over my mat.

A loud whistle sounded behind me. "Spandex is God's gift to man."

Without turning around, I knew who it was. A smile upturned my lips. "And briefs are God's gift to women."

Kyle came to my side wearing a sleeveless shirt that he cut up himself. His defined arms and shoulders were on display. And that happy grin was on his face, like always. "Five pounds?" He laughed at the sight of my weights. "Come on, we both know you can upgrade."

"I'm doing abdominal exercises."

"Use a fifteen pound plate. I know you can handle it."

"I'm not as strong as you think."

He pulled his ear buds out of his ear and stuffed them into his pocket. "I haven't seen you here in a while."

"Yeah, I've been working a lot."

"And planning that wedding."

"Yep. I love Marie, but I'm excited for the wedding to be over. It constantly weighs over my head."

"Imagine how she must feel."

Hawke bought her a twenty thousand dollar wedding dress. She was in heaven right now. "What's new with you?"

"I have a date tonight."

"Oh." I didn't expect to feel hurt by that, but I somehow was. "That's nice."

"Yeah, she came on to me when I was at the bar a few days ago. She's nice and pretty but..." He shrugged. "Honestly, I'm not really into it. But since she had the courage to make the move and execute it so well, I couldn't say no."

"She sounds like my kind of girl."

"You'd like her. But I'm not feeling it."

"Keep an open mind." I wanted Kyle to be happy, especially after the way I hurt him.

"That's what I'm doing. Maybe getting laid will make me feel better."

Even that made me a little jealous, but I hid my reaction. I had no right to feel anything toward him, especially jealousy. And if I showed any sign of that, it might confuse Kyle. "If she has that kind of confidence, I'm sure she's amazing in bed."

"Yeah, probably." But he still sounded indifferent to the idea.

A man approached us from our left but I didn't turn his way. He was probably heading to the free weights against the wall.

Kyle glanced at him then turned back to me.

Once we realized the guy was standing right beside us and had no intention of leaving, we both turned to him.

It was Hawke, wearing a gray t-shirt that fit his body perfectly. It highlighted his powerful chest, and the curve of his pectoral muscles. Even his shoulders were defined in the fabric. His shorts were loose on his legs, but his calf muscles were ripped. He had the physique you would see in a Calvin Klein magazine.

Why was he here? We didn't go to the same gym.

"Hi…" Every time I saw him, I sounded like an idiot. He always put me on alert when he was near, and that made me stutter like I lacked any ounce of confidence. He made me nervous, but some would say in a good way.

"Hi." His eyes were glued to my face, and he didn't blink while he examined me. The looks he always gave me were intense, strong enough to make anyone blink. While his eyes were blue, they took on a darker hue depending on his mood.

Kyle glanced back and forth between us, unsure what was going on.

I was frozen to the spot, unsure what to say. Hawke and I couldn't work out our relationship, but he showed up on my doorstep the other night and cooked me dinner. The sudden change in behavior threw me off, and when I asked him about it, he didn't give me a sufficient answer.

And now he was here—at my gym.

Kyle turned to Hawke and extended his hand. "Uh, hi. I'm Kyle. You are?"

I forgot my manners in light of my surprise.

Hawke eyed Kyle's hand but didn't take it. The recognition in his eyes said he recognized Kyle's name. He knew exactly who he was. "Hawke."

Kyle slowly lowered his hand when he put two and two together.

Damn, this was awkward.

I remembered how terrible I felt when I saw that girl standing outside his apartment. Her hair was messy like she'd been rolling around in his bed all night. My stomach fell and the vomit rose.

I'm sure both of them felt that way now.

I crossed my arms over my chest and continued to let the tension rise. One of them needed to walk away, but neither one of them was willing to make the first move. Hawke stared at Kyle without blinking, and Kyle returned that look with his own stoic expression.

This was a nightmare.

Kyle finally stepped up. "I'll see you around, Frankie." He walked away and didn't continue his workout. He left the gym, his bag over his shoulder.

Hawke didn't watch him walk away. The second Kyle left our presence, Hawke's eyes turned to me, burning me with their gaze.

The sound of weights dropping, and the hum of the workout machines played in our ear. Music from the aerobics room upstairs was distantly heard.

I refused to speak first because I didn't know why Hawke was there.

Hawke made the first move. "You and Kyle are still close?" He asked a different question without actually asking it. His eyes drilled into mine, the fear evident if you looked hard enough.

"No. We just go to the same gym." I wasn't obligated to answer his question, and frankly, it was none of his business. But I wanted Hawke to know I wasn't sleeping with Kyle anymore…for some reason.

"You don't see him outside of it?"

I shouldn't answer him. My personal life was none of his business. "He came into the bakery one time. We chitchatted then he left. He has a date tonight, actually."

Hawke didn't nod in approval or look relieved. His intense gaze still burned the skin of my cheeks. "I haven't been with anyone since before I told you how I felt. And I won't be with anyone else again."

His words came out of left field and I didn't know what to make of them. Of course, I loved hearing that. Even though I couldn't work it out with him, I liked knowing he kept his hands to himself—even though I shouldn't.

"Have you been seeing anyone else?"

I should stand my ground and not answer the question. But I caved. "No."

"Are you going to see anyone else?"

Why did I melt right before his eyes? Why did I crumble every time? "No."

"Including Kyle?"

The smartass inside me rose. "Why would I leave him if that were the case?"

Hawke's expression didn't change—at all.

"I don't see why it matters, Hawke. I told you how I felt, and nothing has changed."

"Everything has changed."

Why were we having this conversation inside a gym? "Why are you making me hurt you again? I don't enjoy it."

"I deserve to be hurt." The sincerity in his voice shocked me. It was so raw. "And I don't deserve you. But I want you anyway."

I tightened my arms around my chest. "Why are you making this so hard for me?"

"I'm not trying to," he said quietly. "I was going to walk away and leave you in peace. But then I realized I couldn't do that. I couldn't give up—not on you." The sound of barbells crashing against the ground echoed in the room, but Hawke didn't seem to notice. "We're forever. And we're still forever."

***

We rented a party bus and hit up Chippendale's for Marie's bachelorette party. While I wanted to get wasted and have a good time, I was a good maid of honor and only allowed myself to get buzzed. Axel made it very clear that Marie needed to be looked after.

Like I didn't know that.

Marie was a fun drunk, but when she had one too many, it wasn't cute anymore. She stumbled with every step and slurred every word. She was a pain in the ass, actually.

"Oh my god." She covered her mouth and gasped. "Look at that bulge. Axel is big but not that big."

I tried not to throw up. "These dancers stuff it down there."

"I don't know…" Marie took another shot. "I'd like to see for myself." She stood up from her seat then cupped her hands around her mouth. "I want to see your junk!"

I covered my face. "Oh my god…"

The dancer, a tall blond, came to the end of the stage. "Hey, sweetheart."

The other girls held up their drinks and cheered Marie on. "Take off his G-string with your teeth."

I hated to be the party pooper but I had to be. "No touching, Marie." If I were getting married, I wouldn't want my man to touch anybody. He could look all he wanted, but that was it.

"Come on," she whined. "Don't be lame."

"I'm saving your ass."

Marie climbed on stage then started dancing with the stripper. She backed her ass into him then turned around and spanked him right on the ass.

"Pull up your camera," Veronica said to Janice.

Janice held up her phone.

I don't think so. I snatched it away and shoved it in my pocket. "Friends don't tape each other and put it on Facebook."

Veronica stuck her tongue out at me.

Marie kept dancing with the stripper, and I had a feeling the stripper genuinely liked her. He kept smiling at her and putting his hands on her waist. "So, can I see your package?"

"Sure." He smiled then pulled his G-string out slightly.

"Oh my." Marie gasped and turned beet red. "You don't stuff."

I took another drink because I couldn't handle this sober.

***

We rode the party bus around town and bar hopped. Marie was wasted, beyond wasted, but she wanted to keep going. When I handed her water, she took a drink then spit it out. "This is the worst vodka I've ever had."

"Because it's water, idiot."

She pushed the drink at me. "Well, I don't want this water vodka."

"It's just water." I set it on the counter.

"Let's get this party started." Marie clapped her hands and moved to the center of the room and started dancing. There was music on, but no dance floor. "I'm getting married!"

The other girls joined in, holding their glasses up while they shook their hips.

I ordered a drink and enjoyed it while I watched them stumble in their heels. At least Marie was having fun, and that's all that mattered. I suddenly felt a piercing gaze penetrate my skin. It was simmering with heat, and without looking, I knew exactly who it was.

Hawke.

I turned to the source of the stare and saw him sitting at a table with three guys. They all wore jeans and t-shirts, but they had an aristocratic air to them, like they wore suits on a daily basis.

Hawke took a long drink of his scotch as he held my gaze. There was no surprise in his eyes, like he'd been staring at me for the past thirty minutes. Instead of being surrounded by pretty girls, he was alone.

The guys were having a conversation, laughing together. Hawke didn't participate because all he was focusing on was me. When he set his glass down, he kept his fingers tightly around it. One ankle rested on the opposite knee.

I finally broke the trance and forced my gaze on Marie. I suddenly felt self-conscious in the tight cocktail dress I wore. It was black and backless. The heels were killing my feet, but Marie insisted I wear them. I wasn't against dresses, but I had intended to wear skinny jeans and a t-shirt.

If Hawke were going to speak to me, he probably would have done it when he first spotted me. But I quickly realized I was wrong when the scent of his cologne entered my nose. He stood beside me at the bar, his glass of scotch still in his hand.

I finally turned to him, hating the way my body hummed for him. The inexplicable needed to wrap my body around his overtook me. Like magnet and steel, we were constantly being tugged together. Some would call it physical attraction or even lust, but it was something else entirely.

"You look…stunning." He set his glass on the bar and stood close to me. He leaned his face close to mine, and the scruff on his cheeks made him even sexier. I liked it when he didn't shave for a few days.

"Thanks."

"I really like this." His eyes took in my bare back, practically devouring it with just the look.

"I like that I got it on clearance."

"Worth every penny."

I focused on Marie in the middle of the floor. She was still dancing around, shaking her ass like Shakira.

"Why aren't you out there?"

"I'm being the responsible one so they don't have to be."

"Sounds boring."

"A little," I said. "But I have to make sure everyone gets home okay."

"I'm assuming this is the bachelorette party."

"Yeah."

"How about I keep an eye on all of you, so you can go out there and let loose?"

It was a tempting offer. "So you can take advantage of me later?" It was a flirtatious joke but judging the pissed expression on Hawke's face, he didn't take it that way.

"I'm not even going to respond to that." He downed the rest of his scotch.

"It was a joke."

"A terrible one." He turned his eyes to Marie. "Go out there, and I'll make sure you guys make it back."

"It's okay," I said. "I told Marie I would do this. Also, I promised Axel."

"You should be out there shaking your ass too." He gave me a smolder along with a smirk. "I'd love to watch that."

"This dress is already too short. Something might pop out."

"Ooh…even better."

My breathing had changed since he came near, and my chest was tighter than usual. Adrenaline coursed through me in powerful waves. As much as I'd like to say I didn't want him anymore, it was impossible to deny. My heart would always beat for his. My soul would always sing when his was near.

"Can I buy you a drink?"

"I'm okay. I'm still a little buzzed from the strip joint."

"Strip joint?" he asked.

I realized I spilled Marie's secret. "I didn't tell you that."

He chuckled. "Whatever happens tonight stays between us. I wouldn't rat out Marie."

Marie pulled a random guy onto the floor and started dancing with him. The other girls joined in. The guy looked like he was having the time of his life, surrounded by beautiful women.

"I didn't know Marie was so much fun." He rapped his knuckle on the bar and ordered another scotch.

"She's a hoot."

"So, see anything you like at Chippendales?"

"Not really."

"I could put that place out of business if I wanted to."

I rolled my eyes. "So full of yourself…like always."

He held my gaze and leaned closer to me, almost like he might kiss me.

If he did, I would kiss him back. I wish that weren't the case but it was. If he made the move, I would be powerless to stop it. He knew I was defenseless against him, so hopefully he would be a gentleman and not make the move at all.

He didn't. He just leaned close to me, his breath falling on my cheek.

I needed to break the tension. It was making my thighs ache. "Are those your boys?"

Hawke moved away slightly. "I work with them."

"At your company?"

"Yeah, they're employees."

"They actually like their boss?"

"What can I say?" he asked before he took a drink. "I'm a great boss."

I could picture Hawke being the most terrifying boss on the planet.

"I'm not really their boss. They work as hard as they want and make the salary they desire. I just get a percentage of it. So, it works out for everyone involved."

"That's interesting." He never told me about his job before. I wasn't even sure how he got started. After we went our separate ways, I never asked Axel a single question about him. "Do you like your job?"

"I love it."

"What do you do all day?"

"It's complicated, but I basically decide how to invest people's money. When they get a return, I get a return. It's that simple."

"And they trust you?"

"I'm a pretty smart guy. I've never lost anything."

"Ever?" That was hard to believe.

"At least not yet," he answered. "About a year ago, I had a really high profile client. We actually met on the town. He gave me a lot of money to invest in smaller markets. I turned it around and made him five times what he put into it. And I got an enormous payout because of it. He told his fellow billionaires and word spread. Now a lot of people turn to me."

"That's impressive," I said. "I'm proud of you."

His lids became hooded, and the emotion in his eyes gave him away. "Thank you, Muffin."

He kept using my nickname. I wished he wouldn't but I couldn't tell him that. Actually, I liked hearing it, in a twisted and complicated way.

"I can give you the world—if you let me."

"I don't want the world, Hawke. I've never wanted it." There's only one thing I've ever wanted, and he was standing right beside me. Rich or poor, it had no bearing on the man Hawke was. I'd fallen in love with him because of his soul, not because of his success.

He tilted his head slightly as he regarded me, his lips looking kissable. I wanted to suck his bottom lip then give him my tongue. "What do you want, Francesca? Name it and I'll give it to you."

Unless he had a time machine, it was impossible. "You can't give it to me, Hawke. No one can." I turned away and watched Marie. She gave me comfort while I had this dark conversation with Hawke.

His hand moved to my cheek, and he forced my gaze on him. His thumb brushed across my skin then stopped at the corner of my mouth. He stared at me possessively, like I was his.

I melted at his touch, pathetically. My body and heart were his for the taking. I couldn't protect them no matter how hard I tried. He could take anything he wanted, even if it was all of me.

"I love you."

The words echoed in my mind, and my stomach did somersaults. I already knew he loved me even if he never said it. When we used to be together, we hardly ever said those words to each other. But we didn't need to. It was so obvious that it was practically redundant to say.

Hawke stared into my eyes as he waited for me to say it back. The need was there, burning right on the surface. He leaned closer to me, his thighs pressing against my knees. He was pressuring me silently, commanding me without giving an order.

"I'm desperately and pathetically in love with you."

***

When Marie had enough and could barely keep her eyes open, the night was over.

"I need to get her home." She was slumped in a chair, practically a corpse that could still vomit.

"Are you sure you can handle it on your own?" Hawke asked. "Because I can help."

"No, it's okay." I shook Marie's arm. "Babe, wake up. It's time to go home."

Her face was on the table and her eyes were closed. Her mouth was gaping open.

"Marie, come on." The rest of the girls left, so I was stuck with the big girl job.

She didn't move.

Hawke eyed her unresponsive body. "I think you need my help."

I hated admitting I needed help from anyone.

He took off his jacket and wrapped it around her body. She didn't seem cold, so I wasn't sure why he did it. When he lifted her from the chair and cradled her in his arms, I understood. He was covering the opening of her dress, where her ass would be sticking out. "Where am I taking her?"

"To her apartment."

"You think Axel should see her like this?"

"He knows what to expect," I said. "Besides, he can take care of her in the morning."

"Okay."

Together, we walked up the street and headed to her apartment. It was just a few blocks away so we walked in comfortable silence. Marie was passed out on his shoulder and oblivious to everything around her.

"Is she heavy?"

"Lighter than air." Hawke walked in stride like he wasn't carrying a human being at all. He was a solid slab of muscle so it shouldn't be surprising.

We arrived at her apartment building then knocked on the door. It was three in the morning so Axel was probably asleep.

"Are her keys in her bag?" Hawke asked.

"I'm sure they are but I'd rather have Axel answer the door."

Axel opened it a moment later, his hair messy and his sweatpants on. He wasn't wearing a shirt, and his eyes were squinted like he'd just woken up. "Is she okay?"

"Just drunk off her ass," I explained.

Axel stepped aside. "Put her on the bed."

Hawke carried her into the bedroom then returned. His jacket was back on.

"Wait," Axel said. "Why were you there?"

"We ran into each other," Hawke explained. "And Frankie needed help carrying Marie."

"She's gonna be a pain in the ass tomorrow," Axel said as he ran his fingers through his hair. "But I'm glad she's okay. Did she have a good time?"

"She had too much fun," I said.

"I'm not gonna ask." Axel began to close the door. "Thanks for bringing her home."

"No problem," I said.

Axel shut the door and left us alone on the threshold.

Hawke turned to me, and the look in his eye told me our night wasn't over yet even though it was three in the morning. "My place is just a block over. Let's go."

"Whoa... Who said I was coming over?"

Hawke grabbed my hand, encompassing my small fingers in his. It was the first time he gave me this kind of affection, something innocent but intimate. "I did."

***

A slave to my emotions, I walked into his bedroom and kicked off my heels. I knew I should leave. No good would come from staying there. My heart was still broken from the last time he shattered it, and I was making myself vulnerable all over again.

But I stayed.

I sat at the edge of the bed still in my tight dress. I would have to borrow clothes from him.

Hawke removed his shoes and jeans. But he didn't stop there and kept going. Slowly, he pulled his shirt off until he was just in his boxers. The bulge in the front was distinct and noticeable.

My throat went dry.

He stood in front of me without breaking eye contact. Then he grabbed the brim of his shorts and pulled them down his long legs. He stood in front of me completely naked, looking like a Greek god chiseled in stone.

I squeezed my thighs together. He was the most beautiful thing I'd ever seen. His stomach was tight with muscles, and the endless lines and grooves made him into a work of art. His thighs were thick and toned, and his chest was as hard as steel.

I knew I was wet without even checking.

Hawke inched toward the bed until he kneeled before me.

I stopped breathing. We were face-to-face, and he was on his knees. This kind of contact made me burn hotter than the sun. I kept my hands in my lap but I desperately wanted to touch him. I purposely squeezed my thighs together in an effort to stop them.

Hawke gripped my thighs with his hands then gently guided them apart, opening my legs to him.

I could have kept them closed. He was guiding me but I still had the control. But I allowed him to do it.

When they were parted, he moved between them until his chest almost touched mine. His face hovered near me, and his lips were just an inch away. Every breath he exhaled landed on me. I tried to control my breathing and pretend I was calm but it wasn't working. My chest rose and fell rapidly because I was both excited and scared.

One hand left my thigh and snaked up my dress. When it traveled over the bare skin, it made me shiver. He felt every inch of my skin, concentrating on the area between my shoulder blades. Then he reached the back of my neck where he unclasped the top.

My dress became loose and the straps fell, but my chest was still covered.

Then he moved to the zipper at the top of my ass and pulled it down as far as my body would permit. The fabric slowly slid down my chest, falling below my breasts and my stomach until it rested in my lap.

I took an involuntary breath when I was exposed to him.

Hawke moved his gaze to my chest and stared at it without any shame. My body was his as far as he was concerned. He studied it like an artist judges a painting. Then he slowly guided me onto my back and pulled the dress down the rest of the way. It slid off my hips until it was past my ankles. Then it was gone. All I wore was a tiny black thong that hardly covered anything.

Hawke stared down at it without blinking before he gripped it with a single hand and pulled it off.

I continued to let him undress me even though the logical part of me knew I shouldn't. This would only make it more difficult for me to live without him. It was a mistake, and I knew it was a mistake. But I wanted to make it anyway.

Hawke looked down at my naked body with appreciation. His eyes didn't burn in desire like mine did for him. He looked completely different, and his thoughts were unreadable to me. His cock was rock-hard and practically throbbing, but that was all I could make out.

Seeing him naked intensified my desperation. I wanted him so much, just like I did in every dream. I missed the way our bodies moved together in the throes of passion. I already knew how it felt because we'd made love so many times, but it still felt like the first time.

Hawke wrapped his arm around my waist then guided me up the bed until my head rested on a pillow. He still hadn't kissed me yet, and I was anxiously waiting for it. This had disaster written all over it, but I would deal with the regret in the morning.

Instead of positioning himself on top of me, he lay beside me. He turned on his side then yanked me into him. My leg was pulled over his hip, and his arm hooked around my waist possessively. Our faces were pressed close together, but no kiss followed.

Touching his body like this felt so good…it actually made me writhe. He wasn't doing anything to me, not the things I liked, but I was still in agony. Just feelings his skin against mine gave me more satisfaction than sex with anyone else.

Hawke took a deep breath like he felt it too, like he desperately wanted me but was satisfied with this at the same time. The intimacy and vulnerability was taxing to both of us. There was nowhere to hide. Our hearts and souls were laid bare, nothing obstructing them from reaching each other.

The anticipation before a kiss was sometimes better than the kiss itself, and feeling our bodies tangled together, pressing up against one another, was making me squirm. But I loved how in tune we were. It was just him and I and nothing else.

He pulled me closer to him, and we became a single being. My tits were pressed into his chest and my nipples were hard from the touch. His face was close enough for a kiss but he never leaned in. His eyes were wide open and he stared at me, not looking at my naked body. He just stared into me, seeing my soul. Only he could recognize it because it was identical to his own.

And when I stared into his eyes, I saw his too.

Tuesday

CHAPTER NINETEEN

Breakfast

Hawke

I was up early because it was impossible for me to sleep in. No matter how late I was up, I was still awake by eight the following morning. Francesca was the opposite of me. She could sleep forever if no one disturbed her.

I went for a morning jog, and when I got back, I made breakfast. I cooked French toast, eggs, and bacon. But it sat out for nearly an hour because she hadn't woken up yet so I ate without her.

At noon, she finally woke up.

She came into the living room with messy hair and smeared make up. She wore one of my t-shirts, and her beautiful body was covered. She squinted as she ran her fingers through her hair. "What time is it?"

"12:30."

She cringed. "The day is already gone."

"Hungry?"

She rubbed her flat stomach. "I skipped a meal today. I'm starving."

I reheated the food then set it on the table.

She plopped down, still a little hung over. "This looks good."

"Thanks."

"Aren't you going to eat?"

"I already did."

"Oh..." Her face fell in embarrassment. She picked up her fork and kept her gaze averted as she ate.

I sat beside her at the table and watched her.

"When did you wake up?"

"Eight"

"What have you been doing?"

"I went for a jog then did some work from my laptop."

"Geez...you're making me feel lazy."

"You are lazy." I gave her a teasing look before I touched her foot with mine under the table.

She kept eating until her plate was wiped clean. "That was good. Thank you."

"I don't mind cooking for a beautiful woman."

She stilled at that comment, and I wasn't sure why. Then she took the plate to the sink where she rinsed it before placing it in the dishwasher. "Do you mind if I use your shower?"

"Of course not."

She walked into the bathroom then locked the door behind her.

Knowing she was in the shower made me think of her naked body. Her skin was flawless like it'd never been exposed to the elements. It was smooth, and feeling my body pressed against it was naturally soothing. But it was arousing at the same time. I had a hard-on pretty much the entire night. While I was insanely attracted to her, all I'd wanted was to feel that connection between us. It wasn't about sex. It was about feeling at home. She grounded me, gave me a world where I could feel safe. I'd lived without it for so long, and now I couldn't handle it anymore.

I needed it.

When she came out of the shower, her hair was still a little damp, but her face was clean. She changed in the bedroom then came out wearing the cocktail dress she wore the night before. Her legs were simply stunning. "Well, thanks for breakfast..." She grabbed her clutch then turned to the door.

She thought she was leaving?

I left the table then came to her side. "I was going to watch a Katharine Hepburn movie. Want to join me?" Francesca liked watching old movies. I was indifferent to them, but I thought it was cute she enjoyed them so much.

She gripped her clutch like she was uncomfortable. Regret was written all over her face. She wished she hadn't stayed here the night before, hadn't lain naked with me in that bed. Nothing happened, but in actuality, a lot did. Now, she was backpedaling, knowing our relationship was becoming too much for her. She needed to keep her distance, and she knew she wasn't succeeding at that. "I really should get going. I have laundry to do…"

"I can go over there." I had her cornered.

"I need to do some bookkeeping too—for the shop."

This time, I gripped her hips and positioned her in front of me. "Francesca, stay with me." I didn't want her to slip through my fingers. Every time she questioned what she was doing, I had to erase her doubt. I wouldn't be another mistake. She could trust me.

When my hands were on her, she struggled to resist me. The defeat was in her eyes. She didn't want to be anywhere else but here—with me. "I can't stay too long."

I smiled because I knew that wasn't true either. She'd spend the night again.

***

We curled up together on the couch, with her lying on top of my chest. The blanket covered both of us, and while the world continued on around us, we sat frozen in time.

Instead of watching the movie, I watched her. My hand fisted her hair while the other remained hooked around her waist. The small of her back was so prominent. It was one of the things I was most attracted to. I used to kiss that area while she lay on her stomach, and the touch would drive her wild. I still remembered all the little things she loved…like I could ever forget.

The movie just ended when her phone started to ring.

I wanted to turn it off.

Francesca glanced at the screen. "It's Marie."

My hand was still in her hair, anchoring her to me.

She answered it. "Hey, how are you feeling?" She listened to her response on the other line. "That bad, huh? I can't say I'm surprised. You got a little crazy there." She listened again. "Sure, I'll swing by and bring you something."

Goddammit, Marie.

Francesca disconnected then sat up. "Marie wants me to bring her some soup."

"Axel is busy?"

"He says he doesn't want to leave her."

Fucking pussy.

"It's just as well," she said as she stood up. "I should get going anyway." She pulled her heels on. The same regret came into her eyes when she realized she spent the entire afternoon with me. She wanted to be close to me, but she also wanted to move on from me.

"Want me to walk you home?"

"I can handle it." She grabbed her clutch and fluffed her now dry hair. "I'll see you later." She avoided eye contact and headed for the door.

I grabbed her by the elbow before she could leave. I turned her toward me, keeping my hand on her. "I'll see you later."

A slight expression of surprise moved into her eyes. She clearly expected me to ask her to stay. As much as I wanted to hold her down and never allow her to leave, I knew that wouldn't get me anywhere—not with her.

***

Cassandra texted me. *What are you doing tonight?*

I met Cassandra a few weeks ago at a bar. We hooked up, and since she was surprisingly good in bed, I invited her over a few more times. It surprised me how many women were okay with a purely physical relationship. Perhaps good sex was hard to come by.

I didn't respond because Axel immediately texted me afterward. *Lunch?*

I eyed the clock and realized it was noon. When I was working, the time flew by. *Where?*

Firebrick?

It was an Italian place just a block over from my office. *K.*

I hadn't spoken to Axel since I dropped Marie off. He didn't know what was going on between Francesca and me or that I was getting close to regaining her trust.

I walked into the restaurant and took a seat at the table. "Hey, how's it going?" I grabbed the menu and browsed.

"Marie is back on her feet. Took her a while though."

"I said what's new with *you*."

"She is me, idiot. And I thought she had alcohol poisoning for a second."

"She's fine now?" I asked, genuinely concerned.

"Yeah, I took care of her. I love having sex with her when she's drunk, but she was way too drunk for that."

TMI.

His phone rang and he answered it. "Hey, baby. What's up?"

Of course, it was Marie. I kept looking through the selections since I had nothing else to do. I would probably get a salad. It's what I usually got.

"You want to join us?" he asked. "We're at Firebrick."

The only time it was just he and I was when we were playing basketball and that was because Marie didn't play basketball.

"Yeah," he said into the phone. "Bring Francesca too."

That caught my attention.

"Alright, see you soon. Love you."

I tried not to roll my eyes.

"Bye." He hung up and set the phone on the table. "My fiancée is coming."

"So I heard."

"She's bringing Francesca."

"I heard that too."

"Any progress with her?"

It was tense when I talked about other women, but it was particularly awkward when I talked about his sister. "A little. She slept over last night."

Axel's eyes widened slightly but he didn't look angry. "Yeah?" He didn't ask for the details.

"We just slept together, nothing else." Whenever a girl spent the night, it usually meant sex was involved, and I didn't want Axel to get the wrong idea.

"And you just slept?"

Well, we were buck-naked but the details were irrelevant. "Yeah."

"Then why was she there?"

I shrugged. "Haven't you ever just slept with Marie? You know, cuddled?"

"Yeah, but I'm marrying her. I assumed that a couple getting back together would be hot and bothered for each other."

We are. We definitely are. "She and I are different. We just like to be together sometimes."

"So, is there a reconciliation on the horizon?"

"Yes, but I don't think it's going to happen overnight. I don't mind being patient. I know I really hurt her."

Axel didn't agree with me, which was a first. And he wasn't so protective of her either. Maybe he was beginning to realize that she was an independent woman and capable of taking care of herself.

Marie and Francesca walked into the restaurant and headed to our table. Francesca wore a leather jacket over her t-shirt, trying to cover up the flour on her clothes. Her hair was in a loose bun. I liked it when she pulled her hair back. She had a beautiful face with nice cheekbones. Our eyes locked when she approached, and a silent conversation happened between us.

"Hey, baby." Axel immediately jumped out of his chair and kissed Marie. "You're looking really hot in that dress."

"Thanks." Like always, color tinted her cheeks.

I noticed Axel complimented her left and right, but his words didn't seem empty.

Francesca came to my side of the table and watched me with hesitation.

I stood up but didn't touch her. "Hi."

"Hi."

Our greetings were still awkward, even after everything that happened over the past few months. "Managed to get away from work for a little bit?"

"Yeah, I was starving."

I pulled out the chair for her without thinking twice about it.

She eyed it before she sat down.

I pulled in my chair and sat beside her, aware of how close we were. I wanted to grab her hand and hold it on my thigh but I managed not to. This weird relationship, being friends and almost lovers, was confusing. Sometimes, I thought it was okay if I gave her public affection, but when I read her mood, I knew it wasn't.

After Axel and Marie finished their smooch-fest, they sat down.

"Want to split something?" Axel asked.

This guy couldn't be more whipped.

"Sure," Marie said. "How about the spaghetti?"

"Perfect," he answered. Then he asked her about her day.

Francesca and I were pretty much ignored.

I cleared my throat. "How are things?"

"Good," she said. "You?"

I just saw her the other day and there wasn't anything new to discuss. "Good. All work and no play."

"You're at lunch. It looks like you have some leeway."

"Only because my boss is a decent guy." I smiled at my own joke.

"I don't know...he seems like a real jerk to me."

"But a hot one, right?"

"He's okay," she said with a shrug.

I playfully brushed her leg with mine under the table. "You're full of it."

"He's named after a bird," she said. "How cool could he be?"

I tried not to laugh. "You're lucky you're cute."

"Or what?" she challenged.

I wanted to grab her face and kiss her hard on the mouth. The need gripped me by the throat and squeezed. When she sassed me back like that, it turned me on. She was so sexy and adorable at the same time. "Or the next time you sleep over we won't actually sleep."

Her teasing nature immediately disappeared. A look of desire replaced it, and when she realized her feelings were on display, she sipped her water to hide it.

The waiter came to our table, and our eye contact was broken by his presence. When it was my turn to order, I looked at the menu as I made my selection. My phone vibrated on the table with a text message but I didn't look at it. "I'll take the seafood pasta."

"Very good, sir." He took our menus before he walked away.

Once he was gone, I glanced at my phone. To my horror, it was Cassandra.

I want you to give it to me like you did last time. XOXO. And to top it off, there was a scandalous picture of her. She lay on her bed with the camera pointed down. Her blonde hair was sprawled out on the sheets, and her perfect body was covered in only a push-up bra and a thong.

I immediately locked the screen in the hope that Francesca didn't see it.

But she did.

I could tell by the sudden coldness emanating from her. She wouldn't make eye contact with me, and she purposely looked out the window, keeping her shoulders slightly turned away from me.

Fuck. My. Life.

I wanted to fix it then and there, but I couldn't with Marie and Axel sitting across from us. I couldn't afford any setbacks right now, not when Francesca was so fragile. It was one thing for Cassandra to ask me to hook up, but why did she have to send a picture? She had nothing on

Francesca, but of course, Francesca would feel threatened by a beautiful woman who had the confidence to take a picture like that.

I was screwed.

***

At the end of lunch, we said goodbye on the sidewalk.

"Baby, I'll walk you to the office." Axel put his arm around her waist.

"I can make it on my own," Marie said.

"Come on," Axel said. "You're going to be my wife soon. I don't mind."

Yes, just walk away.

"I'll see you guys later." Francesca made a quick wave before she darted down the sidewalk, clearly trying to get away from me.

I didn't bother saying goodbye to them when I followed after her. "Francesca."

She quickened her pace.

I wasn't going to chase her down. That wasn't my style.

She didn't look back, but she stopped at a cross walk because she needed to get across the street. She pressed the button, and when the light didn't change, she pressed it again anxiously.

I stopped by her side. "It's not what you think."

She pressed the button again like that would make me go away. "I don't know what you're talking about."

"I'm not sleeping with her anymore."

"She's gorgeous. Maybe you should start again."

I gritted my teeth and managed not to growl. Francesca was never the jealous type, and I loved that about her. "How could you possibly be threatened by her? I'm in love with you, but she'll always be some chick that I won't remember."

Francesca tapped her foot as she waited for the light to change.

"I'm sorry that she texted me but that was out of my control."

The light finally turned green and she immediately took off.

I matched her pace. When we reached the opposite side, I grabbed her by the arm and pulled her out of the way of the crowd. "It happened over a month ago. End of story."

She crossed her arms over her chest and watched the people walk by.

"Aren't you going to say something?"

She slowly turned to me, the anger in her eyes. "I am going to say something. You're wrong."

"I'm wrong?" About what?

"I have every right to be threatened by her. Because while I was curled up in a ball in my bed every single day after you left, you were spending your nights with nobodies just like her. You say you love me, but you leave. You never leave those girls. Anytime they come back for another round, you're available. So, yes. I should be threatened by a gorgeous supermodel that sends racy photos to you." Her eyes welled up with tears and her voice cracked with emotion.

I felt like shit.

"You know what? I stand by what I said before. This is never going to work. Maybe I need to get over what happened and stop living in the past, but that's not so simple to accomplish. Not once did you call or check on me. You just disappeared. My mom was taken from me, and then my dad abandoned me. Then you did the same thing. I'm not going through that again, Hawke. We're done—for good."

***

Why did she have to text me?

Why did this entire thing blow up in my face?

Why did I have to leave Francesca to begin with?

I gave Francesca space because I knew how upset she was. She needed time to calm down and ground herself. She was the kind of person who needed to lick her own wounds. No one could do it for her.

I was terrified I would never fix us. Too much damage had been done. She was constantly scared she was going to lose me again, so she always kept me at a distance. When I got too close, she found a reason to leave.

I didn't know what to do.

After a week of silence, I showed up at her door. I stood outside for a long time before I finally had the courage to knock. She would probably look through the peephole and realize it was me. Then she wouldn't answer it.

But she did answer it.

Her walls were up the minute she looked at me. Eyes void of all emotion stared back at me, and her normally jubilant attitude had disappeared. She wasn't ready to talk to me. A week wasn't long enough.

"Can I come in?"

She didn't open the door wider. In fact, she didn't say anything at all.

"There's something I'd like to say, but I'd rather not do it in the hallway."

Francesca considered my request before stepping aside.

I entered her apartment and no longer felt collected like usual. I was actually scared that I would fail. If I never made this right, I would never have the one thing I wanted.

Everything was on the line.

"I just wanted to say—"

"I realized how deep I'd gotten in with you," she crossed her arms over her chest as she stood in the middle of her living room, "when I saw her name on your phone and what she said… Well, I died inside. I know you aren't mine but knowing you were someone else's, even for a short period of time, kills me. And that's what scares me. The fact I've fallen so hard all over again terrifies me. That's why I flipped out. That's why I got upset. It wasn't because I was jealous. It was just because I hated myself for letting you in."

I put my hands in my pockets and let seconds of silence pass. I wanted to make sure she was finished before I spoke. When I realized she was done, I took my turn. "I understand that. It makes perfect sense."

Her hair was in a braid over one shoulder and it reached past her chest. I loved it when she wore her hair like that. It was so innocent and so sexy at the same time.

"You were right about what you said before. I never called, and I never came back for you. You've never really had a chance to tell me how you felt. You never told me what you went through. I want you to tell me. I want you to scream at me. I want you to let it out."

She slowly turned to me, her gaze unreadable.

"Francesca, tell me." I sat down on the couch and watched her. "I want to know."

She moved to the seat beside me and rested her hands in her lap.

I wanted to wrap my arm around her waist but I kept it to myself. I wanted to pull her into my lap but I managed not to. She needed me to listen, and that's what I would do.

"You want to listen to me whine?" she asked incredulously.

"It's not whining. Talk to me." We could never move on unless she put the past behind her. She needed to confront me, to get all the ill feelings off her chest. I knew it would hurt me, but I deserved to be hurt.

"My life was a bit of a blur. I repressed most of it, honestly. Every night, I would go to sleep and hope I wouldn't wake up the next morning. I'm not trying to be dramatic, like losing a boyfriend is something to make you stop living. But you filled the hole that formed when I lost my parents. My mom left involuntarily, but my dad…chose to leave. You fixed all of that. And when you left…I went through that loss all over again.

"I lost my faith in love. I lost my faith in everything. Marie and Axel looked after me the best they could, but I gave into the darkness and took Marie's pain killers…the entire bottle."

I wasn't sure if I could listen to this. It broke my heart—literally.

"I passed out and can't remember the rest. When I woke up, I was in the hospital. Marie said they pumped my stomach and got everything out before it was too late. Her shift ended early that night. If it hadn't…I wouldn't be here right now."

I closed my eyes in anguish.

"Marie and Axel paid more attention to me after that. When I wasn't with one, the other was there. They traded shifts, working out a schedule to be with me. After the episode with the painkillers, I didn't try anything else. I wasn't suicidal. I just had a bad night when I spotted the pills in the bathroom."

No wonder why Axel was so hard on me.

Francesca continued talking about her life after I was gone. It was lonely and cold, and she didn't know how to go on after the fire died out. There was no blame in her tone. In fact, she judged herself for collapsing so hard. "I was angry with my father for leaving us…but then I did the same thing to Axel. I can't believe I put him through that." Droplets formed on her eyes then they fell down her cheeks. She sniffed loudly and tried to stop herself. Her fingers wiped the moisture away, and her chest heaved because it wanted to release everything inside.

"Let it out." I moved my hand to hers.

She blinked quickly and kept trying to stop herself.

"Muffin, don't keep it bottled inside." I pulled her into my lap and pressed her face into my neck. Once she was against me, she sobbed. Her body convulsed in my arms and she cried her heart out. I'd seen her teary-eyed a few times, but she never bawled like this.

I ran my hand through her hair and down her back to soothe her, but nothing could fix a broken heart. I knew I did this. It was my fault. When I turned around and left, I knew it would hurt her. But I didn't understand the destruction in my wake. I thought I was saving her, but in reality, I was destroying her.

An hour passed before her tears started to dwindle. She sniffed and wiped her cheeks, and there was a long pause before her eyes were finally dry. She clung to me and didn't break her hold. Eventually, she fell asleep. Her chest rose and fell at a steady rate. Her body was exhausted from the emotional hit.

I gathered her in my arms and carried her into the bedroom. When I lay her down, she didn't wake up. Her hair cascaded across the pillow, and she looked like a mermaid lying on the beach.

I removed my clothes, except my boxers, then got into bed beside her. My arms formed a protective cage around her, and my eyes took in the beautiful features of her face. The skin around her eyes was slightly red from constantly rubbing the area, and her nose was irritated too. Even when she cried, she still looked beautiful.

My absence caused her unnecessary pain, and I would always regret that. I didn't trust myself to be the man she deserved, to control my anger and sheath it rather than unleash it. But I had to do it for her. If I just focused and channeled my anger into a positive outlet, I could do it. If I just left the situation whenever I was angry, there should never be an issue. When I saw Kyle at the gym, I wanted to break his neck, but I managed to keep my arms by my sides. I didn't say a word because I knew that would open the gates of my rage. Thankfully, he left the situation so I didn't have to.

There was no other option. If I couldn't make this work, I would lose Francesca forever. My life would be hollow and empty, and the beauty that filled it would disappear. I'd been with hundreds of gorgeous women and there wasn't a single flaw in any of them. But never once did I feel anything more than lust. Not once did I want something more.

But when I met Francesca, I did.

Axel could call me a pussy for thinking she was my soul mate. People could judge me all they wanted. I knew how crazy it sounded. But it was the truth. I recognized it a long time ago. There was a connection between us, and even when we were hundreds of miles apart, that connection still rang true.

This was where I was meant to be.

Tuesday

CHAPTER TWENTY

New Beginnings

Francesca

When I woke up the following morning, I felt weightless. The baggage sitting on my shoulders had disappeared. Somehow, I felt better. I felt different.

I felt whole.

I didn't want to cry in front of Hawke. It was something I was always self-conscious about. But he wouldn't allow me to hide any longer. So I sobbed into his shoulder, reliving the painful way he abandoned me.

Now I felt like a new person.

I opened my eyes and looked at Hawke. He was still asleep, his hair messy from rolling around on my sheets. The hair on his chin was more prominent because he hadn't shaved in over a week.

His hard body was still defined even though he was fast asleep.

He was beautiful.

My reservations disappeared last night. It was hard for me to trust Hawke again after what he did, but my heart still yearned for him. Keeping him at bay was like asking a gray cloud not to rain.

It was impossible.

He seemed to know I was awake because his eyes fluttered open. He stared at me with squinted eyes as he came back to reality. His arm was around my waist, and when he felt me, he squeezed me gently. A quiet sigh escaped his lips, masculine in tone. "Hi."

"Hi…" My hand glided up his arm until it settled in his hair. I felt a strand then twisted it in my fingers, an action I used to do years ago. His hair was slightly curly, and I loved to feel it in my hands.

Hawke watched me, his eyes glued to my face. He noticed the change in atmosphere, and the fact there wasn't a concrete wall erected around my heart. He didn't blink as he watched me, not wanting to miss a single thing.

My fingers stopped twisting his hair then rested on the side of his face. I noted the rough texture of his incoming beard. The touch was sexy, manly.

Hawke stared at me like he was waiting for something.

I was tired of pushing him away. I was tired of keeping us apart. I could keep running from this, but no matter how far I ran or where I went, I would always end up back here.

I pressed my face close to his then let the tips of our lips touch. I eased into it, not wanting all of it at once. Hawke's lips moved slightly against mine, an involuntary reaction. I brushed my lips past his, feeling the build up in my heart. I was anxious for this kiss. I knew where it would lead and what it would mean.

But I wanted it anyway.

I leaned in and pressed my mouth to his. His soft lips felt warm against mine, and the second we touched, I felt the heat sear me like a blue flame. It felt so good it hurt. I gasped into his mouth because every nerve was stimulated. Neither one of us had brushed our teeth but I didn't notice. I had a feeling he didn't either.

Hawke tightened his hold on me and pulled me closer, practically gripping me. He breathed into my mouth, his shoulders tensing like the affection was enough to make him break.

After the initial kiss, I slowly moved my mouth against his. I took my time because it felt so incredible. My body coiled up like a wire in intensity. My hand snaked to his chest and moved to the area over his heart. I felt it beat for me, not the falter.

Hawke kissed me harder, his restraint waning. His hand fisted the back of my hair and he gripped it tightly so I couldn't slip away. He kissed me just the way he used to, but somehow, it was more intense than ever before. He worshipped me with his mouth, and despite the heat both of our bodies generated, there was no lust.

There was just need.

Hawke rolled me to my back and held himself over me, kissing me lovingly. Our lips moved against each other, making quiet noises. Soft moans came from deep in our throats as we embraced. My legs wrapped around his hips, and he hooked one arm around my waist and his hand rested on the small of my back.

Without saying a word, we put ourselves back together. I told him I was his, and that I'd always been his.

And he told me he was mine.

***

I shoved the pan into the oven then set the timer. My body was yearning for the clock to hit five o' clock. I never watched the time when I was at work, either because I was too busy or I didn't care, but now I desperately wanted to get the hell out of there.

I couldn't stop smiling.

I wanted to see Hawke, to run into his arms and never leave. All the pain I carried disappeared when he held me as I cried. When I realized he wouldn't give up on me, that he was going to be there whether I took him back or not, I knew he wouldn't hurt me the way he did in the past.

He was truly sorry.

Hawke was the only man I wanted, and I was tired of denying him. I needed him, and he needed me. Most people would give out a second chance after what he did, but I wasn't most people.

Arms circled me from behind, and large hands moved across my stomach. The scent of his cologne reached my nose, and my heart suddenly danced. His hard chest was pressed against my back, and I could feel the definition of his tie. "Hey, Muffin." He pressed his lips to my ear, and his voice came out raspy.

I leaned my head back and looked up at him. "Hey, Grizzly." I hadn't used that nickname in a long time. Now it felt like I'd been using it forever.

He smiled as he stared down at me, his perfect teeth showing. Then he released a quiet growl.

My hand moved to the back of his neck, and I pulled his lips toward mine. I gave him a slow kiss as my ass dug into his hips. He cock hardened, and I could feel it through his slacks and my jeans.

He breathed into my mouth and pulled me harder into him.

I shook my ass slightly, being a tease.

He bit my lip gently. "Baby…don't torture me."

I pulled away and turned around, and then I realized I got flour all over his black suit. "Shit, I'm sorry." I started to wipe it away but that only made it worse. I knew his clothes were expensive even though he never told me that.

"Hey, it's fine." He grabbed my hand and yanked it off his chest. "It's nothing the drycleaner can't fix."

I still felt guilty for making him look like a mess.

"When are you off?" His hands circled my waist and he gripped my hips.

"At five."

"Well, it's 4:59. Can you take off early?" He rubbed his nose against mine then stared at my lips.

"I guess I could slack off for once..."

"Good. You work too hard as it is."

"I have a feeling we'll be working when we get home..."

He grinned widely, and even his eyes sparkled. "Interesting. I have the same hunch."

***

"Let's go to my place." I pulled him in the opposite direction.

"Why not mine?" he asked. "It's closer. And frankly, it's bigger."

His apartment was far superior to mine. It was in a much nicer neighborhood and the view was to die for. It was the type of apartment you saw in the movies. Mine was barely superior to a janitor's closet. "But, all my cooking supplies are at my place."

"I've proved to you I can cook." He yanked me toward him.

There was an entirely different reason why I didn't want to stay at his place. And it was childish, immature, and stupid. "Let's just go to my place. Come on, I'm tired of arguing."

Hawke caught on to my out of place behavior. "Muffin, what is it?"

"Nothing. I just—"

"Don't bullshit with me." His eyes smoldered in aggression. He only did that when he was irritated, but he somehow came off as sexy.

I avoided his gaze when I spoke. "I don't want to fuck on the bed you've fucked everyone else on. I know it's stupid but…it just bothers me." I hated thinking about all the women who entertained him while I was fighting to breathe. He was mine, even when he wasn't. I could sleep with him in that bed, but there was no way I could do anything physical without thinking of the others. It was unfair because I'd had men in my bed but I wasn't giving him the same courtesy.

"You're right," he said. "It is stupid."

My eyes found his.

"But I wouldn't be fucking you, Francesca. I never fuck you."

I crossed my arms over my chest.

"It's completely different with you and you know that. But if you're more comfortable at your place, then fine. I'm okay with that." He snaked his arm around my waist. "Now let's go."

***

Hawke took his time getting my clothes off. He peeled them away slowly, removing every article of clothing like it was fragile. More and more of my skin was exposed, and when he saw my bare flesh, his eyes smoldered in desire.

When he unclasped my bra, his mouth moved to the valley between my breasts. He kissed the skin softly, moving his tongue along the sensitive area.

My head rolled back, and I gasped at how good it felt. His tongue touched me in just the right way. My nipples automatically hardened in response. The skin of my chest started to blush in arousal.

Hawke moved his kisses to my neck. He sucked the skin aggressively before he sprinkled it with delicate kisses. Then he made his way to my jawbone, where he followed it all the way to my lips. He gave me a heated kiss, swirling his tongue with mine.

My hands automatically gripped his jacket and yanked it down his arms. He helped me get it off while he continued kissing me. Once it was on the floor, he moved down again. He gripped one tit in his massive hand and sucked the nipple. His tongue moved across it before he blew on it. Then he did it again—and again.

After he loved the other tit, he moved his lips down my stomach. When we reached the skin of my ribs, I automatically arched my back. I was practically writhing on the bed even though we hadn't even begun.

He kissed my belly button and then my hips. Then he moved down to my jeans where he unbuttoned them and got them off. They slid down my legs until they fell into a heap on the floor.

Hawke held my gaze as he fingered the lace of my thong. Both of his hands touched the material on either side of my hips. A hungry look was in his eyes as he slowly pulled the lace down my thighs. He had the resistance to go slow. I didn't have a clue where he found the willpower.

When my panties hit the floor, he pressed his lips to the skin beneath my belly button and moved down, inching his way closer to the center of my arousal. As he moved lower, my breathing became deep and raspy. My body ached for release, and not just from anybody, but from him.

When his lips pressed against my clitoris, I practically screamed.

So. Good.

Hawke kissed the area like it was my mouth, using his tongue to smother it with love. His tongue moved inside me before it returned to my clitoris. My back arched because my nerves were firing endlessly. It was just so damn good. Hawke used to do this to me all the time, and I couldn't believe I actually forgot how incredible it was.

I felt my core clench tightly as the unbridled passion took over. I was on the edge of an amazing high. Part of me wanted it desperately, but another part resisted it. "Hawke…I'm going to come."

He sucked my clitoris harder.

"That's not what I meant." I scooted myself away from his lips. That wasn't how I wanted to convulse. I wanted him inside me, not his tongue. I wanted our bodies to be joined together, his massive, sweaty, and yummy chest on top of mine.

He didn't move on top of me. He stayed where he was, completely clothed.

What the hell was he doing? "Come here."

He remained kneeling at the bed. "I'd rather stay here." He dragged my hips back to him, and his mouth was on me again.

The wave of pleasure overtook me, and I fell back as the writhing goodness spread through my body again. Hawke was making me feel amazing, and I wanted to make him feel the same way. "Hawke, stop."

"I know you don't mean that, Muffin." He kept going.

Somehow, I found the strength to pull away. "Make love to me."

His lips were shiny from juice, and his hair was messed up where I gripped it. His collared shirt was still on, but his tie was loosened around the neck. "I am."

I pulled his tie then began unbuttoning his shirt. "If I go, I want you to go with me."

He watched me undress him, his eyes never leaving my face.

I pushed his shirt off and saw his rock-hard chest.

"No."

I flinched in response. "No, what?"

"I don't want to rush into this."

"There's nothing to rush into. You better not make me wait like last time." That was pure torture.

"Sorry, Muffin."

"Give me one good reason why." I knew I was acting like a brat but I didn't care.

He held my gaze for a full minute without speaking. "Because we have the rest of our lives." He pushed me back onto the bed then pressed his face between my legs. He kissed me and did amazing things with his tongue. Then he brought me to the edge, making me whimper in pleasure.

My nails dug into the sheets, and I held on as the orgasm rocked through me. Everything was on fire, but I loved the burn. "Hawke…" I kept saying his name over and over, living out my greatest fantasy. The man between my legs was the only man I'd ever loved, and he was on his knees pleasing me. My back ached because I was arching it so strenuously, and I was trying to keep my legs apart so they wouldn't press against his head.

Hawke kept kissing me as I winded down. My body slowly relaxed as the high disappeared. His hands gripped my hips as he lavished me down below.

"Hawke."

He moved back onto the balls of his feet. "Francesca."

I sat up and undid his slacks, knocking my knuckles against the hard definition of his abs. The fabric started to slide down, and I yanked on his boxers. Once he was naked, I leaned down to press my lips against his tip.

But he stopped me. He threw me back then guided me up the bed. "I'd rather kiss you."

"Why?"

"Because I love it." He pulled my naked body against his and leaned toward me.

"I'd rather please you the way you like."

"There will be time for that later." He tucked my hair behind my ear. "I'd rather kiss you like a teenager in high school. It's amateurish and anticlimactic, but I love it. I want to do it for the rest of the night, and as soon as you shut up, I'll get started."

I zipped my lips.

CHAPTER TWENTY-ONE

New Look

Hawke

Want to play ball after work? Axel texted me at the end of the workday.

Can't. Have a hot date.

He texted back quicker than I could put my phone down. *With who?*

Who do you think?

He stopped texting me and called me instead. "You guys are back together?"

"You know, you don't look like a girl but you sure act like one."

Axel ignored the jab. "Answer the question."

I smiled and felt odd doing it. Smiling wasn't in my nature—unless Francesca was involved. "Yeah."

"Why did she take you back?"

"I think I proved how sorry I was." And I showed her I would never leave her again.

"Can I tell Marie?"

I laughed into the phone. "I'm sure she already knows."

"If she does, she hasn't told me yet," he said. "Can you do me a favor and not fuck it up this time?" His tone was teasing, but it was clear he was being serious.

"I won't."

"Good. So, basketball?"

"I told you I'm going out with Francesca."

"Oh yeah. I forgot. Looks like you'll be busy from this point onward..."

"I'm sure I can squeeze you in if you don't piss me off."

"What are you guys doing?"

"I'm taking her out to a fancy dinner."

"And then?"

Axel was a little slow sometimes. "I have a surprise for her at my apartment."

Axel steered clear of the topic once he understood what I meant. "Well, I'm happy for you. You guys are the most complicated people I know, which is why I think you should stick together."

"I think we should stick together for a lot of reasons."

"Well, I'll see you later."

"Bye."

***

When I picked her up, she was wearing a tight navy blue dress that pushed her tits together and made a noticeable cleavage line.

Lucky me.

I whistled quietly. "You look nice."

"Thanks." She placed her clutch under her arm. "You look nice too." She pressed her body to mine and gave me a long kiss. When her tits were pressed against me like that, my mind thought of things I shouldn't. I suspected that was her goal, and she succeeded.

I ended the touch and put my arm around her waist. "Hungry?"

"Always. You know me."

I pulled her to my side and felt the happiness wash over me. I had the girl of my dreams on my arm, and everything in the world was right again. When I had her, nothing could bring me down. I was exactly where I should be, and I could be myself when I was with her.

"I missed you today."

"Yeah?" I asked. "I always miss you."

"Always?" she pressed.

"Yeah." I was being dead serious. The entire time I was without her, she was all I ever thought about.

"So, when you went home this morning, did you miss me then?" She walked beside me, her heels clanking against the ground.

I knew what she was referring to. I went down on her and made her come in my mouth, but I hadn't let her do the same to me. I was so hard up for her but couldn't find a release. "I did."

"Did you jerk off in the shower?"

That statement brought me back to our time together in the past. She said it turned her on when I touched myself in the shower, and hearing her say that made my dick hard. "Yeah."

"Did you think about me?"

"I always think about you." I placed a kiss on the shell of her ear.

"I would have loved to see that."

She was flirting with me, and she was doing a good job. My dick was hard in my jeans, and I kept thinking about how sweet her pussy tasted. "I'll show you sometime."

"Yeah? I'll hold you to it."

"I hope you do."

We reached the restaurant and took our seats. I ordered a bottle of wine for the table, and after I glanced at my menu and decided what I wanted, I stared at her. It was a favorite pastime of mine. She had the most beautiful features but she was never vain about them. But she wasn't oblivious to her charms either.

She rubbed her leg against mine under the table.

I grabbed her hand and interlocked our fingers together. I didn't mind going out in public and taking her to a nice dinner, but I preferred to be home. When it was just she and I, I could touch her all I wanted. If I had it my way, she'd be in my lap right now. But I would be a shitty boyfriend if I didn't take her out on the town and show her off. We hardly went out together before, but things were different now.

After we ordered, we made small talk about work. She asked me about my investment strategy and seemed genuinely interested in it. Most women didn't care about my line of work—just how much money was in my wallet. I asked her about the bakery, and her response was the same as it usually was.

When the food arrived, we ate it quietly. Neither one of us ate much, probably because we would rather be eating each other. Francesca was eager to jump back into bed, and I was too. But I wanted to do things right. I really hurt her, and I had a lot of making up to do even though she already forgave me.

"Coming back to my place?" she asked after I paid the check.

"Actually, let's go to mine." She hated the fact my bed had many visitors before she came back into my life. It was understandable to a certain extent, but she didn't truly understand how meaningless they were. She was with Kyle for six months in her bed, and I thought that was completely different. But since I'd dragged her through the mud for so long, I gave her leeway in a lot of things.

She immediately tensed like that didn't sound the least bit appealing to her.

"There's something I want to show you."

"At your apartment?" she asked incredulously.

"Yeah." She'll understand it when she sees it.

"You better let me watch you beat off."

"Actually, I have something better in mind."

***

We walked into the apartment, and I didn't bother turning on the lights. It was dark, but you could still see inside the apartment. A distant glow came from down the hallway, the surprise I'd made for Francesca.

I took her hand. "Come with me."

She didn't object as I pulled her away.

I guided her into my bedroom, and on the nightstands and dressers were white candles flickering in the dark. They glowed dimly, and the shadows they made stretched across the walls.

Francesca took it in then eyed my bed. White rose petals were sprinkled on the brand-new comforter. New sheets were on the bed, as well as pillows. In fact, everything in the room was new. I'd replaced the bed frame, the mattress, and the remaining furniture.

"You're the only woman who will ever sleep in this bed." I came behind her and wrapped my arms around her waist. I kissed her neck then the shell of her ear. I tightened her against my chest and felt her breathing increase.

Her objection to my old furniture, the stuff the others had been on, was childish. But Francesca didn't ask for much, so I would give her whatever she wanted. I felt her body tremble in my arms at the gesture, and it picked up a few degrees. She and I were starting over, getting the future we should have had two years ago.

My lips found her hairline, and I pressed a gentle kiss there. I was a very sexual person, needing good sex on a regular basis. Perhaps it was just my nature, but it was the one thing that subdued my anger. I liked it dirty and kinky, and I liked it hard and fast.

But I never wanted that with Francesca.

What we had was so much better than that. When we touched, so did everything else. Without the use of words, we communicated. She made me feel whole—deep inside, in places I never thought I could reach. With her, it was about a lot more than sex.

I continued to kiss her neck as I slowly unzipped the back of her dress. Her breathing hitched slightly as I pulled it all the way down. When I reached the small of her back, my fingers grazed the skin, just inches from her ass. Then I pulled the top of the dress down, revealing her body in just her black bra. My fingers pulled her hair over one shoulder, and I kissed the area between her shoulder blades. Her skin tasted like honey, and her hair smelled like vanilla. My lips were drawn to her like a moth to a flame. I loved kissing her everywhere. It was my favorite thing in the world.

My hands pulled the dress the rest of the way, and it slid to her ankles. She remained absolutely still, letting me worship her body with just her lips. With a single hand, I unclasped her bra.

The straps came loose and I pushed them off her shoulders and watched it fall.

The only thing left was the black thong. My fingers played with the lace, and I stared at the definition of her tight ass. She had a beautiful body with endless curves. I wasn't sure why Cassandra intimated her. In actuality, all women should be intimidated by Francesca.

"You're beautiful." I pulled the lace off her hips.

She took a deep breath, showing her excitement.

I pulled it down to her ankles then helped her step out of them. When we were fooling around the other night, I didn't want to keep my guard up and wait. But I didn't want to give in to my physical desires when Francesca deserved something more. She deserved a perfect night, not a hook up. I wanted her to know, without a doubt, that she was different than all the others.

She was the one.

Francesca turned around and faced me. Her features were cast in shadow, but they could still be distinguished. Her perfect tits were just below my chest, and her tight little stomach had an hourglass shape. She grabbed the bottom of my shirt then slowly pulled it over my head, revealing my naked chest. When it was off, she stared at it lovingly, desire and appreciation in her eyes. Then she leaned in and pressed a kiss to the center of my chest. It wasn't sexual, but intimate.

And it made me come alive.

She undid my belt and zipper then pulled down my jeans. When she got to her knees in front of me, I pictured her sucking me off. But I shook the thoughts away because I knew there would be time for that later. Francesca and I had a strong physical relationship when we used to be together but that developed later on.

When she pulled my boxers down, my cock popped out. I was proud of my size, and I knew every woman I'd been with was impressed by it. Whoever said size didn't matter was full of it.

She licked her lips as she stared at it.

Fuck.

I wrapped my hand around her neck then pulled her lips to mine. I kissed her fiercely, savoring every moment because I wanted it to last forever. When we made out for hours the other night, I loved every second of it. Most guys wouldn't, but then again, most guys weren't head-over-heels in love like I was.

I guided her to the bed then lay her down on it. The rose petals were soft against her skin, and they smelled like a garden. I lay my body on top of hers, holding myself up by my arms. Francesca's legs wrapped around my waist, and she held me against her, like she was eager for the connection we were about to feel.

I was too.

There wasn't any hesitation in her eyes like there used to be. After she opened up to me, she seemed to have forgotten all her reservations. Like steam, it evaporated. Now she looked at me just the way she used to, like I was the single most important thing to her. Trust was in her eyes, and she was in love with me.

I didn't ask her if she was on the pill. I didn't ask if it was okay if I went bareback. She didn't ask if I was clean. We didn't have that conversation. Even if she wasn't on the pill and became pregnant, I wouldn't care. That was bound to happen someday anyway. And she knew I would never be with someone without protection, besides her.

My lips were desperate to kiss her but I restrained myself. My gaze was focused on hers, and my heart hammered in my chest. I pointed myself at her entrance, and the second my tip felt her warm skin, I wanted to moan. When I pushed slightly against her, I felt the moisture between her lips. The sensation wasn't just pleasurable. It was so much more—because it was Francesca.

I pushed against her gently, forcing myself between her legs. When I was barely inside her, Francesca bit her bottom lip then gripped my arms. Her eyes were bright with fire and her nipples were harder than the tip of a diamond.

I kept going and felt her familiar tightness. She constricted me like a python, and to say it felt good was an understatement. Just the knowledge that I was inside her, feeling her, made my muscles tense in satisfaction.

"Hawke..." Her hair was scattered around her on the pillow, and she had a dreamy look in her eyes. Her lips were parted like she wanted my tongue, and her tits shook with every move I made.

When I sheathed myself completely inside her, I didn't want to move. I wanted to stay just like that, buried deep within her. I breathed harder than I wished and felt my restraints give way. Whenever I was with her, my cold exterior melted. I was in a different universe, one where just she and I existed.

Francesca ran her fingers through my hair and tightened her legs around my hips. Then she kissed me slowly, not rushing the embrace. She took her time, savoring every caress of my tongue.

I rocked into her slowly, caring more about the interaction of our hearts instead of our bodies. She was underneath me, and she was mine. The pain disappeared when she cradled me like this. I was turned on and so hot for her, but I was also so deeply and pathetically in love.

Francesca's kiss became immobile and she breathed into my mouth as the pleasure overtook her. She arched her back and writhed on the bed like she couldn't handle how good I felt. Her nails trailed down my back, leaving marks where she gripped me. "Oh shit..."

I loved pleasing her. It was my favorite thing in the entire world. Watching her spin out of control gave me the greatest sense of satisfaction. I usually only cared about my own pleasure, but with her, she was the only thing that mattered.

"You're going to make me come." She said it with a tone of surprise like she couldn't believe that could happen so quickly.

I wanted to release at the same time, but that was too soon. I wanted this to last all night—until the end of time. "Muffin." I sucked her bottom lip then brushed my lips across hers. She constricted around me, preparing to explode.

And then she ignited.

"Hawke..." She gripped my shoulders and held on. "Oh my god."

She came all over my dick. I felt the moisture flood around me, and that made my cock twitch. I kept thrusting, hitting her in the right spot so she could enjoy it as long as possible.

She was out of breath and covered in sweat. Her chest had a flushed color to it, and her eyes were somewhere else. She ran her hands up my chest, feeling the grooves and lines of muscle.

I loved being inside her.

"I love you." She held my gaze as she moved underneath me. Her hands were pressed against my chest, and her fingers dug into me slightly.

So many women had hit my sheets, and I couldn't remember what a single one looked like. It was all a blur, a meaningless escapade. I may as well have been alone because I was never truly there. But with Francesca, I was in the moment. I was thankful to be alive. "I love you."

CHAPTER TWENTY-TWO

Gossip

Francesca

Marie stormed into the back of the bakery where I was working. "Spill it. I know something is going on and you better tell me what it is. I'll snatch that spatula and shove it so far up your—"

"Calm down, woman." I set my stuff down and removed my apron. "Damn, you should be an interrogator."

"It was one of my options." She crossed her arms over her chest. "Now fess up. Axel has been acting weird lately. Anytime Hawke comes up, he gets this weird look on his face, like he's trying not to smile but it comes off as a cringe. Believe me when I say, it's not sexy."

The only reason why I hadn't told Marie was because I hadn't seen her much. She was busy with work and the wedding, and when I wasn't working,

I was with Hawke. "Hawke and I got back together." I laid it out and didn't add any filters to it.

"What?" she asked in surprise. "When?"

"About two weeks ago."

"Why didn't you tell me?" She stomped her foot.

"I wanted to do it in person."

Marie's irritation didn't last long. When she saw the smile on my face, she couldn't keep her anger. "Are you happy?"

"You can see all my teeth, can't you?" I was over the moon.

She smiled against her will. "Yes, I can. And it's really surprising that you never had braces."

"Why, thank you."

She dropped her arms to her sides and came closer to me. "Tell me the details."

"Remember when I said he wanted to get back together but I said no?"

"Clearly," she said. "Because it didn't make any sense."

"Well, he didn't accept that answer and tried to win me back anyway. He cooked me dinner and spent time with me...and I slept over a few times."

Her eyes widened and she opened her mouth to speak.

"We didn't have sex," I said quickly. "Just slept together. He told me he wasn't going to give up until he got what he wanted. I didn't trust him for a long time, and that didn't change until I told him exactly how I felt…and about everything that happened after he left."

Marie's eyes fell in sadness when she understood what I was referring to.

"And I cried my eyes out for a long time until I fell asleep. When I woke up the next morning…all that pain was gone. I let it go and Hawke and I moved forward."

Marie pressed her lips tightly together. "You think this is it? You don't think he's going to do the same thing to you?"

"No." There was no hesitation. He wouldn't do that to me, not again.

Marie took my word for it because she smiled. "Then I'm very happy for you."

I smiled again, melting at the thought of him.

Marie hugged me. "Now we can go on double dates."

"We've been going on double dates," I said with a laugh.

"The other girls are going to be so disappointed," she said. "Every single one of them has a crush on Hawke."

"That's too bad," I said. "Because he's mine."

"They didn't have a chance anyway." She pulled away with a hint of a smile on her lips. "So, have you guys...?"

"Oh yeah," I said. "The other night."

"Was it as good as it used to be?"

"It was better, actually."

"I'm a little jealous..."

"Axel isn't good?"

"No, he is. But we haven't had make up sex in a long time...maybe I should pick a fight with him later." A mischievous grin was on her lips.

"Just make sure you don't break up for two years."

***

Marie and I walked into the restaurant and spotted Hawke and Axel sitting at a table. They were across from each other, the seats beside them vacant.

"Look at those hunky men," Marie said into my ear.

"Yeah..." Hawke wore a charcoal gray suit, and it outlined his strong shoulders and massive chest. It matched the scruff on his cheeks, and he looked appetizing.

When Hawke noticed me, he stood up and discreetly buttoned his suit with a single hand. He watched me and didn't smile. He just stared at me, commanding me to come to him with just a look.

"Let's go." Marie pulled me with her.

I didn't need to be told twice.

Marie got to Axel first, and he embraced her like a man deeply in love.

As I came closer to Hawke, his eyes were glued to me. He watched every move I made with intensity. When I finally reached him, his hand moved to the small of my back and he pulled me against his chest. He looked down at me without kissing me, but he made love to me with just the look.

My knees felt weak.

Hawke pressed his lips against mine and gave me a slow kiss. He had to bend his neck to reach me, and I had to stand on my tiptoes because of his six foot three height. The kiss went on longer than necessary, and Hawke had to force himself to pull away even though it was clear he didn't want to.

We didn't say a single word to each other, but with a connection like ours, words were unnecessary. Hawke pulled the chair out for me before he sat in his own. When I took my seat, his hand automatically moved to my thigh.

Axel eyed us back and forth. "About fucking time."

Hawke shrugged.

I didn't say anything at all.

"Don't tease them," Marie said under her breath, like she hoped we wouldn't hear her.

"No, I'm gonna," Axel said. "Their relationship has been a damn soap opera. And I don't watch soap operas for a reason."

Marie slapped his wrist. "Knock it off. Hawke might be your brother-in-law someday. You should be happy."

He will be Axel's brother-in-law.

Hawke squeezed my thigh.

"Now that it's out in the open," I said. "Can we just move on and act normal?"

Axel looked at his menu in response.

"So, what's left for the wedding?" I asked. "Anything else we need to do? Party favors? Centerpieces?"

"No," Marie said. "Everything is ready. Now we just need to get married."

"The sooner the better." Axel kissed the top of her hand.

It still surprised me when he did sweet things like that. It was so out of character for him.

Marie didn't react to his affection like she used to.

"Can you believe you guys are getting married in two weeks?" I asked.

"I can't believe it," Marie said. "This engagement went by so fast."

"I'm excited for the honeymoon," Axel said.

"I bet," Hawke said with a grin. "Best part of the wedding. Where are you going?"

"The Caribbean," Axel answered. "Marie is gonna wear a thong bikini." He grinned wide like an idiot.

"In front of people?" Hawke asked. Hawke was the polar opposite. He didn't tell me what to wear, but he wouldn't want my ass exposed to the world. My body was his and he didn't want anyone else to enjoy it—even if it was just with their eyes.

"Oh yeah," Axel said. "They'll wish they were fucking her instead of me. But they can't because she's my lady."

"Let's change the subject before you make everyone throw up," Marie said.

"Throw up?" Axel asked. "You have a gorgeous ass. That wouldn't make anyone throw up."

"He's right," I said. "You do."

Marie shrugged in agreement.

Hawke leaned toward me. "I'd love to see your ass in a thong right now."

"We can arrange it." I wasn't joking. "There's a bathroom here."

His eyebrow rose in interest.

I held his gaze without backing down.

"How about in my office after lunch?"

Being bent over his desk sounded innately appealing, but then I thought about all the other girls who'd done the same thing. I shouldn't think like that and I wish it would stop but I just couldn't. I broke eye contact and looked at the menu, silently answering his question.

***

After we said goodbye to Axel and Marie, we faced each other on the sidewalk. Hawke hooked his arm around my waist, resting his hand on the small of my back, his favorite place. "My office is just a block away. And I'm pretty sure you haven't seen it."

"Or we could walk a few extra blocks to my apartment."

Like always, Hawke could read me with just a simple look. "Why don't you want to see my office?"

I felt childish just thinking about the answer.

After a few more seconds of staring, Hawke figured it out. "I've never fucked a woman in my office before."

I found that hard to believe, and my expression showed it.

"Why would I lie?"

I knew he wouldn't.

"Now, do you want to see my office?" He pulled me harder into his chest and dangled his lips near mine.

My knees felt weak again. "I'd love to."

***

His office was on the tenth floor of the building, and it was beautiful. It was modern, with pristine white walls, glass doors, and elegant furniture. A secretary sat in the front of the double doors. She was blonde and pretty, and there were people waiting in the chairs.

"Hello, Mr. Taylor. Have a good lunch?" She glanced at me with interest then turned back to him.

"I did, Abby. Thank you." Hawke opened the glass door and allowed me to walk inside first.

I felt out of place with my dirty t-shirt and old jeans. My hair was in a braid over one shoulder. I didn't look anywhere near as classy as that secretary.

Hawke took my hand and guided me to his office. There were others along the wall, and men wearing suits were inside each of them. Some were on their computers and others were on the phone.

"It's really nice." I was truly impressed.

"Thank you." He said hello to his secretary, another blonde, and then walked inside with me. Instead of glass doors like everyone else had, his were black.

I surveyed his office and looked at the gray bookshelves against the wall. Two red armchairs faced his large mahogany desk. On the end table were a few pictures. One was of him and me.

Had that always been there? Or did he put it there after we got back together?

My fingers touched the frame, and when I felt the dust on my fingertips, I knew it'd been sitting there for over a year.

Hawke leaned against his desk and crossed his arms over his chest. "What do you think?"

"I love it," I answered. "It's very...you."

"Dark, foreboding, and terrifying?"

"No," I answered. "Beautiful."

He didn't blink.

I came to his desk and stood in front of him. I didn't touch him, keeping my hands to myself. "Why haven't you had a girl in here?" I wasn't sure why I asked the question. I wish I didn't care about the others. When we first got together, I didn't care. But after he left, I did.

"Because this is my office." The tone of his voice suggested that was all he needed to say. "I have an image I need to protect. People don't need to know my personal life."

"Then why did you bring me here?"

He tilted his head slightly. "You're different, Francesca. And you know that."

My heart swelled to two times its size, and it thudded painfully in my chest. My fingers found my shirt, and I slowly pulled it over my head, taking my hair with it. Then I tossed it on the ground.

Hawke's eyes left mine, and he stared at my tits in my bra.

I unclasped it and let it fall.

Hawke gripped the edge of the desk.

My fingers undid the button and zipper of my jeans, and I pulled them down my thighs and over my Converse. I left the shoes on, just to be different.

He eyed my thong darkly.

I pulled that off too. Then I stood naked before him, in just my Converse.

He swallowed the lump in his throat before he rose to his full height. Then he pulled his jacket off and tossed it on the armchair. Slowly, his fingers undid every button of his collared shirt. He pulled it off and let it slide down his arms until it hit the floor.

I would never grow tired of seeing his perfect chest.

He slowly approached me as he undid his belt and slacks. With a quick shove, he pushed them down until they fell around his ankles. Then he kicked them aside, his shoes still on too.

All that was left were his boxers.

He held my gaze as he pulled them off his slender hips and down his powerful thighs. Once they were gone, he was naked. With a smoldering look in his eyes, he grabbed my hips and pressed me into his body. My tits rubbed against his hard chest, and I felt my breathing hitch.

Hawke pressed a soft kiss to my lips before he guided me to the desk. My back was pressed against it, and he was about to lift me up and place me on the surface. Instead, I turned around, giving him my ass.

He dropped his touch and stared at my behind.

"You said that's what you wanted to see." I looked at him over my shoulder.

He gripped one cheek with his palm and massaged it. "It's as beautiful as I remember." He kneeled down then placed both palms on my ass.

My body tightened in anticipation.

He pressed his face between my cheeks then kissed the area between my legs. He licked and sucked the area, devouring it like every taste was turning him on even more.

I remained bent over the desk, breathing hard and enjoying every second of it. He was so good at everything involving sex, and I felt like the luckiest girl in the world for unromantic reasons.

He was hot.

He kissed the area for a few more minutes before he rose back to his feet, his hard cock pressed in between my cheeks. I had a large ass for my size. I hated it because it was difficult to fit into jeans, but every guy I'd ever been with was obsessed with it.

Hawke pressed his lips to my ear and he moved his cock between my cheeks. "Damn…"

I arched my back in anticipation.

He leaned over, his arms on either side of me on top of the desk. Then he inserted himself slowly, feeling no resistance because I was wet. I was soaked, actually. It was my own fluids and his saliva. When he was completely inside me, he moaned in my ear.

I rocked my ass and sheathed him over and over, too anxious to wait for him.

He released another moan then started to move with me. He kept his lips against my ear so I could listen to every breath and sound he made. That was an even bigger turn on, listening to him enjoy me.

I pressed my palms against the surface of his desk as an anchor but my hands kept slipping because they were covered in sweat.

Hawke wrapped his arm across my chest, right against my tits. He gripped me and used me as an anchor to move himself inside me. He was so long and thick, and every stroke made me want to crumble.

I was already barely holding on, and I gripped his arm and dug my nails into his skin as the explosion began. It was searing hot and my body could hardly contain it.

Hawke leaned over me and pressed his mouth against mine, silencing my moans and making me come harder at the same time. His tongue danced with mine, and he pounded into me as I rode my high. It lasted so long, and it was so strong. My back arched, and I released a moan louder than I meant to.

Hawke pulled his lips from mine after I was finished, and then he kissed the back of my neck and the area between my shoulder blades. He continued to thrust into me at the same time. Then he moved his lips back to my ear as he pumped into me harder, moaning quietly in my ear. I knew he was about to explode because his body was tensing against mine. His breathing quickened and he gripped me so tightly he was practically squeezing me.

Then he released. "Francesca…" His cock twitched inside me as it spilled everything it possessed. He made his final thrusts before he buried his face into my neck and inhaled my scent. The sweat on his chest rubbed against my back. He remained there for a long time, just holding me.

"Is this the first time you've defiled your desk?" I asked as he kept his body on top of mine.

He chuckled. "Defiled?"

"Yeah. You know, did something naughty on it."

"Yes, it's the first time. But defiled isn't the right word. Beautiful. That's the word you're looking for."

***

I heard footsteps behind me when I was in the rear of the bakery. Without turning around, I knew who it was. The footsteps sounded heavy, like a large man was behind me.

And that could only mean one thing.

I turned around with a smile plastered on my face, expecting to see the man of my dreams.

But it was Kyle instead. "Hey, is this a bad time?" He wore jeans and a long-sleeved gray shirt. His biceps were defined, and the hardness of his chest was visible to anyone, even if they were blind.

"Uh…" I wish I could think quicker on my feet. "No, you just surprised me."

"Sorry, I know I shouldn't be here." He rubbed the back of his neck and released a sigh. "There's just something I need to know, and I think your answer might help me."

What did he want to know? I set my supplies down then removed my apron. "What's up?"

"Hawke." He said the name like it explained everything.

"What about him?"

"A few weeks ago, he was at our gym…and I was just curious what that meant. Are you back together?" He cringed slightly like he didn't want to hear my answer—at least the one that would hurt him.

I didn't want to be honest, not because I wanted to lead him on. I just didn't want to break his heart all over again. "Why are you asking?"

"Because…if you are, then I know there's absolutely no hope for us. But if you aren't…maybe we can work things out. I haven't enjoyed my single life, not the way I used to. I would much rather settle for half your heart than storm this existence."

Was he trying to rip me apart?

"So…are you?" He put his hands in his pockets and waited for the answer.

Either way, I lost. There was no answer I could give that would make him feel better. So, I went with the truth. "Yes."

The pain moved into his eyes and he couldn't hide it. He nodded his head slightly then cleared his throat. "Okay. I can move on now."

I hate myself.

"Congratulations." Despite his pain, he seemed sincere. "I know this is what you wanted. You always said he was your soul mate and everything."

"He is my soul mate." I didn't want to drive the nail into the coffin but I wanted him to walk out of there feeling a little better than he did when he walked in.

"Well…I guess that's it." He rubbed the back of his neck and shrugged at the same time.

"Kyle, you're such a great guy. You're going to find a woman a million times better than me, and she's going to love you like no other."

"Thanks." He didn't make eye contact with me, telling me he didn't believe a word I said.

"I really mean that."

"I'm sure you do," he said with a sigh. "I've just never felt this way toward anyone before. What are the odds of me feeling that again? And, there's no one else better than you, Francesca. You're wrong about that." He returned his hand to his pocket then backed away to the door. "I'm sorry for bothering you. I won't do it anymore."

I wanted to hug him and comfort him in any way that I could. But showing him any type of affection would just make it harder. I would much rather see him walk out hating me than heartbroken over me. I wished I'd seen the signs earlier. I wished I ended things before he fell for me.

It was entirely my fault.

"Good bye, Francesca." Kyle turned around and headed to the hallway, but he stopped when he realized someone was in the way.

Hawke stood there, threat burning in his eyes.

I hadn't even noticed him. He wore a suit and tie like he did every workday. His size and presence should have alerted me, but I was so absorbed in Kyle that I hadn't noticed.

Kyle stared him down without the slightest hint of fear.

Hawke didn't blink.

It was tense as hell. Neither one of them said a word, but they did all the talking with just their eyes. Their muscles were flexed, and they were both ready for a fight. Hawke didn't talk much, but his thoughts were visible in his eyes. Right now, he wanted to rip Kyle's throat out for even looking at me.

I waited for the moment to pass, for one of them to walk away.

Finally, Kyle walked into the hallway without turning back.

Hawke watched him go until he was out of sight. Then he turned to me, that anger still burning deep inside his soul. His shoulders were stiff, and his arms didn't move by his sides. He gave me the same death threat, jealous and angry.

I didn't do anything wrong and neither did Kyle, so I had nothing to apologize for. He could growl at me all he wanted but that wouldn't change anything. I had to sit by and watch his phone light up with explicit messages and see chicks waiting outside his door.

He could get over this.

Hawke finally closed the distance between us, his body still rigid. "Do you need me to kill him?"

"No. That won't be necessary."

"Can I kill him anyway?" He kept a straight face.

"No."

Hawke was about to burst. The anger was about to erupt out of his eyes. "Then what the fuck is he doing here? Who the hell does he think he is? He has no right coming here and talking to you. You. Are. Mine."

I put one hand on my hip and met his gaze without blinking. "He's a human being and he's my friend. He didn't touch me, he didn't come on to me, and he just wanted to talk. There's nothing wrong with that."

"Like hell, there's nothing wrong with that. I won't let some guy harass my girlfriend."

"He wasn't harassing me."

"He still has no right coming in here. What the hell did he want?"

"None of your business."

The vein in Hawke's forehead started to twitch. "It is my business. I don't want him anywhere near you."

"I can take care of myself, Hawke. And you should trust me."

"I do trust you. It's him I don't trust."

"Well, just deal with it."

"Excuse me?" he hissed.

"I've had to deal with all your skanks and hoes. You can deal with this."

"Those skanks and hoes never meant a damn thing to me. You actually had a relationship with this guy. You met his family for god's sake. I have every reason to be pissed, Frankie. You're with me now, which means you aren't allowed to talk to him."

He just said the wrong thing. "I'm not allowed?" Now I put my other hand on my hip.

Hawke knew he messed up. "If you're with me, there's no reason you should be talking to him. That's all I'm saying. I don't have a relationship with any of my bimbos. Exes can never be friends."

"Kyle is a great guy. You should be nicer to him."

"That's exactly why I'm not nice to him." His arms shook by his sides.

I crossed my arms over my chest. "You either trust me or you don't. In case you've forgotten, I left him because I was so hung up on you. There's not a single reason in the world you should feel threatened by him. If I'm your soul mate, then it shouldn't matter that he was here."

Hawke pressed his lips tightly together. "What did he want, anyway?"

"He wanted to know if you and I got back together."

"He didn't know that before?" he snapped.

"Why would he?" I asked calmly. "I don't talk to him on a regular basis."

His anger dimmed slightly.

"And I told him we did."

"What does it matter?" Hawke asked. "You aren't with him regardless."

"Because he said it would help him move on." I felt bad saying the words out loud. I knew what it was like to want someone you could never have.

Hawke's expression didn't change, but it was clear he didn't like that answer.

"Now let it go and stop jumping down my throat." I turned back to my table and put my apron on. I was too irritated to kiss Hawke and pretend everything was perfectly fine. I didn't appreciate being interrogated like that, especially when I had never faltered in our relationship.

Hawke sighed from behind me and didn't leave.

I kept my back to him and waited for him to leave.

"I'm sorry." The words cut through the air like a knife, his sincerity acting as the blunt edge.

I didn't turn around.

"I overreacted. I'm never sane when it comes to you."

I knew that all too well. I remembered how crazy things got when he saw Aaron kissing me at the bar. Hawke almost killed him—literally.

"I know I shouldn't be jealous—not ever. There's no reason to be, not with you."

It was becoming more difficult for me to hold on to my anger. When he admitted he was wrong, something extremely rare, it was impossible for me to turn him away.

His hands moved around my waist and he guided me to turn around.

I fought it at first, not ready to see his face.

But he won and turned me toward him. When he saw my features, he gave me a ghost of a smile. His eyes brightened slightly as he moved his hand to my neck. His fingers rested in my hair and his thumb touched the corner of my mouth.

Yep. I was lost.

"Muffin, I'm sorry." He looked down at me, his forehead almost touching mine.

"I forgive you."

He smiled when he knew he had me. Then he gave me a soft kiss that would make any girl grow weak. My lower stomach burned in desire, and I felt light-headed and even a little dizzy.

When he pulled away, I didn't want it to end. "Want to get lunch?"

I forgot he came down here for a reason. "Not really."

"You aren't hungry?"

"I am," I said. "I just would rather do something else than eat."

His hands tightened on my waist. "We can arrange that. Do people come back here often?"

"Sometimes…but no one goes into the pantry but me."

He brushed his lips against mine. "Things are about to get messy."

"Good thing I like messy."

***

Marie's wedding was just days away. The pressure and stress started to kick in.

"Okay, I need to get the photo album—"

"Got it." I took care of that weeks ago.

Marie went down the list. "I need to tell the DJ the music we're having at cocktail hour."

"Took care of that too."

Her eyes were glued to the paper. "Shit, I forgot—"

"I got your something old, something new, something borrowed, and something blue."

She finally put the list down. "You're the maid of honor of the year, you know that?"

"I do." I wasn't going to be humble about it. I was at Marie's beck and call and did everything she asked. Actually, I did things without her asking.

"What about the cake?"

"What about it?" I asked incredulously. "Marie, your cake will be perfect. Don't give it a second thought."

"But you already have so many things going on—"

"Girl, this is what I do best. Shut up and chill."

She smiled. "You've made this so easy on me. I'm so glad you shared this experience with me."

"I'm honored to be by your side, Marie."

"And I'm so relieved I'm not getting crazy in-laws."

"Are you sure about that?" I asked with a smirk.

"You're crazy, Frankie. But in a good way. So, how's it going with Hawke?"

"Perfect." There was no other way to describe it.

"You guys are still living in a fairytale?"

"It's like we picked up where we left off…but better." Because I knew this would end happily. He wouldn't take off and leave me again. He wouldn't hurt me again. Like he said, we were forever.

***

I wanted to do something reckless—with Hawke.

I was head-over-heels, so happy it should be illegal, type of in love. Hawke and I spent time together every night after work. We would stay at his place or mine, and we cuddled on the couch and stared into each other's eyes. Sometimes, we didn't say anything at all and just communicated with a simple look.

Just the other night, Hawke grabbed my hand and kissed every knuckle while he held my gaze. The touch was innocent, but it made me hotter than I'd ever been before. With him, I was whole. With him, I was home.

But I wanted to do something adventurous and crazy. We'd been taking things slow ever since we got back together. Hawke was always gentle with me, and when he made love to me, it always felt like the first time.

But now I wanted something more.

I stepped onto Hawke's floor and walked past the secretary. She raised an eyebrow like she wanted to say something to me, but when she recognized who I was, she let me pass.

When I reached his assistant's desk, she didn't say a word to me. Judging the frown on her face, she wasn't happy that I was Hawke's girlfriend. Come to think of it, I didn't think any single woman was.

I knocked on his door.

"Come in," he said with an indifferent voice.

When I walked inside, he was typing on his iPad. He didn't look up at me, like he thought I was his assistant or someone else who didn't matter.

"What's up?" He raised an eyebrow but kept typing.

I walked further into the room then undid my trench coat. I wore nothing underneath except black lingerie. It wasn't something I would normally do, but I wanted to surprise Hawke.

When I didn't say anything, he looked up. He almost did a double take, like he couldn't believe I was standing in front of him—in lingerie. His fingers slipped and he dropped the iPad on the desk. "Francesca..." He stared at me with greed and swallowed the lump in his throat.

Trying to keep my confidence, I walked around the desk and kneeled at his feet.

He looked down at me, more surprised than ever.

I undid the top of his pants and pulled his dick out. It was long and hard.

He stared at me without saying a word.

I tossed my trench coat aside then licked the tip of his cock.

He took an involuntary breath and moaned.

Slowly, I licked the shaft and sucked the tip. Then I massaged his balls before I shoved him deep into my throat. I gave him the best head I was capable of giving, and soon, he was digging his hand in my hair and moaning uncontrollably. He flexed his hips and moved himself further inside me, gripping my hair by the scalp. "Francesca…"

I controlled my gag reflex and took it like a soldier. He was thick and long, and his size was intimidating. But he did so much for me, and I wanted to do something for him.

"Muffin, I'm about to come." He moved his hand to my neck.

I pulled my mouth away briefly. "Then come." I inserted him back into my mouth and watched him as I moved up and down. My hand gently rubbed his sack, something I knew he loved.

"Fuck." He did a few more pumps before he exploded inside my mouth. He watched my face as he filled me, his eyes burning in desire. He squirted a few times before he finished. He leaned back into the chair and released a satisfied sigh.

I swallowed everything he gave me, and then put my trench coat back on and prepared to leave.

Hawke watched me with tired eyes. "What was that about?"

I grabbed my purse and headed to the door. "Bye."

"Whoa…what?"

"See you later, Grizzly."

He stood up even though his pants were still undone. "Francesca, what are you doing?"

I blew him a kiss. "Enjoy the rest of your day at work."

***

Hawke knocked before he entered my apartment. "There she is. The mysterious sucker."

I placed the pan inside the oven. "That's what they're calling me these days?"

"They?" he asked. "I hope it's just me." He wrapped his arms around me and gave me a kiss. He wore jeans and a t-shirt.

"It is."

"So, what was that about today?" He cradled me to his chest.

"What do you mean?"

"You've never done something like that before."

"I've gone down on you plenty of times. And I want credit for that."

He chuckled. "That's not what I meant and you know it." He searched my gaze as he waited for a response.

"I just wanted to surprise you...do something adventurous."

He nodded slowly. "While I enjoyed it and appreciated it, you don't have to do stuff like that to keep me around. I'm thinking about you all day whether your lips are around my dick or not."

I smiled then pressed my face into his chest.

His lips pressed a kiss to my forehead. "How was your day?"

"It was okay."

"Ready for Saturday?"

"I'm ready to get this over with."

"Nervous?" he asked.

"I'm not the one getting married."

"It's still nerve-racking," he said.

"How's Axel doing?"

"Fine," he answered. "I think he wants to get married more than Marie."

"Pussy..."

He laughed then kissed my forehead again. "I want to marry you. Does that make me a pussy?"

I looked into his eyes and searched for sincerity.

His smile faded away and he gave me a serious look, like he dared me to question his words.

"No."

"Good. Because I'm anything but a pussy." He kissed the corner of my mouth then peeked inside the oven. "What do we have here?"

"Stuffed mushrooms and squash raviolis."

"Sounds good."

"Who said anything about you joining?" I teased.

That sexy smile returned and he pulled me to his chest again. "I'm joining—whether you like it or not."

Tuesday

CHAPTER TWENTY-THREE

The Rehearsal Dinner

Francesca

"This is the order." Rodolfo lined the girls up at the altar.

I knew my place was beside Marie, so that was easy.

The girls toward the end of the line had pissed looks on their faces, and the ones closer to the center acted like they belonged there. I liked most of Marie's friends, but honestly, some of them were just bitchy.

"Now the men." Rodolfo was the emcee for the wedding, so it was his responsibility to make sure everything flowed well. "Hawke, you're here." He grabbed his t-shirt and shifted him.

Hawke didn't like to be touched.

Then Rodolfo lined up the rest of the guys.

"Damn, he's so gorgeous," Cheyenne whispered to Kayla.

I knew they were talking about Hawke.

"And his arms look so good," Kayla whispered back.

They obviously didn't know Hawke and I were an item, and if they did, they must not think it's very serious.

I'll straighten that out.

"Let's practice from the top. Go to your starting places."

We walked back to the entryway to the ballroom and waited for the music to start. I was walking with Hawke, which was a relief. I didn't want one of Axel's perverted friends touching me, and I didn't want any of Marie's slutty friends touching Hawke.

The music started, and I walked to the center of the room, where Hawke met me. He gave me his arm, and I took it. He watched me as we slowly walked down the aisle together.

"What?" I whispered to him.

"I feel bad for Marie."

"Why?" Did he know something I didn't?

"You're going to outshine her."

My cheeks blushed, and I shook my head. "No, that's not true."

Hawke smiled knowingly. "Always the perfect maid of honor…"

We took our places at the end of the aisle and waited for everyone else to finish. The entire time we stood there, Hawke stared at me. He was oblivious to everyone else around him.

Axel and Marie faced each other, and that's when I noticed something off with Axel. He wasn't frowning, but he didn't seem his normal self. He didn't make a single joke all night about the honeymoon or how nice Marie's ass would look in her dress.

It was odd.

"Are we done yet?" Shane, one of Axel's friends, asked. "I'm starving."

"That's a wrap," Rodolfo said. "Good job, everyone. We'll see you tomorrow for the big day."

Axel looked pale.

"Where are we eating?" Veronica asked.

"Here," Marie said. "In the restaurant."

"Nice," Kayla said. "Good thing I wore a nice dress."

Hawke moved toward me and put his arm around my waist. "Want to sit next to me?"

"Please." I glanced over my shoulder and saw Axel looking faint. "Is Axel okay?"

"Yeah," Hawke answered. "Why?"

"He just seems...like he's about to pass out."

"I'm sure everything is hitting him right now. He probably just needs a few minutes to soak it in."

"I hope that's it...and not food poisoning."

"I'll talk to him later when no one's around."

"Good idea."

***

Hawke had his arm over the back of my chair the entire night. "You look beautiful tonight." His lips were pressed to my ear, and as he talked, I could feel his lips move slightly.

"Thanks...you already said that."

"I can't say it more than once?" He only had eyes for me.

I knew Marie's friends officially hated me. "You can say it as many times as you want."

Hawke grabbed his wine and took a drink.

I glanced at Axel and noticed how quiet he was. He wasn't talking with his groomsmen but he wasn't talking with Marie either. Fortunately, Marie didn't seem to notice anything was off because she was talking to her bridesmaids.

I couldn't picture Axel leaving Marie at the alter so that was the last thing on my mind. But there was definitely something bothering him, eating him alive. Was he having second thoughts? Or did he simply drink too much the night before?

At the end of dinner, Hawke gave me a PG kiss. "I'm sorry I can't stay with you tonight."

"What?" I blurted. "Why aren't you?"

"I'm going to stay with Axel. You know, keep him calm."

I wanted to ask him to stay but that would be selfish. "That's a good idea."

He shrugged. "I'm the best man, right?"

"I'll miss you."

He seemed pleased by that response. "I'll miss you, Muffin." He gave me a final kiss goodnight.

I wrapped my arms around his neck and hugged him, not wanting to let him go. I would miss him more than I cared to admit, and even though it was just one night apart, it was too much for me.

Hawke allowed the affection to linger and he pressed his lips against my forehead. "I'll be dancing with you all night tomorrow, Francesca. And I'll dance all my dances with you forever."

Tuesday

CHAPTER TWENTY-FOUR

Trouble

Hawke

I wasn't looking forward to staying with Axel. It was nothing against him personally. I just wanted to be with Francesca, to feel her small body wrapped around mine while we slept. I wanted to open my eyes and see her first thing in the morning.

I wanted her.

Axel and I walked back to my apartment. He was dead quiet, walking with his hands in his pockets.

"Everything alright, man?" I didn't confront him directly. Instead, I tried to go about it casually so he wouldn't feel like he was on trial.

"I'm fine." He kept up the quick pace like he desperately needed to get inside.

"You're sure?" I asked. "You didn't eat spoiled meat or something?"

"No."

There was definitely something wrong but he wasn't sharing.

We entered my apartment and turned on the lights.

"I'll take the sofa. You can have the bed."

"I'm good," he said. "I prefer the living room."

"I washed all the bedding." Maybe he was grossed out by the idea of Francesca and I doing it on that mattress.

"Honestly, I prefer the couch." He took off his jacket and tossed it over the back of the couch. Then he kicked off his shoes. When he sat down on the cushion, he released a deep sigh.

I sat beside him. "Axel, I know marriage is scary. It would scare anyone. You don't have to shut me down. I don't think less of you."

Axel rested his hands on his knees. "Marriage doesn't scare me."

"Then what's up?"

"Nothing."

Why was he being such a pain in the ass? "Dude, you can tell me. I'll take your secrets to the grave."

He remained quiet like he was considering his answer. But then he abruptly stood up and headed to the bathroom. "I'm going to shower. Good night."

I officially gave up.

***

I had a hard time sleeping that night, and I knew it was because Francesca wasn't there. I missed her scent on my sheets. I missed the way she kissed me on the chest first thing in the morning. Her slender legs would wrap around my body, and she would cling to me like she needed me to survive.

Without her, I was just a man alone in a bed.

Just when I dozed off, my phone rang.

I anxiously grabbed it because I hoped it was Francesca calling to tell me she missed me. But it wasn't her.

It was my mom.

I immediately answered it. "Mom?"

There was an unrecognizable sound in the background, like something was moving. I couldn't make it out.

"Mom?"

Finally, her voice came to the phone. "Hawke?" She sounded distressed, like she was in danger.

"Mom, are you okay?"

"Hawke—"

The line went dead.

I listened to the dial tone as the panic kicked in. I was on the other side of the country and had no way of getting to her. The only option I had was calling the police, and of course, I would do it even if my mom didn't like it. I ended the call then pressed 9-1-1.

My phone rang again, my mom's name on the screen.

I answered it and shoved it against my ear. "Mom, I'm calling the cops. They'll be there in a second."

"The cops?" Her voice was nothing like it was before. Now she sounded calm, almost happy. It was like the previous conversation never happened. "Why would you do that?"

Was I missing something? "When you called earlier, it sounded like something was wrong. Are you okay?"

"Oh that?" She laughed into the phone. "I dropped my cell on the counter and it almost fell in the sink. So stupid of me."

I sat up in bed and kept listening.

"I was just calling because I remembered Axel is getting married tomorrow. Are you excited?"

"Yeah." Not really. Axel was acting strange, and I knew the wedding would be stressful.

"Good. I'm sure you'll look handsome in your suit."

"Thanks, Mom."

"Well, I'll let you go. I just realized how late it was there."

Something in my gut told me to keep her on the phone. "Are you sure you're okay?"

"Yes, sweetheart." She breathed into the phone and remained quiet. "I miss you." Her voice was full of emotion, like her heart would give out.

"I miss you too."

"I love you so much, Hawke. You're the best son a mom could ask for."

I didn't get emotional very often but those words filled me with warmth. "I love you too, Mom."

***

The next morning, I headed into the kitchen to make some coffee. I didn't get any sleep last night and my eyes were practically bloodshot. I'd need some serious caffeine if I were going to get through this day.

"How do you take it?" I asked as I put on the coffee pot.

No response.

I walked to the couch and looked at the scattered blankets and the pillow that fell on the ground. "Axel?" My eyes immediately moved to the bathroom, but the door was wide open. I looked for his bag on the ground but that wasn't there either.

Shit.

I turned to grab my phone when I noticed the note on the table.

Hawke,

Tell Marie I'm sorry.

***

Francesca answered on the first ring. "Miss me?"

I did, but there wasn't time for that conversation. "Go somewhere where no one can hear you."

Instead of asking questions, the phone became muffled as she moved. Then her voice came into the receiver. "What's up?"

"Can anyone hear you?"

"I'm at the end of the hallway by the stairs. Marie is in the apartment. What's up, Hawke?"

It was a long shot but I had to ask. "Is Axel there? Have you seen him today?"

"No... Why?"

I didn't want to bring her into this, but I needed help. "Axel took off."

"As in...he went out for coffee?" There was hope in her voice, but also doubt.

"No. He left, Francesca. He left a note on the table."

Now she started to panic. "What did it say? Tell me word for word."

"He said tell Marie I'm sorry."

"Oh my god." She gasped into the phone. "What the hell is he thinking?"

"I don't have a clue."

"This is just so…unexpected. He loves Marie."

I rubbed the back of my neck. "I knew something was bothering him last night."

"I did too," she said. "But I thought he just ate something bad."

"Francesca, I don't know what to do."

"Did you call him?"

"His phone is off."

"That piece of shit," she hissed. "Hawke, you have to find him."

"I don't even know where to look. He might be on a plane to Tuscany for all I know."

She sighed into the phone. "I'm not letting him do this to Marie. And I'm not letting Axel make the biggest mistake of his life."

"Then what do we do?"

"I'll stall Marie as much as I can while you find him."

I rubbed my temple. "I don't even know where to look."

"Check all his regular places, like bars and restaurants. If he's not there, check his office and his gym."

"You really think he'd run out on his wedding day and hit the gym?" Now wasn't the time to be sarcastic but I was too stressed to filter my words.

"Just check," she snapped. "And let me know when you do."

***

I checked every place I could think of, and like I expected, he was nowhere in sight. If I were going to run for it, I'd be on a plane somewhere beautiful. I wouldn't stay in town and risk the possibility of being found.

We were running out of time, and the fear was turning into pure panic. I didn't know why Axel took off, but I knew it wasn't because he stopped loving Marie. He loved that woman more than anything on the planet. I couldn't let him throw his relationship away. A girl could forgive a man for a lot of things, but leaving her at the alter in front of her friends and family was not one of them.

Francesca called me. "Please tell me you found him."

I sighed in response.

"Goddammit, Axel."

"I'm sorry. I looked everywhere."

"Okay, what did he say to you? What was the last thing he said? Think, Hawke."

"I told him it was okay to be scared of marriage. It's common."

"Why the hell would you say that?"

"Because I knew something was bothering him," I snapped. "I was trying to make him feel better."

"Whatever," she said. "What did he say to that?"

"He said he wasn't afraid of marriage then he got into the shower."

"What?" she asked in surprise. "He said he wasn't afraid of marriage?"

"Yeah."

"You're sure?"

"I know what I heard, Francesca." Butting heads with her would get me nowhere but the frustration was getting to me.

"Now this makes even less sense."

"I know." I tried to think of somewhere else he would be, and I had a strong suspicion he was over the Atlantic Ocean by now. "We aren't going to find him in time. You need to tell Marie."

"No. We have a few hours."

"Even if I find him, I'm going to need a few hours just to convince him he's making a mistake. If he left Marie like this, he's probably set in his decision."

"Keep looking."

"Where?" I demanded. "If his phone was on, I could have a friend trace it but that's not an option."

Francesca was silent on the phone. She was probably pacing in the hallway. "Marie is about to put her dress on. I can't let her put it on then watch her take it off while she's in tears."

I didn't want that for her either. "We're out of options."

Francesca continued pacing. "Wait...I think I have an idea."

I already didn't have much faith in it. "What?"

"Go to my shop."

"Why?" I asked. "You want me to bring you some muffins?"

"No," she hissed. "I bet Axel is hiding there, in my office."

"Why?"

"Because that's the one place we wouldn't look."

I highly doubted that. "I don't know..."

"He has a key to get inside. I bet he's there."

"Uh…"

"Hawke, just check. If he's not there…then I'll tell Marie."

Axel better be there. Otherwise, this was going to be the worst day of Marie's life…and Francesca's. "Okay."

***

I headed into the back of the shop and passed the workers. They recognized me so they didn't question why I was there when Francesca wasn't. If they did ask, I would say she left something behind for the cake.

I'd never been to Francesca's office but I found it easily. The door was closed so I opened it without knocking. Unable to believe my eyes, I froze on the spot. Just as Francesca predicted, Axel was sitting in the chair behind the desk looking like hell.

He stared at me with equal surprise.

Now that I was face-to-face with him, I didn't know what to say. I closed the door behind me and leaned against it so he couldn't make a run for it.

Axel covered his face and sighed. "How did you find me?"

"Francesca."

"That brat."

I crossed my arms over my chest. "Axel, what the hell are you doing? You're getting married in two hours."

"I'm not getting married." He lowered his hands and rested them against his lips.

"Why the hell not?" I moved to the chair facing the desk because it was clear he wasn't going to take off. "You were so excited about it last week. Don't get scared, Axel. You love Marie, and she loves you."

"Of course I love her." He stared at the surface of the table and didn't meet my gaze.

"Then don't let the fear scare you off. Marriage is a big commitment, but it's a good kind of commitment. You get to spend the rest of your life with the one woman you love." It wasn't easy for me to spit out mushy shit like this, but I was doing it for him. "I know this is what you want. You want to be with her forever. I've seen you with her, Axel. Even if you never said you loved her, it's obvious—to the world."

"Shut up."

My eyes narrowed on his face, and I felt my hands form fists. If he said that to me under a different circumstance, he'd have a bloody lip. But since the situation was so tense, I let it slide. "Excuse me?"

"I told you I loved her. That's not the problem."

"Then what the hell is?" I snapped. "What could possibly make you run out on Marie on her wedding day? You're going to break her heart and no one will ever put it back together."

He kept his knuckles against his lips.

"Talk to me."

"It's…hard to say out loud."

I had no idea what he was referring to. What could possibly be weighing on him? If the commitment wasn't holding him back, and love wasn't an issue, what could it be? "It's me, Axel. You can tell me anything."

He covered his face again then slowly lowered his hands. He released a deep sigh before he spoke. "I cheated on Marie."

What?

Holy shit.

Did he really just say that?

I stared at him blankly because I couldn't believe it. He was head-over-heels for Marie. Why would he sneak around? "You cheated on her?"

He closed his eyes in shame. "Yeah."

I leaned back in the chair and rested my chin on my knuckles, unable to believe this. This was the last thing I expected him to say.

"I can't marry her. I don't deserve her."

I wish I could say otherwise but I couldn't. A lot of things were forgivable but cheating wasn't one of them. And I knew Marie wouldn't turn her cheek and let it slide. I would judge her if she did. "You should have said something to her before...not waited until your wedding day."

"I know." He rubbed his temple. "I thought I could just forget about it and move on but...the guilt has been killing me. I hate myself, Hawke. I really do. I wish I could take it back."

I do too.

"I'm not marrying her. I'm not going to even speak to her...because I don't deserve to."

This was how it ended? The couple I believed in most called it quits? Axel, a man I thought was madly in love, betrayed the one person he cared most about. It actually broke my heart a little bit. "What happened? Were you drunk?" That was the only scenario I could think of.

"Yeah...really drunk."

It didn't justify his behavior but at least it was better than him purposely having an affair. I didn't know what to say so I sat there in silence.

Axel continued to rub his temple.

"Did you sleep with her just one time?"

"Sleep with her?" he asked. "I didn't sleep with her."

Both of my eyebrows shot up. "Come again?"

"I didn't sleep with her." He rested his hands on the desk.

"Then what did you do?"

"We made out for a few minutes. Then I realized how stupid I was being and I left."

This changed everything. "So, you just kissed someone?"

"What do you mean *just* kissed someone?" he asked. "Cheating is cheating."

"What else happened?" I asked. "When did this go down?"

"About two years ago."

This was getting even more confusing. "Two years ago?"

"Yeah, it was when Marie and I were first getting together. We got into a bad fight and I stormed off and went to a bar. I was pissed at Marie so I did something really stupid."

This changed everything. "When you guys first got together? Didn't that take months to happen?"

"Yeah. We weren't in a relationship but we were still seeing each other…I still fucked up."

"Axel, hold on. You didn't cheat on her."

"I made out with some chick that wasn't her," he said with a deadpan voice. "Yes, it was cheating."

"But she wasn't even your girlfriend."

"Not officially, no."

"Then you didn't do anything wrong."

"I still never told her about it."

"And you think today is the best day to spill the beans?" I asked incredulously. "Marie wouldn't leave you for that. It happened two years ago and you weren't even together yet. You weren't the same person then as you are now. Axel, it's irrelevant."

"Can I really marry her and never tell her?" he asked. "I don't think I can."

"You're just going to ruin the day by telling her."

"What if I marry her then tell her and she never forgives me?" he asked. "Wouldn't that be worse?"

"Why tell her at all?" I asked. "She would forgive you if she knew. It's not even worth talking about. It was so long ago."

Axel shook his head slightly.

"Axel, don't run out on Marie because of that. We all know you love her."

"I do," he said sadly.

"Then let's get you ready for the ceremony."

He didn't move from his chair.

"Axel, come on."

He bowed his head. "Hawke, I have to tell her. I don't want this marriage to be her biggest regret."

It wasn't a good idea but it was the only way I could stop him from running. "Okay."

***

Francesca opened the door wearing her deep purple bridesmaid dress. It was strapless and showed her toned and rounded shoulders. Her brown hair was in a pretty updo. She looked beautiful, to say the least.

She spotted Axel beside me. "Oh, thank god. You found him."

"He was at the bakery."

"Thank goodness." She clutched her heart. "What are you guys doing here? You aren't even dressed."

"Is Marie here?" Axel's voice came out broken.

"Yeah," Francesca said. "She just put on her dress. Why?"

"I need to talk to her." The tone of his voice implied it wasn't good.

Francesca shut the door behind her. "Axel, you aren't leaving her. You're just being ridiculous right now—"

"I'm not leaving her," he said quietly. "But I need to tell her something."

Francesca turned to me for guidance.

I just nodded.

"Well, you can't see her," Francesca said. "She's already in her gown."

"I don't need to see her," Axel said. "She just needs to be able to hear me."

"Okay…" Francesca couldn't hide the panic in her eyes.

"Does she have a changing divider?" I asked.

"Yeah," Francesca said.

"They can use that." It was thin enough that they wouldn't have to yell to be heard, but it was thick enough so they couldn't see each other.

"Okay. Hold on." Francesca walked back inside.

I turned to Axel. "Are you sure you want to do this?"

He nodded. "I have to. What would you do if you were in my shoes?"

"I wouldn't have made out with some girl to begin with."

He didn't laugh.

When I thought about it, I knew I would do the same thing. I wouldn't be able to lie to Francesca. "I would do the same thing."

Axel didn't gloat when I agreed with him.

"Okay, she's ready." Francesca opened the door and ushered us inside.

Axel slowly approached the tan and white changing divider, his hands in his pockets. He stopped in front of the wood and stared at it even though he couldn't see Marie.

Francesca and I stayed near the door, able to see and hear everything.

"Axel?" Marie's voice was full of emotion. Fear hung with every word. "You're scaring me. What's wrong?"

"There's something I need to tell you," he said quietly. "I couldn't let you marry me unless you knew the truth. For what it's worth, I really do love you. I've never loved anyone so much in my entire life. I'm not the same man I used to be. You've made me into a better person, a better version of myself I never thought was possible. It's because of you that I'm so happy. It's because of you that I'm whole."

Marie's voice came out weak. "What is it?"

"I did something stupid. I wish I could take it back."

Marie's deep breathing echoed in the room.

"Two years ago, you and I got into that big fight at the house. You told me we shouldn't see each other anymore, and I agreed...because I couldn't give you what you deserved. I went out that night and got drunk then kissed some girl. I'm so sorry."

Marie didn't say anything for a long time. "Did you sleep with her?"

"No, I just kissed her. It went on for a few minutes before I realized what I was doing and left."

Marie said nothing.

"Marie, I'm so sorry. I was stupid and reckless. I've felt guilty ever since and I knew I needed to tell you before you made a mistake. We both know I don't deserve you. We both know you're too good for me. If you don't want to marry me anymore, I completely understand." Axel breathed deeply then blinked his eyes like he was trying to fight the incoming tears. He was scared, and I'd never seen him scared before.

"Close your eyes."

Axel stared at the ground. "What?"

"Close your eyes," Marie repeated.

Axel continued to stare at nothing before he did as she asked.

"Are your eyes closed?" she whispered.

"Yes," he answered.

Marie came around the divider, holding up the bottom of her gown. She looked like a princess covered in jewels. Her hair was in big curls, and her make up made her eyes look bigger than they really were.

Axel didn't open his eyes.

Marie stopped in front of him and stared, emotion written all over her face. Then she wrapped her arms around his neck and pressed her mouth against his. She gave him a slow kiss, just using her lips.

Francesca didn't look away like she normally would. She clutched her hands to her chest and tried not to cry.

Axel kissed her back but kept his hands to himself.

Marie pulled away, her arms still around his neck. "There's no one else I'd rather spend forever with."

Axel's shoulders immediately relaxed and he released the breath he was holding. "You forgive me?"

"Axel, there's nothing to forgive." Her finger twirled a strand of his hair.

"I don't agree."

"It was a long time ago when we both didn't know what we were doing. What we have now is so much different. I don't care what you did then. All I care about is the man I know now."

"Really?" he whispered.

"Really."

"So, we're still getting married?"

"I'm not giving you a choice in the matter."

Axel smiled for the first time. "I love you, Marie. I promise I'll spend the rest of my life making you happy."

"I know you will."

Axel pulled her into his chest and hugged her, his eyes closed the entire time. "I can't wait to see you walk down the aisle."

"And I can't wait to say I do."

Axel held her for a long time, and the sadness finally drained from his face. He buried himself in her neck while his arms remained locked around her waist. It didn't seem like he wanted to break their hold. And neither did she.

Francesca sniffed loudly from beside me.

I turned to her and saw tears fall down her cheeks.

She wiped them away quickly and tried to compose herself. "Sorry…they're just so cute."

I put my arm around her waist and pulled her against my chest. "I got a little teary-eyed too."

"Did you really?" she asked.

"No," I said with a chuckle. "But I almost did."

CHAPTER TWENTY-SIX

Wedding Bells

Francesca

Hawke and I were the last couple to walk down the aisle before Marie. My arm hooked through his as he guided the way. Everyone stared at us, and as I passed Yaya, I saw her wipe her tears away.

Before Hawke released me at the end, he kissed me on the cheek.

I smiled then took my place.

Axel stood with his hands held in front of his waist. His face was indecipherable but his gaze was glued to the entryway where Marie would make her appearance.

The music changed and it was time for Marie to emerge. Wearing the beautiful dress that hardly anyone could afford, she walked down the aisle with her arm tucked under her father's. She wore a flower headpiece with two ribbons that trailed down the back of her hair. The pink bouquet she held was alive with color.

She held herself with grace as she came closer to Axel. Everyone had their eyes glued on her, unable to believe such a beautiful bride existed.

I turned to Axel to see the expression on his face. Instead, I caught Hawke staring at me. He didn't look at Marie at all. I managed to look away and see Axel's face. His eyes were coated with moisture, but the tears didn't fall. His chest rose with a heavy breath.

I smiled and returned my gaze to Marie.

Her father kissed her on the cheek before he finally let her go. Then she moved to Axel, her eyes just as wet as his.

They hadn't even begun the ceremony, and I was in tears. Mom would be so proud of Axel for becoming such an honest man. He got me through the hard times, and now he was marrying the perfect woman. Dad would be proud too, and I knew they would both be here if they could.

I took a deep breath and stilled the tears. But like the ocean tide, they came back in full force. I kept my voice down so no one would hear the quiet sobs I made.

And I watched my brother get married.

***

After the dinner and speeches, Marie and Axel had their first dance as husband and wife. We gathered around and watched them move together on the floor. Axel looked into her eyes the entire time like he never wanted to look away. And Marie looked like the happiest girl in the world.

Hawke snaked his arm around my waist. "We saved the day."

"Yeah, we did." Axel deserved this moment. If he took off, Marie never would have forgiven him. I wouldn't have forgiven him either. "Actually, you did. You were the one who talked some sense into him."

"And if I had failed, you would have been the second line of defense." He pressed a kiss to my temple. "We both put them back together."

I melted into his side and realized just how happy I was. I'd been happy several times throughout my life, but right now was the climax. My brother was dancing with his wife just feet away, and his new bride happened to be my best friend. And the love of my life, my soul mate, was right next to me. He stared at me just the way he used to, like a man desperately in love. It reminded me of the way Axel looked at Marie, but somehow stronger.

When their song ended, everyone else was invited to the dance floor. It was a slow song, and Hawke grabbed my hand and pulled me toward the center. "May I have this dance?"

"You can have all my dances."

"Good answer." He spun me around before he pulled me against his chest. Together, we moved. Hawke stared into my eyes without blinking. Sometimes, he glanced at my lips, and at other times, he looked deep into my eyes. He wanted the whole picture and all the parts at the same time.

Sometimes, I wasn't sure if my life was real. It was too perfect to comprehend. The two years we'd been apart were unbearable. They were so difficult I couldn't think straight. But the second we were reunited, all that pain went away. All that was left was joy. He was the missing piece of me, the part of my soul that lived outside my body.

And I knew he felt the same way.

One day, we would get our happily ever after. One day, he would get down on one knee and ask me to spend my life with him. It would be the happiest day of my life, and all other days would pale in comparison. But today was not that day.

Hopefully, it would be soon.

I hoped you enjoyed reading TUESDAY as much as I enjoyed writing it. It would mean the world to me if you could leave a short review. It's the best kind of support you can give an author. Thank you so much.

Is that really the end of Hawke and Francesca? Or is there still hope? Find out in the next installment of the series WEDNESDAY.

Tuesday

Want To Stalk Me?

Subscribe to my newsletter for updates on new releases, giveaways, and for my comical monthly newsletter. You'll get all the dirt you need to know. Sign up today.
www.eltoddbooks.com

Facebook:

https://www.facebook.com/ELTodd42

Twitter:

@E_L_Todd

Now you have no reason not to stalk me. You better get on that.

Tuesday

EL's Elites

I know I'm lucky enough to have super fans, you know, the kind that would dive off a cliff for you. They have my back through and through. They love my books and they love spreading the word. Their biggest goal is to see me on the New York Times bestsellers list and they'll stop at nothing to make it happen. While it's a lot of work, it's also a lot of fun. What better way to make friendships than to connect with people who love the same thing you do?

Are you one of these super fans?

If so, send a request to join the Facebook group. It's closed so you'll have a hard time finding it without the link. Here it is:

https://www.facebook.com/groups/1192326920784373/

Hope to see you there, ELITE!

Tuesday

Made in the USA
Columbia, SC
31 July 2018